Praise for

Were Chronicles

I love how the plot line is progressing as each story adds new characters while continuing the earlier character's lives... The story ended with a cliffhanger leaving me impatiently waiting for the next book in the Were Chronicles series. ~ *Fallen Angel Reviews*

Plenty of hot bedroom play between truly well-drawn characters, you should enjoy this story.
~ *Whipped Cream*

I0607500

Total-E-Bound Publishing books by Crissy Smith:

Corporate Wolves
The Favour
Losing Control

Secrets
The Shifter and the Dreamer

Were Chronicles Volume One
Pack Alpha
Pack Enforcer
Pack Territory

Seduced by the Neighbour
Lacey's Seduction
Eternal
Bid High
Fated Love
Vamps in the City

Anthologies
Caught in the Middle: Magical Ménage

Seasonal Collections
Bite Me: Savage Love
Summer Seductions: Summers' Girl
Cloaks and Daggers: Vapmire Hunter

WERE CHRONICLES
Volume Two

Pack Rogue

Pack Community

Pack Mates

CRISSY SMITH

Were Chronicles Volume Two
ISBN # 978-1-78184-610-0
©Copyright Crissy Smith 2013
Cover Art by Posh Gosh ©Copyright 2013
Interior text design by Claire Siemaszkiewicz
Total-E-Bound Publishing

Published in 2013 by Total-E-Bound Publishing, Think Tank, Ruston Way, Lincoln, LN6 7FL, United Kingdom.

Total-E-Bound Publishing is an imprint of Total-E-Ntwined Limited.

PACK ROGUE

Dedication

For my family, whom I love and cherish even through
the tough times.

Chapter One

Kiley Palmer sat scrunched down inside her SUV, well-hidden by the tinted windows as she held a camera up and snapped off pictures. The old man had been right. The fourth Mrs. Douglas was having a visitor every morning as soon as her husband left for work.

"Gotcha," she whispered to empty air as she snapped off four more pictures before the front door of the large house closed.

She set the camera down and prepared herself for the wait. All week she had been staking out the home of her client, Edward Franklin Douglas the Third. The man knew his young thirty-year old wife was cheating on him, and Kiley had just finished collecting the reminder of the evidence to provide to her client. She would snap off a few more pictures as the man left then she would be done with the job.

As private detective work went, this had been simple. Easy money. Mr. Douglas had known his wife was not being faithful and, to protect his money, he had needed proof.

Kiley reached for her coffee and found the cup empty. *Damn*, she thought as she sat back with a sigh. She was contemplating running to the closest convenience store to grab another cup when a knock on the passenger window startled her.

She jumped, her hand going to her heart. The grin from the man on the other side of the glass annoyed and amused her at the same time. She rolled her window down.

"Detective," she greeted.

Detective Gray Mason continued to grin as he leant against her door. "Kiley, how's it going?"

Kiley shrugged. "Fine, until you scared the living daylights out of me."

He chuckled in response.

Kiley crossed her arms over her chest and gave him her best pout.

Unfazed, he continued to smile. "All done here?" he asked.

Kiley looked at the house and back at him. As Gray turned serious, she knew it wasn't so much a question as him telling her she was done. She nodded.

He opened her door and held out a hand. "I need you to come with me."

She rolled her shoulders and stepped from her vehicle, ignoring his hand. He stepped back, giving her room as another man stepped up and drew her attention. Kiley frowned at the guard. She didn't know Wyatt well but he had a reputation for being a hardcore fighter.

"What's going on?" she asked Gray, her eyes snapping from one man to the other. Dread scrawled up her spine as unease settled in her stomach. This couldn't be good.

"He needs to see you," Gray told her quietly.

Kiley shook her head and started to back towards her SUV. "No." She knew what this weekend was about. She'd seen the many cars which had driven through town on their way up to the compound.

Gray's hand on her elbow stopped her. "It'll be okay. I'll stay with you," he promised.

Kiley's heart sank. It had been months since her presence had been requested at the local Alpha's residence. Always it had been when few people had been around.

"Come on," Gray urged with a gentle tug.

Kiley tried to plant her feet. "I'll follow you."

Gray shook his head, knowing the game. "I don't think so," he quipped.

Kiley bit her bottom lip. Damn, she'd already used that trick. It wasn't that she didn't like the Alpha—the new Alpha anyway—it was just that she had too many bad memories of the old one, and the guests he always had over.

"Wyatt will drive your vehicle and follow," Gray explained. "You won't be without a way home."

Kiley knew she should be grateful. At least they were giving her a way out without depending on one of the Pack members. It was a small thing but it made her relax a little, just as Gray probably knew it would. In the year the man had lived in her city, he had got to know her better than anyone else.

One foot in front of the other, she let Gray lead her to the big Hummer parked behind her SUV.

"This new?" she inquired. It had to be since she'd never seen it before—damn, it was huge.

Gray just shrugged, and she grinned. "Over-compensating much?" she teased.

Gray growled as he opened the passenger door. "Get in."

Kiley giggled. "Oh yes, sir," she said innocently. She relaxed enough to really enjoy teasing Gray. It had, after all, become one of her favourite activities.

Gray's lips twitched as if he was holding back a smile. Kiley settled in the seat and had pulled her seat belt on by the time he made it to the driver's door and got in. She glanced at him out of the corner of her eye.

Gray was one of the few Pack members she would actually call a friend. As a police detective, he matched her ideal of the perfect strong male. He was well built. The play of muscles under his dress shirt, the wide shoulders, and just the plain bulk of the man both intimidated and aroused her. His kind heart and quick wit were just added bonuses.

There had been numerous times in the past that she had wished she could fall in love with him. They'd fooled around a few times, but as good as it was, it wasn't what either of them were looking for. They were not destined to be mates.

Which saddened her. She had never expected to be given the chance to find her mate. At one time it had been forbidden, in fact. She was already spoken for, or she had been until the Alpha had finally come across someone he couldn't threaten or beat into submission.

Lost in her thoughts, she hadn't realised they'd started to move until Gray reached over and intertwined his fingers with hers. Kiley leant her head back and closed her eyes. "What does he want to see me for?"

Since the night she had been released from her own living hell, she had tried to avoid contact with other shifters. The new Alpha had left her alone, only calling on her to check how she was doing and sometimes asking her to watch his child. But when he needed a babysitter, he'd always called. Not sent guards after her.

Gray lifted her hand to his face and ran his cheek over her knuckles before kissing the back of her hand. "I believe he has a job for you."

Kiley was beginning to get lost in the sensations Gray caused. She shivered as her body instantly began to heat. "A job?" she breathed.

"You heard about the Wolf council wanting to go public," Gray started to explain. "They are sending someone to meet with him and another Alpha. There've been threats."

Kiley blinked in surprise and pulled her hand away so she could concentrate. "Threats?"

"Yes," Gray said with a frown. "Against any Pack members who might agree to the publicity."

"Why does he need me?" Kiley wondered aloud. The Pack had their own investigators.

"Always so suspicious," Gray commented.

Kiley grunted but didn't reply.

Gray's heavy sighed sounded loudly through the vehicle. "It's complicated."

Kiley nodded, even though he wasn't looking at her. Had it only been a year since the new Alpha had come to Clear Water, Colorado? It seemed like so long ago. In a matter of hours, her life had changed. Her Pack leader had been killed and another Alpha now led. He had granted anyone who wanted to stay Pack status and allowed the others to leave. Kiley hadn't wanted to do either,so she was caught somewhere in the middle.

Kiley had the feeling that the new Alpha gave her odd jobs here and there to keep her in his territory without smothering her. No pressure to join the Pack, but letting her know she would be welcome if she chose to. For that reason alone, Kiley vowed to help in any way she could.

As they left the city behind and started towards the secluded woods where the Alpha's home was located, Kiley could felt the tension invade her body. Too many memories haunted her for her to be able to control her fear.

Tyler Adams was one of the best and most honest Alphas in the country. The day he'd walked into the small bedroom she's been imprisoned in and demanded her release was one that would forever stay with her. She owed him more than she would ever be able to pay back. She knew that, but he never made her feel bad about it. He was one of the few people in the world who had earned her respect.

As if he could feel her growing nervousness, Gray started to tell her about the last full moon run and the antics of the cubs who had shifted for the first time. It made her miss being Pack even more, but she held that feeling inside. It wouldn't help anything.

Kiley grinned as Gray went into great detail about one of the boys, who had only got his paws and tail to shift until one of the guards had scared him and he had finally fully shifted in self-defence.

By the time they reached the outside of the stone gates barring the road that led to the Alpha house, she was wiping tears of laughter from her eyes.

A young, handsome guard waved Gray inside as the gates slowly opened.

"Breathe, Kiley," Gray urged quietly.

She took a deep breath and counted to ten. Kiley knew she was safe here. She was almost calm by the time they pulled into the circular drive and parked in front of the house. Several unknown vehicles were there and she took stock of each one. She liked to be prepared in case she needed to make a quick exit. If one of these vehicles followed her, she would know. Several yards from the compound, she saw a new house in the process of being built.

The beautiful brickwork and large glass windows looked welcoming and secure at the same time.

"What's that?" she asked Gray with a nod to the building.

"Tyler's having a new main house built."

"Really?" Kiley asked, shocked. The compound was big and solid. She hated it but thought that was where an Alpha belonged.

"He hates the compound. Says it's like living in a tomb. He wants a happy place to raise the cubs and welcome the Pack," Gray informed her.

"Wow!" Kiley couldn't help the awe in her voice. So much change.

Gray turned in his seat after he cut the engine. As he cupped her check, she leant into his touch. "Maybe I can take you out to dinner after this?" he inquired.

It had been a few months since they'd been together and Kiley was more than ready to reconnect with him. Even if they would never be mates, she still had strong feelings for the man.

She turned her head and kissed his palm. "I'd like that," she agreed.

He smiled once more at her, his eyes warm and inviting as he reached for the door handle on his side. "Well then, let's get this party started so we can get to the good stuff."

Kiley just shook her head, grinning as she followed his lead and climbed from the monster vehicle. She had to jump to get down.

The front door opened before they reached it, and Kiley barely had enough time to brace herself before her arms were full of a small six year old girl.

"Daddy said you were coming!" she squealed as she hugged Kiley's neck tight.

Kiley patted the little cub's back. "Hey sunshine, miss me?"

"Uh huh," Jesse, the Alpha's daughter, said excitedly. "I've been waiting for hours!"

Gray chuckled as he pressed his hand against the small of Kiley's back, urging her forwards. "It didn't take that long."

Jesse rolled her eyes as only a young child could. "Seemed like it to me."

"I tried to tell Gray to hurry," Kiley teased. "But you know cops. They gotta obey all the rules."

Gray growled playfully but the two females ignored him.

"Yeah, he never goes fast. Not like Dominic," Jesse whispered.

Dominic Adams, the Alpha's Beta and brother, stepped out from the shadows at the mention of his name. "Are you telling my secrets?" he asked Jesse, winking at Kiley.

Jesse clapped a hand over her mouth and shook her head.

Everyone laughed at her antics.

"Come now." He held his arms out for Jesse. "Let Kiley see your daddy and then you can hang all over her."

Bright, innocent eyes looked up at her. "Promise?"

Immediately, guilt flooded Kiley. She didn't see Jesse enough. The young girl had attached herself to Kiley on her first visit. There was nothing like the heart-melting feeling of the total love the cub gave.

Jesse had quickly become one of her favourite people in the world.

"I promise," she told Jesse with one last hug before she allowed Dominic to take her.

"They are waiting for the two of you in the study," he said with a more business-like tone than he'd used with Jesse.

Gray nodded and took Kiley's elbow to lead her. Kiley concentrated on remaining calm as they walked down the long hall. Gray knocked on the door, and they waited for the command to enter.

As Gray pushed the door open, Kiley remained behind him. As she stepped into the room, she was suddenly hit with the strongest, most intoxicating scent she'd ever been around.

She gasped as her body responded quickly and she became light-headed.

Gray blocked her view of the room but even without looking, she knew she was in deep trouble.

Her mate was here.

Chapter Two

Austin Winters' head snapped up a moment before the knock sounded on the study door. By the time it opened, he was already on his feet. His mate's scent hit him hard and he took a step forward even before she entered.

He couldn't see her, but the gasp of breath and the overwhelming emotions he felt combined to almost make his knees buckle. His Beta and best friend, Colt, grabbed his arm.

The room was silent as the others recognised the mating scent that saturated the room. The man in front of his mate half-turned and said something too low for him to hear.

Austin didn't like that the man stood between him and his mate. A growl started deep in his throat and there was no way to hold it back. The man looked over his shoulder at him with an expression that surprised Austin.

Instead of fear of the Alpha, his look was one of sympathy. He nodded and stepped to the side. Austin understood immediately. The expression on his mate's face was one of panic.

Austin took a step towards her, dislodging Colt's hand, his only thought to comfort his mate. Her eyes widened and she took a step back. Austin paused, confused.

He heard Tyler sigh before he cleared his throat. It was hard, but he took his eyes off his mate and looked at the other Alpha.

"Austin, you've met Grayson, and this is Kiley Palmer," he introduced.

Austin wasn't sure what was going on. Tyler's eyes were trying to convey something to him but he wasn't picking it up. He wanted to cross the room and grab his mate. His fingers literally itched to touch her. She was his mate, his one, and he didn't know why everyone looked so worried. It was a cause for celebration.

Tyler walked to him and clasped him on the shoulder. "Kiley, this is Austin Winters—a good friend of mine and Alpha of a Pack further south."

"She is very uneasy with being around any shifter, much less powerful ones." Tyler murmured quietly to him. "Your being an Alpha is not good."

Austin frowned and looked back to the woman. She remained frozen just inside the doorway. He breathed in deeply, pulling her scent into him. She was a shifter. More and more shifters were finding mates among humans. He didn't mind, but some of his friends had told him how hard it was to tell a human mate about their...unique abilities. Kiley—his mate's name was Kiley—was a shifter, so that wasn't the problem.

The room was filled with members of both his Pack and Tyler's. While the meeting had already started, the only thing he cared about was getting to his mate. But if she was uneasy around shifters, being in a roomful of them wouldn't be comforting.

Tyler must have thought the same thing, because the order from the other Alpha was given only a moment later. "Gentlemen, if you could please give us a minute. Grayson will take you to get a drink and I'm sure we have some snacks made in the kitchen."

As soon as everyone was on their feet and heading to the door, Kiley glanced back at him. Her intent was clear, and Austin tensed. He would chase her. He met her eyes squarely and tried to convey that to her. If she ran he would follow.

"Kiley…" Tyler called in warning.

Her expression didn't change. She shifted to the balls of her feet.

"Kiley, I would like to speak with you for a minute. I'll allow Tyler to stay with you if you'd like," Austin tried speaking softly.

Confusion and doubt covered her face. She obviously wasn't sure about trusting him. The room had cleared out, and Austin watched as Gray pushed her gently further into the room before closing the door behind him.

Terror began to set in as soon as she was alone with them, Austin noticed. Trying to put her at ease, Austin sat back in the overstuffed chair he'd occupied earlier and gestured to the couch. "Would you like to have a seat?"

She watched him warily as she walked around the room so she wouldn't pass in front of him. Tyler, to his relief, stood behind him, giving him the opportunity to address only her.

She sat. Too far away in his opinion, but at least she did face him.

"I'm sure this comes as much as a shock to you as it does me. But I've waited my entire life to find my mate," Austin started to explain. "It's very nice to meet you, Kiley."

Kiley was biting her bottom lip. "I'm not your mate!" she blurted.

Austin felt his mouth drop open and it was all he could do to stay seated. When he recovered, his voice came out more harshly than he intended. "You most certainly are."

She shook her head. "No! No, I can't be."

Austin leant forward. "There is no doubt and we both know it. *You are my mate.*"

She dropped her head and Austin watched her try to calm herself. After several minutes, she looked up at him. Her eyes were clear and he could see her resolve. He felt proud of her for being able to get her emotions under control. That would be very important as mate to an Alpha.

"You are mistaken," she said boldly.

"One of us is," he practically growled. "Even the members of my Pack recognised you when you came in."

"Pack will form the same opinion as the Alpha. They were just following your lead," she told him with a sad smile.

"Not my Pack. They can think for themselves," he argued. "What kind of Alpha would I be if I didn't let them form their own opinions?"

She sighed.

"You'll get to know them and find out for yourself I guess. The Pack scented you as their female Alpha."

"I am sure you are a wonderful Alpha," she told him. "Unfortunately, at this time I do not wish to join any Pack, even yours."

Austin snorted. That wasn't even an issue. "Oh, you'll be joining my Pack, all right."

She opened her mouth but he cut her off. "It would be impossible to be the mate of the Alpha and not be a member of the Pack. It has never been done," he informed her.

"Then it would be impossible to be your mate," she said quietly.

Austin jumped to his feet. He'd tried to stay calm. Really, he had. But this was his life and he couldn't allow a scared female to throw away what they should have together. Despite his best intentions, his emotions got the better of him. "You would deny me my mate?" he demanded loudly.

She jerked back.

"Answer me," he said as he stood to tower over her. His hands shook so badly he had to stuff them in his pockets. His whole life he had waited for his mate—the one person who would complete him. A mate was the most valued and loved person a shifter could have. His heart breaking, he asked one last time, "Do you deny me as your mate?"

Austin held his breath. She had every right to deny him. Whether she was Pack or not, a female could make the decision not to be with their mate. He'd never met anyone who had denied their mate but he'd heard stories.

God, it was just so frustrating. He would be good to her. If she would just give him a chance, he could prove she would be cherished and loved. He just needed her to agree.

"No," she responded quietly. "I don't deny you."

His breath rushed out. *Oh, thank God!*

"I...just...you can't be my mate."

Austin went from relieved to irritated. "I am," he repeated for what felt like the hundredth time.

"I need to think...I just need time to think," she told him honestly as she met his gaze.

"Time," he repeated. "I can give you time."

Kiley smiled a small smile and her blue eyes sparkled. Austin knew he would never deny her anything.

He tried to convey honesty and caring as he cupped her chin. She gasped but didn't pull away. "I will do anything for you," he whispered. "Just ask." Austin released her and took his seat. "Hopefully you will agree to spend some time getting to know me," he said as he sat back and relaxed. Yes, that would be best. Give her time in her own territory to feel comfortable with him. "There is quite a bit of Pack stuff going on, but I would like to see you later, if that's all right. You will be staying here at the house, won't you?"

Kiley frowned. "I have my own place off Pack land."

Austin shrugged a shoulder. "But I thought..."

Tyler cleared his throat, drawing Austin's attention. "I haven't had a chance to speak with her before this. She doesn't know anything about the call."

"I apologise, Alpha," Austin said formally.

Tyler just grinned. Usually they weren't very formal or worried about Alpha protocol. They'd been friends for too many years. Austin hadn't spent a lot of time in Tyler's territory, though, so he didn't want to assume their relationship would stay the same in front of Tyler's Pack members. An Alpha deserved respect, and Austin wanted the other man to know he had Austin's.

"Thank you, but unnecessary," Tyler told him before speaking directly to Kiley. "Kiley, I asked you to the house because I need a favour."

She nodded. "Gray said you had a job for me."

Austin bit back a growl at the casual way she said Tyler's Enforcer's name. While she was wary of him—her mate—she spoke the other man's name naturally. Austin wondered how close they were.

The wolf inside him started to get agitated, so he took several deep breaths to calm himself while Tyler continued to talk.

"You may have heard that we have meetings set up to discuss the issue of going public. I have a few guests coming to speak with Austin and myself about it. It's been planned for several months."

Austin watched Kiley take in the information. He could practically see the wheels turning in her head. Her eyes were sharp and she nodded, showing she was listening.

"We started getting anonymous calls as soon as the meetings were set. Austin was already planning to come down to be in the meetings with us, and he also started to get threatening phone calls," Tyler told her.

Kiley glanced over at him, and he sent her a reassuring smile.

She nodded and gave her attention back to Tyler.

"I can't *not* have the meetings. It doesn't matter if we choose to go public or not, I cannot back down. It would put the entire Pack in danger," Tyler explained.

Kiley nodded. "Makes sense. What do you need from me?"

"Jesse," Tyler said simply.

"Oh God!" Kiley exclaimed. "The threats aren't against her, are they?"

Tyler frowned. "They're against all of us. I just can't take the chance of something happening to her."

"I'll do anything for Jesse, you know that."

Austin grinned. That boded well for their future together. He wanted cubs, lots and lots of cubs.

"I want you to stay here with her as her guard. You can spend time with her and keep her from getting worried and hopefully out of trouble."

"Yeah," Kiley laughed. "No problem there."

Tyler shook his head with a wide smile. "I know you'll try your best. So will you help? "I'll help," she agreed.

"Wonderful," Austin commented, standing. "And that will give us some time together too." Austin thought of all the possibilities. He had meetings to concentrate on but nothing would keep him from getting to know his mate. And letting her get to know him.

Chapter Three

Kiley lifted Jesse into her arms and carried her aeroplane-style into the kitchen. Thanks to her wolf shifter abilities, she could easily hold the girl above her head without too much strain.

Jesse giggled happily as they stepped through the open doorway.

Kiley stopped short when her gaze fell on the men that occupied the kitchen. She lowered Jesse to her side and wrapped her arm around the girl's shoulders — more for her benefit than Jesse's. Not paying close enough attention to her senses, she hadn't realised the men had taken a break from their meeting.

Austin, Gray, Dominic, and two other men sat around the large oak table. The men had stopped talking and looked over when they'd entered. Kiley shifted from foot to foot, trying to think of something to say.

Right after she'd left Tyler's office earlier so the men could take a phone call, she'd gone up to Jesse's room with her. She'd been able to avoid everyone else in the house. Jesse had kept her occupied and she hadn't had time to dwell too much on her problem.

Now it seemed she had run out of luck. Not only was her new mate in the room with her, but so were a few others. Strangers—she hated strangers.

When she didn't say anything, Gray started to stand. Austin growled, freezing the other man in place. Kiley glanced between the two. She could feel the tension from Austin. It seemed nothing had been settled earlier. She'd tried to convince Austin that he wasn't her mate—she'd tried to protect him—but he wouldn't buy it. Gray looked to be another problem.

Gray looked unsure, while Austin had his teeth clenched. Immediately Kiley knew Austin was aware she and Gray had a relationship and that she needed to calm her mate down before the situation exploded. She might still be uncertain about him, but she didn't want Austin unhappy or Gray hurt.

She swallowed hard and offered a smile to Austin. "Hi," she greeted him.

He seemed to make an effort to relax and nodded. "Hello, ladies," he replied.

Jesse, who was unaware of any tension, escaped from Kiley's hold and ran to her uncle. "Uncle Dom! Uncle Dom!" And just like that all the tension left the room.

"Yes?" Dominic answered the little girl.

"Kiley is going to stay the whole weekend with me!" Jesse exclaimed happily.

Dominic chuckled and lifted Jesse into his lap. "I heard that. What do you girls have planned?"

"Kiley said we could make cookies!" Jesse shared enthusiastically.

All eyes turned to her. Kiley shrugged a shoulder. "It shouldn't be too hard."

Dominic and Gray groaned in unison.

"It's just cookies," Kiley growled in reply.

Dominic grinned at her, not saying anything. Kiley glared back and then looked around the table. "I'm sure I can handle cookies."

"I'll be sure to keep the fire extinguisher handy," Gray quipped.

Austin and the two strangers didn't say anything, but Kiley could tell they were amused too. She huffed out a breath and fisted her hands on her hips. "Oh, ha ha," she muttered.

Austin stood and walked over, swinging his arm around her shoulder. It took everything she had not to pull away. She didn't want to embarrass him. "I'm sure you can do whatever you set your mind to."

The compliment from her mate was unexpected but made her heart swell. She knew the others were just teasing her, but it felt good to have someone on her side for once. She found herself leaning in to Austin's embrace.

So close to her mate, she could feel the contentment and care coming from the man. A sudden surge of emotion hit her. She made him feel that way. Trying to hide her feelings, she cleared her throat.

"Thank you," she whispered for his ears only.

He tightened his arm for just a second then pulled her forwards. "I'd like you to meet some people," he told her.

Kiley let him lead her over to the table where the men sat and Jesse was happily swinging her legs in her uncle's lap.

"Kiley, this is my Beta, Colt," he introduced an attractive blond man. Like the other wolf shifters, he was big but the smile lines around his eyes and broad grin on his face made him a little more approachable.

"Hi," she said awkwardly.

His smile still in place, he bowed his head. "It's a pleasure to finally meet you," he responded.

Kiley knew he wasn't talking about her so much as about his Alpha's mate. Strangely that didn't bother her.

"And this is Tony. He is visiting from the Blue Ridge Pack in Oklahoma," Austin continued.

The other man at the table was just as big as Colt but much more serious. His eyes held so much worry in them that Kiley felt a strong urge to offer him a hug. And she never wanted to do that. It surprised her, so she simply dipped her chin in respect.

If she had to guess, this man was the one who had come to talk about the wolf shifters going public. Kiley wasn't sure of what that would entail, but she'd heard others talk about it for the last few months.

Being Rogue, she didn't have to worry about whether or not her Pack would choose to agree. Or, she *hadn't* been worried about it. But Austin had been right earlier—if she mated with him she would have to join his Pack.

She lifted her face up to her mate's to ask what he planned, but they were interrupted before she could.

"Daddy!" Jesse yelled and was out of Dominic's lap and across the room.

Tyler laughed and bent to scoop her up as she ran to him. "Hey, baby girl."

"Me and Kiley…"

"Kiley and I," Tyler corrected before she could finish her sentence.

Jesse scrunched up her face and sighed heavily. "Kiley and I…" she repeated. "We're gonna make cookies!"

The Alpha's eyes darted to her. "I don't know if I carry that much home insurance."

Kiley's mouth dropped open. *Oh no, he had not just said that!* She threw her arms up in the air. "One time!" she cried. "And it wasn't even my fault!"

"Kiley, you caught a table on fire," Gray reminded her.

She glared over her shoulder at him before looking up at Austin. "It wasn't my fault."

He nodded in agreement.

She sighed and relaxed against him again, thinking about the day they were talking about.

Kiley had avoided going up to the main house as much as she could. But it had been Jesse's birthday, and she couldn't have missed it for any reason. Somehow while she was there, Gray and Dominic had put her in charge of the grill while they went to get Jesse's new bike out of the house.

And that was when all hell had broken loose. The flame had somehow caught on a tablecloth, which had blazed up so quickly that Kiley was still staring at it when it moved to the chairs.

No one had been hurt and the guys had been able to put the fire out quickly, but to this day they still teased her. She didn't mind too much—except it made her feel like family, like Pack. And she wasn't either of those things.

Kiley shivered when Austin's mouth pressed close to her ear. "I have plenty of home insurance," he promised.

It felt so good to have his arm around his mate, Austin could have died and gone to heaven happy. It surprised him a little that Kiley allowed him the privilege, but he wasn't going to complain.

When the teasing had started from the others, he could feel her embarassment, amusement and, surprisingly, sadness. He didn't know what about it made her sad, but he never wanted her to feel that way again.

As soon as they had finished with the meetings scheduled for the day, he planned to spend some alone time with his mate, getting to know her better.

He liked the fact that she seemed to have a strong will. He'd hoped for a mate who would be able to stand up and challenge him when she needed to. He had never been attracted to submissive women. He worried Kiley might be just a bit too stubborn but knew he could handle any conflicts that might come up. He couldn't wait to take her home and see how she would get along with his Pack.

His Pack was so small that they were more like an extended family. While Tyler had over two hundred members, Austin was very happy with his intimate fifty or so. Okay, fifty-three, to be exact.

He wasn't paying much attention to the conversation around him until he heard Kiley say she would head to her apartment to pack a couple of bags.

"One of my men will accompany you," he told her automatically.

She stiffened. Instantly he knew he should have phrased that better.

"It will be safer for you to have an escort," he tried.

She whirled on him, eyebrows raised and hands on her hips. "An escort? For me to drive ten minutes, pack a bag, and drive back. Thirty minutes tops?"

Austin nodded, glad she understood.

"Will I sit in the back like a good little pup while my chauffeur makes any stops I want?" she asked.

Okay, the sarcasm was not lost on him.

"Umm...well," Austin was at a loss for what to say.

"So the little bitty woman needs a strong man to act as her guard?" Kiley continued to taunt.

Austin glanced at Tyler and saw the other man's lips twitch. No help there. He looked over at Gray, hoping that since the other man knew her so well he would maybe convey something to him. But Gray had his head bent to the table. The one time he needed the other man's experience, he didn't get anything. Beside Gray, Tony was avoiding looking at him. Dominic was turned away, with Jesse on his lap staring at them. He darted his gaze to his best friend, but Colt just sat there with his eyes wide and mouth open.

"No, that's not what I meant..."

Kiley cut him off. "Of course it was. Get one thing straight. I may be your mate but that does not mean you get to dictate everything I do. We are either equal partners or we're nothing."

Austin opened his mouth to tell her he wanted them to be equal but Kiley didn't even slow down her rant.

"I don't know what it is about Alpha men who think they can just issue orders and expect them to be followed, but that is so not going to happen," Kiley stated loudly.

Austin shook his head. "I didn't..."

Kiley huffed and quickly walked over to Jesse, picking the girl up in her arms. She headed for the door then turned back once more.

"We'll make cookies later. I believe you gentlemen have a meeting."

Austin just stared at her. He didn't know what to say.

"I'll get my bags, don't you worry about that. Right now Jesse and I are going upstairs to work on a puzzle."

And with that, his mate sashayed out of the kitchen.

Austin continued to stare at the empty doorway for several minutes before he turned to the other men. "What in the hell just happened?" he asked.

The entire room burst out laughing. Austin wasn't amused.

"She did just admit to being your mate," Colt pointed out.

Austin grinned. "She did, didn't she?"

Chapter Four

Kiley couldn't believe it. She'd gone off on her mate! In front of a full room—including another Alpha. God, she was so ashamed. And yet that hadn't stopped her from going on her own to her apartment. Every woman needed to have a limit, and hers was to not blindly follow orders.

She hadn't missed the tail she'd picked up, either. Since leaving Tyler's house, another vehicle had been following at a slower pace. She circled her block a couple of times just to make sure.

It had to be one of Austin's men because Tyler's would already know where she lived.

Giving up on losing her follower, she pulled into the parking garage and parked in her designated spot.

She exited her SUV and waited. It didn't take long for the big black truck to show up. Kiley waved at the driver. The truck pulled in front of her and the passenger window rolled down. She was surprised to see her mate.

"Austin?" she asked, surprised. It wasn't a real question but he nodded anyway. "What are you doing?"

"You know what I'm doing. I'm keeping an eye on my mate," he stated sternly.

Kiley supposed he hadn't got over the encounter in the kitchen either. She blew out a breath and counted to ten—slowly. "Park over there," she told him, waving to the nearest visitors' spot. "You might as well come up."

He pressed his lips together and sat quietly for a moment before rolling the window up and complying.

Kiley waited until he'd got out of the truck and joined her before she led the way up the stairs and into her building. Neither spoke, and Kiley's nerves were frayed. She didn't know how to act with him. Didn't know how to be a good mate. She was at a complete loss for what to say to make everything better. So she said nothing.

Austin followed her to the elevator and she pressed four to be taken to her floor. The ride up was quick but she was still relieved to get out. Being so close to Austin made her feel uneasy. Not in a bad way—she wasn't sure *how* she felt. She wanted him—there was no question about that—but she didn't know how they could possibly get along.

She needed to warn him. She needed to let him know that being with her could be dangerous. He might leave, she knew that, but she was already starting to crave him near her. If he left later, it would only hurt more.

Even though it was the last thing she thought she'd wanted, she found herself already enjoying the thought of him being hers.

Still, it was a good time for her to find out if he could handle being her mate. At least here they would have privacy. If he left…well, she would get over it. His silence was also nerve racking. She walked down the hall and unlocked her door before she stepped aside and let him enter first.

It was on the tip of her tongue to ask if he wanted to check her closet for monsters or not. But that probably wouldn't help the suitation.

Instead, she watched him take in her small but clean and comfortable apartment. The front door opened into the main room. The living room was to the left, containing a black leather couch and chair. On the right was the open full kitchen with an island in the middle. Straight ahead were the bedroom and bathroom doors. Her style was simple but elegant, or so she thought. She was secretly pleased when he whistled low.

"Nice place," he told her.

"Thanks," she waved him forward. "Would you like a drink?"

Austin shook his head and walked over to the full length windows behind the couch. "Pretty view of the mountains."

Kiley took her eyes from her mate and looked at the scene he was enjoying. It was a wonderful view. Tyler had helped her get the place, and she was glad she'd agreed to take a look. She'd jumped at the chance to move in.

It was a far cry from the museum she'd grown up in. Her father had been a stickler for rules and formality — which was one reason she refused to have a formal dining table. She ate standing in the kitchen, on stools at the island, or even occasionally at the coffee table.

Neither spoke for several minutes. Finally, Kiley couldn't take it any longer. "Will you sit down? We need to talk."

Austin turned and, with a look of apprehension, nodded and sat on the couch. Kiley took the chair across from him and curled her feet under her.

"First, I want to say I'm sorry about what I said in the kitchen," she told him sincerely. "You didn't deserve to be treated like that, especially not in front of the others. I'm sorry."

He looked surprised but slowly nodded.

"I have a tendency to go off sometimes and say things without thinking them through. I overreacted," she added.

"Kiley...I..." Austin started. He leant forward, resting his elbows on his knees, and dropped his head.

She bit her lip, scared that because of her outburst he wouldn't want to mate with her after all.

"We have to figure this out," he said softly. "I won't always say the right thing. I'm going to make mistakes. But if you're my mate, you need to talk to me about these things. You can't walk out every time I say something you don't like."

"I know," she admitted.

"I understand you have a problem with my position. I don't know why, but I can see it bothers you," he continued. Kiley opened her mouth but he held up a hand to stop her. "Just listen for a moment, please."

"Okay." She could let him get out whatever he needed to say. She owed her mate that chance.

"I'm an Alpha. Yes it was by choice, but I was born to do it. My Pack is small compared to most others. We're a family. We have disagreements but that doesn't mean we don't love each other," he told her.

35

"We'll have disagreements, Kiley. But we need to take care of them in private."

She dropped her head. She knew that, really she did. "Yes."

"I want this to work. I promise to try my hardest to give you what you need but you have to talk to me. You're my family now."

She had to blink back the tears that were forming. The last six hours had been the most emotional time for her. She hadn't been such a mess since she'd left the Pack. And she still needed to tell him about that.

"You know I'm Rogue?" she asked.

"Tyler told me that much," he responded gently.

"I left the Pack after Tyler took over. I didn't have the choice to do it before. My father had demanded I marry the son of the Alpha," she explained. "I couldn't stand the man. He was loud and abusive and made my skin crawl."

"Your father didn't know?" he asked.

"Oh, he knew," she assured him. "He just didn't care."

"But why would he…"

Kiley shook her head. "I didn't grow up with a father like Jesse's. Instead of letting me go like I begged, he gave me over to the Alpha when I turned eighteen."

"Fuck."

Kiley sighed. "It wasn't good. I won't go into detail now but it was bad for a really long time. I had no choice in anything I did. I was to follow orders, and that was that."

"I'm sorry." He scooted off the couch and knelt in front of her.

"What are you sorry for?" she asked, confused.

"It upsets you to talk about this."

"It does," she confirmed. "I don't have great memories from my childhood, but as an adult it's even worse. For the first time in my life I'm on my own. I feel like I finally have control of my life," she explained.

"And here I come along. Your mate. An Alpha."

"Fate. A mate is given to us by fate," Kiley clarified.

"So again you have no choice. Is that why you don't want me as a mate?" Austin asked. His voice cracked at the end and the sound pulled at Kiley's heart.

She got up and knelt before him. "No. I still have a choice. I could deny you. You asked me if I did. You gave me a choice. Now I will give you one."

Austin opened his mouth but she put her fingers up to his lips. "Just listen now." She waited until he nodded. "I was told I would never have my mate. At first, I used the excuse of a mate to try to get out of being with Simon. The Alpha, Simon, even my father assured me I had no mate. And if one came looking, he would die before he ever found me."

"What the…" Austin barked out.

Kiley shook her head. "I can't help feeling if I say…if I admit out loud that you are my mate that you will die. They'll find a way to take you from me."

Kiley squealed in surprise when Austin grabbed her and planted her in his lap. "No, baby. You're mine. Nothing is going to happen. I promise."

"Logically I know that. I know the Alpha can't hurt me anymore. Tyler killed him when he fought for the Pack. I even saw the body. I know that, but still…"

"It scares you," Austin finished.

"Yes," she admitted softly.

"It's okay to be afraid. But you can't let that fear rule your life," Austin said, with thick emotion in his voice.

"You have to be sure before you mate with me, Austin," she pleaded. "I can't let you in and then lose you."

"You won't," he promised.

Kiley took a deep breath before she confessed her biggest concern. "I don't know how to be a mate. I don't know if I'll be good at it."

"Oh baby," he said grasping her hands in his. "I know you'll be a great mate."

"How?" she questioned. If she didn't know, how could he? But he sounded so certain.

"Because you're here with me now, sharing your fears. The way you are with Jesse. The goodness I see when I look in your eyes. I couldn't have asked for a better mate."

Kiley laughed uneasily. "You may be building yourself up for a big fall. You don't even know me."

"No, no I'm not. And I do know you. I know what I see when I look in your eyes. I am connected with you even though we just met," he told her before he kissed her.

The kiss was soft, just a meeting of lips. Kiley relaxed into the first intimate touch from her mate. Austin ran his tongue over her bottom lip before he nibbled the soft flesh. She opened with a gasp and he slid his tongue inside.

Her whole body came alive instantly. His taste, spicy and manly, burst in her mouth and she moaned as she wrapped her arms around his neck. She could smell his arousal and it made her body ache with need.

Her panties were catching the liquid that escaped from her sex and she shifted in his arms, trying to relieve the pressure.

He broke the kiss and rested his forehead against hers. "God, Kiley." He didn't need to say any more. She knew exactly what he meant.

"Yes Austin, kiss me again, claim me as yours," she urged, knowing it was now or never.

He growled and slammed his mouth back down on hers. This time the heat came quickly. Her head swam with the passion she felt for him until she found herself straddling his lap, humping him.

"Hot...need," she panted out against his lips. The mating instict was strong and she didn't want to fight it. She was so tired of fighting. In Austin's arms, the arms of her mate, she could let go.

"Yeah," he agreed, his voice low and husky. He stood, picking her up with him. She wrapped her legs around his waist. "Bedroom?"

"First door," she told him before sealing her mouth on his neck. She sucked and nibbled the muscled skin, running her tongue over him and tasting her mate.

His jugular pulsed as she paid special attention to that spot. That was where she would give him the claiming bite. She tested her spot, biting down gently but not breaking the skin. He stumbled before he tightened his arms around her.

"Don't stop," he ordered, his breath coming in short bursts.

Kiley was more than happy to listen to that demand. He made it to the bedroom door and threw it open while she gave him little love bites up and down his neck.

"Good, your mouth is so good," he told her.

"Mmm hum," she murmured.

They didn't turn on any lights. Austin just clumsily made his way to the bed. He fell down on it with her underneath him.

Kiley pulled his shirt over his head. She ran her hands over his strong, wide shoulders. "I've wanted to touch your bare skin since the first moment I saw you."

Austin looked up from where he was pulling off her boots and socks. "I know...I know..."

They undressed each other quickly but still took the time to explore each new piece of flesh that was revealed.

By the time he covered her body with his once again, Kiley was trembling. She wrapped her legs high up on his back, feeling his hard, leaking cock at her pussy.

"Please, I need to feel you inside me," she told him breathlessly. Her entire body was flushed and she knew once he was inside her it wouldn't take long.

He groaned long and loud, filling the quiet room with the sound. He pushed in slowly, but Kiley didn't want him to be gentle. She dropped her feet onto the mattress and bucked her hips, taking him in deep.

They moaned in unison.

"Fuck!" he exclaimed. "So tight. Hot and tight."

Kiley dug her fingernails into his shoulders. "Move, hurry."

He pulled out before plunging back in.

"Yes! Yes!" she cried out. He filled her completely. More than just her body. With him thrusting in and out, she felt their souls connect. Her teeth lengthened, the need to claim Austin strong.

"God...Oh God..." he chanted. His hips pistoned faster and faster.

Kiley was beyond words. Her head thrashed back and forth on the pillow and she arched to meet every stroke. Her body shook, and like an explosion, she came apart.

Dimly she could hear herself scream, his hoarse cry above her, before she sank her canines into his neck. She didn't even feel his bite to her shoulder as they claimed each other.

Chapter Five

Austin nuzzled Kiley's neck as he carried her bags to her vehicle. "Drive back with me," he asked softly. He didn't want her to think he was demanding it, he just wanted her close. The mating bond was strong now and he didn't want her out of arm's reach.

What he had experienced with her had been wonderful. They'd only had a short time alone together but it had been enough for now. She was his. His claim on her had been made and they were tied together forever.

She stopped walking but didn't pull away. "I can't," she whispered. "Please understand, Austin. I can't be without a way to leave. I'm not saying I will leave again but I have to have a way."

He cupped her cheek. Their eyes locked and Austin could see the emotions there, see how important this one thing was to her. "Okay, no problem."

Her relief was so noticeable she actually shook with it. Austin could understand some of how she felt after learning more about her old Pack, but he wanted...no *needed* her to trust him. He knew trust would take time, but the wolf inside him was restless.

The animal part of him didn't want to give her time. He wanted to claim, to conquer, and to have Kiley admit she was his.

In his heart he knew he would have to fight that part of him. His mate was special. He wouldn't do anything to cause her unnecessary worry or heartache.

He still had questions, though. When they had more time together he would ask but for now he knew enough. Home. When he took her home, they could talk and learn each other's pasts. Now was for securing their future.

"Thank you," she told him with a smile and pushed up against him.

Austin bent his head, unable to resist his mate's luscious lips, and sealed his mouth over hers. Kiley responded quickly, wrapping her arms around his neck and opening to him.

He held back a groan as he pulled her body flush with his. It felt so wonderful to hold her. The sudden squeal of tires broke the moment and he pulled away in time to see a big, dark SUV racing towards them.

Instincts kicked in. He threw her bags between two cars, pushed her after them, and jumped to cover her body with his.

Metal hit metal as the SUV hit one of the parked cars. Kiley screamed and his wolf howled inside at her fear. Austin leapt to his feet as the SUV reversed. He couldn't see inside the dark interior but he could smell shifter. He grabbed hold of Kiley's arms and yanked her up.

"Go around the front and get in your car!" he ordered.

Without hesitation she scrambled to comply. She grabbed the bags at her feet and darted in front of the car that had shielded them. Austin stepped back out into the parking lot just as the SUV lurched forwards, as if taunting him.

Austin smiled grimly. He was a pretty easygoing guy but threaten his mate, and he felt like ripping someone's balls off and feeding them to them. He narrowed his eyes and waited. The vehicle was only about fifteen yards from him. Whoever was inside would clearly see his challenge.

As fast as the attack had started, it was done. The SUV sped backwards and was out of sight in seconds. His first instinct was to follow but he needed to check on his mate.

He hurried over to her vehicle. Kiley was scrunched down in the driver's seat, wide eyed, hair dishevelled. He knocked on the window and she jumped.

He offered her a smile, hoping to convey that everything was all right. She fumbled for the lock and opened the door, then launched herself into his arms.

Austin held his trembling mate, whispering sweet nothings in her ear. When she had stopped shaking, he pulled back enough to look at her face.

Tears had streaked down her dirty face but she had never looked better to him. Just the fact that she'd allowed him to comfort her calmed both him and his wolf.

"They tried to kill you already," she whispered so quietly he barely heard.

Austin knew what she was talking about. She thought the attack was because of their mating. "Remember the threats, honey? That's more likely what this was about," he murmured against her cheek as she buried her face in his chest.

She continued to hold onto him, so he eased forwards until she was back in the front seat. He kept one arm around her as he dug in his pocket for his phone.

He punched the first speed dial with his thumb. As soon as Colt answered, he started to bark out orders.

"Get to Kiley's apartment ASAP! Make sure you bring plenty of help. Leave Tyler at the house and make sure Jesse is guarded."

Colt's calm voice assured him he was already on his way and everything would be handled. He didn't ask any questions and Austin was glad. He didn't know if he could explain what had happened and how close his mate had come to being hurt without breaking down.

He needed to get himself together before the others got there. He still had the scent of the shifter who had come after them.

When he found him there would be no mercy for him.

He hadn't been able to see behind the blackened window but his nose had told him all he needed to know. The scent of the one who would now become the prey.

Kiley watched from the front of her SUV while Austin ordered his men around, making sure they got everything they needed from the scene.

He'd been pissed when Tyler had shown up with Colt and Dominic. Kiley could see it in the way he glared at the other Alpha while he watched his men. She would have been amused by the obvious protectiveness of her mate if she wasn't so shaken up.

Even when they'd asked her to guard Jesse she hadn't taken the threat seriously. Who was going to attack two Alphas surrounded by Pack? Kiley'd thought she was just a glorified baby sitter while they held the meetings. That is, if she was to believe the attack was because of the meetings and not her.

She wasn't sure. Which meant she had to be that much more concerned for her mate.

But just in case, she had to change her entire way of thinking. She wouldn't let Jesse get hurt. No, there was no way that little girl would be put in any dangerous situation.

Austin walked over to her and she had to look away since her emotions were so close to the surface. She was still deeply shaken from the whole encounter. Especially from her unexpected reaction to it.

She had been so scared for her mate. He'd put himself in danger to protect her. No one had ever done that for her. It had brought up too many feelings for her to easily be able to separate and process. Feelings she had spent a long time trying to bury.

Austin cupped her cheek and lifted her face before placing a soft kiss on her lips. The sweet gesture was too much and she had to pull away and drop her chin to hide the tears that wanted to fall.

"Shh, it's okay," he murmured, pulling her back into his embrace.

She nodded but didn't trust her voice not to crack if she tried to speak.

"Gray and Tony are on their way. They were across town when we called. As soon as they get here, we'll head back to Tyler's."

Kiley started to relax against him as he gently rubbed circles on the small of her back. "Okay," she managed to whisper.

She allowed him to hold her until Tyler walked over. Then her instinct to show no weakness in front of others kicked in and she pulled away.

Austin let go of her with a heavy sigh. She knew it bothered him but there was nothing she could do about it right then. She would work on it, she promised herself. She was mated to the man and he deserved to have a mate that could handle his affection.

"How are you doing, kid?" Tyler asked.

Kiley rolled her eyes but laughed, which was no doubt the reaction he was trying for. He gave everyone stupid little nicknames. The first time he'd called her kid, she had reminded him he was only about three years older than she was.

He'd responded that it didn't matter because when she was with Jesse, it was like she was a kid herself again.

She'd thought long and hard about that and had eventually agreed. When she was with Jesse it did feel like she was ten, fifteen years younger, getting to do all the things she had never done as a child.

She enjoyed playing games, swimming, and spending time with the little cub. It had even made her think about having her own kids one day. She had been almost certain she wouldn't, but now the possibility was there. She wondered if Austin wanted children.

She hadn't realised she'd gone off on her own thoughts until Austin pressed harder on her back and she looked up to see matching looks of concern on his and Tyler's faces.

"Sorry," she mumbled. "I'm fine. Really."

Tyler nodded while Austin just stared at her. Her mate wasn't buying it.

"I promise, Austin. I was just thinking…" She let her sentence trail off, not wanting to share exactly what she was thinking. Not just then.

"You'd tell me…" he asked, dropping his voice low so only she could hear. "You'd tell me if you weren't okay?"

"Yes," she assured him.

He took a deep breath and she watched the play of his muscles over his stomach. A stomach she wanted to spend hours licking and tasting.

She wanted to have him all around her. Surrounding her, filling her, consuming her. She felt flushed, hot, and needy. She could smell her mate—rich, sweet, and woodsy.

Austin chuckled and she gasped, caught once again lost in her own thoughts. Except this time she'd been busted fantasising about Austin.

But when he turned his body into her, discreetly rubbing his erection against her, she knew she wasn't the only one longing to reconnect as they had earlier.

Chapter Six

Austin paced the bedroom he'd been given, thinking about everything that had happened in the last twenty-four hours.

He'd found his mate. He was thirty-six years old and was just starting to think that he wouldn't be one of the lucky ones. But then, when he'd least expected it, Kiley had walked into his life.

Then, right after he'd claimed her, someone had tried to run them down.

And, of course, that same night someone had tried to kill Tony and Gray.

He couldn't believe it. He'd come to his friend's territory to sit in on some meetings and that was all. He had already pretty much made up his mind that his Pack would not be going public, while Tyler was still undecided.

His visit had been to support his old friend and learn as much as he could about what would be coming in the future. Tony had been working with several government officials who had accidentally found out about the shifter world.

Now, he had a mate, there was a real threat against anyone who was meeting with Tony, and he wasn't even on his own turf to take care of matters the way he would prefer. He wanted to hunt down the shifter who had dared to place his mate in danger and kill them. Even if they had been after him, they'd still placed his mate in jeopardy.

When he'd reached Tyler's, he was ready to gather up his men and go out looking, but no one else had agreed with him. Even Colt, the traitor, had told him he needed to calm down so they could plan their next move.

Luckily Gray and Tony would both recover. Gray's wounds had been superficial—a few cuts and bruises, and a bullet had grazed his arm. Tony hadn't been so lucky. He'd been shot in the leg and chest. Gray had managed to stop the bleeding and they'd called the Pack doctor to the house to look over the man.

Doc Jensen had removed the bullet and bandaged Tony up. Already Tony's brother and some members of his Pack were on the way. So they'd decided to wait until morning when Cain, Tony's brother, would arrive.

That was why Austin was pacing his room. But that didn't explain why he was *alone* in his room.

After they'd got back to Tyler's Kiley had wanted to check on Jesse. Austin had watched her head up the stairs before he joined everyone else in the study. He'd checked on Kiley about an hour later. She was still sitting next to Jesse's bed, looking exhausted. He'd coaxed her into getting up and taking a shower. Then he'd asked her if she would stay in his room but she had shaken her head, saying she needed to stay close to Jesse. The room she'd been given had an adjoining bathroom so she could leave the doors open to listen for the young cub.

It hurt, the fact that she didn't need to be with him as much as he needed her right then. He could understand and respect her concern for the girl, but he felt like he was going out of his mind. He'd thought briefly about going for a run as his wolf but didn't want to chance being away from the house for any amount of time.

So he had time to stew. The attack on Gray and Tony had come less than an hour from the one on him and Kiley, which meant they were dealing with a group of people. A group that was keeping close tabs on them, since while he'd been with his mate at her apartment, Gray had taken Tony to a bar to relax.

Tyler had asked his members to get into Pack territory and stay there for their own safety. Austin agreed with him and would have made the same decision in his place. The compound could be protected more easily. He'd made a call home and warned his own Pack to be on the lookout for anything strange.

He needed to get back and see to them himself but he couldn't leave Kiley. And Kiley wasn't ready to go yet. At the moment, being close to her was all he could do. While she was in her room and he in his, he could at least listen out for trouble. He doubted he would sleep much.

Even if Kiley wasn't with him he knew she was safe inside, so that gave him some reassurance.

Resigning himself to a night alone, he stripped off his clothes before climbing into bed. The cool sheets felt good against his skin. He turned off the lamp and settled against his pillows. He was still painfully hard from thinking about his mate and he lazily stroked himself.

He was just getting into it, lifting his hips and tightening his grip, when there was a soft knock on his door. He could sense his mate in the hallway and it almost sent him over the edge. He held back, barely.

Austin started to lift himself from the bed when his door opened.

"Austin?" Kiley asked in a quiet voice.

He was thrilled. His mate coming to him. It didn't matter what she wanted or needed. If she only wanted to talk, that would be fine with him. Oh, he would like to do a whole lot more, but he would take anything he could get with her right now.

"Come in, Kiley," he encouraged.

She stepped into the room and closed the door behind her. He had no problem seeing her in the dark. She stood next to the door dressed in pyjama bottoms and a tank top, hair still wet from her shower, wringing her hands together.

He reached over to turn the lamp on.

"No," she said quickly.

He froze with his hand still in the air.

"Can I…you said…"

Austin waited, trying to give her time to get out what she wanted to say. He hoped she wanted to spend the night in his bed after all.

She cleared her throat. "Tyler came and got Jesse. Said he wanted to put her in his bed so he could sleep. You know, having her close and all, so he'll sleep better."

Austin knew exactly. That's why he wanted Kiley.

"So I thought, since Jesse's with him, I could come in here. That is, if you still want me to."

Austin pressed his lips together to stop his wide grin from showing. Instead he lifted the edge of the sheet and invited her to join him.

She didn't waste any time climbing into bed with him and cuddling into his arms. Her head resting under his chin, he held her tight against his body.

He closed his eyes, content to have her in his bed. "Thank you for coming to me," he whispered. He would never be able to tell her how much it meant to him that she had wanted to be with him. Not just because of the mating bond, but because he was finally beginning to understand a little about her.

She put her own needs aside for what she thought she should do. She had vowed to protect Jesse and she would. Even when she really wanted to be with him.

Her soft lips brushed against his collarbone. "I didn't want to sleep alone," she confessed softly.

"You never have to again unless you want to," he responded. And it was the truth. He didn't plan to sleep in another bed without Kiley, ever.

She sighed and her body slowly went soft against him. He laid there for a long time just listening to her soft, steady breathing, happy despite everything else that was going on.

Kiley woke up alone in the big bed. And that was not something she was happy about or wanted. She frowned. She was used to sleeping and waking alone, but that was one of the many changes in her life since she'd met Austin.

She would have blamed it on the mating, but deep down she knew that it was because of Austin. Already she cared for him. He was the guy she could grow to love. And wasn't that a scary thought!

She shook her head as she climbed out of the bed and made her way to her own room. She dressed quickly and peeked into Jesse's room. The little girl wasn't there.

Standing in the hall, she used her senses to pick up where the two people she wanted were. They were both in the kitchen. She could smell eggs, bacon, sausage, ham, and coffee. She could hear low voices speaking but couldn't make out what they were saying.

Knowing she would find not only Jesse but her mate as well, she headed for the kitchen. Once at the door, she heard a soft bark. Tyler didn't have a dog.

She entered slowly. The kitchen was full. Gray was standing at the stove managing three large skillets. Jesse was on the floor with a man Kiley didn't know while a brown puppy sat in her lap licking her chin. Both Jesse and the man were laughing. Austin, Tyler, Colt, and an older man sat at the kitchen table.

"Kiley!" Jesse exclaimed. "Look what Cain brought me!"

Kiley looked over at the puppy Jesse held up. It was cute. A small furball with huge paws and big, floppy ears.

"She's a Lab. I'm gonna call her Daisy," Jesse told her.

Kiley knelt in front of the girl and her new puppy. Daisy wiggled around until Jesse released her. The puppy walked clumsily over to Kiley before jumping up and down trying to get in her lap. Kiley picked the little thing up and was surprised by her weight.

"Wow, what a big girl," she said playfully.

The man laughed. "That's just the beginning. She should get to be about seventy pounds."

Kiley's mouth dropped open. "Seventy?"

The man nodded with a wide grin on his face.

"Oh my!" But the puppy was adorable. Kiley cuddled it up to her face. "Hello, Daisy."

"She's my very own dog!" Jesse commented.

Kiley looked over at the table to see Tyler's reaction to that bit of news. The Alpha's attention was taken up by the stranger at the table but Austin caught her eye and winked. Happiness bubbled up inside her. Just seeing him and being in the room with him made her body come alive and her heart swell.

She smiled back at him and looked at Jesse. "This is a very good dog. It's going to take lots of hard work to take care of her, but I know you can do it."

The little girl beamed back.

Kiley was thrilled to see her happy. Peeking up from under her lashes, she looked at the other man on the floor. She could smell the man's mate on him and relaxed just a little.

"I'm Tony's brother, Cain," he told her with a dip of his head when he saw her looking at him.

"Kiley," she responded. She was glad he didn't try to take her hand or touch her.

"I know. Austin hasn't been able to take his eyes off you since you walked in. My father asked him three times if he was okay," Cain said laughing.

Kiley felt herself blush. She could feel Austin's eyes on her.

"It's good to see him happy. Congratulations," he said sincerely.

"Thank you," she murmured in response.

She placed the puppy back in Jesse's arms and stood. Austin was saying something to Colt but held his hand out to her. She carefully made her way to his side and took his outstretched hand. Austin pulled and she ended up on his lap.

She heard Tyler chuckle beside her. She looked over at the Alpha and raised an eyebrow. He quickly looked away but a grin was planted firmly on his face.

The older man looked up and smiled. "You must be Kiley. It is a pleasure to meet Austin's mate."

Kiley blinked at him for several seconds. No one had actually called her his mate out loud before except Austin. She could tell the man was an Alpha but she didn't get an uneasy feeling around him. She actually felt the same ease as she did with Tyler.

"Thank you, sir," she replied respectfully.

He nodded. "Good mate, Austin," he said.

Austin slipped an arm around her stomach. "Thank you and I agree." Then he introduced the strangers. "This is Lamont, Tony's father. The man on the floor with Jesse is Cain."

She'd already met Cain, so she nodded. "I'm sorry Tony was hurt. I hope he gets better soon."

Lamont smiled and his face transformed, making him look twenty years younger. "He is already feeling much better. We'll be taking him home tomorrow, where he can recover fully."

Kiley was relieved to hear Tony was doing well. She didn't know the man well but he seemed decent. Kind of serious, but honest.

Tyler asked Lamont something but Kiley was distracted by Austin's fingers teasing over her body.

She stiffened and held in a moan when he slipped one hand down the front of her pants. She leant back against him, wiggling her hips and rubbing her butt against his erection in payback.

Austin pushed her off his lap and stood. "If you'll excuse us for a few minutes."

No one said anything as Austin practically dragged her from the room. Austin pulled her behind him and back up to the room.

Once inside the room, he slammed the door closed and pushed her back against it. "Need to taste you," he said huskily.

Austin flattened his body against Kiley's, capturing her moan inside his mouth. He was hard under his jeans and he rubbed against her softer body, adding just enough friction. It felt wonderful.

He kissed her breathless before moving his mouth down her neck and nibbling her sensitive flesh. She trembled under him as he ran his hands up her hips and under her shirt.

She arched her back, pressing closer as he cupped her breasts.

"Want you," she said softly.

"Yes," he yanked her shirt over her head and quickly unlatched her bra, letting the garment fall to the floor as he took one pert nipple into his mouth. He teased the tip with his tongue before sealing his lips over the little nub and sucking.

She bucked against him. "Austin!" She cried his name, clawing at his back.

He didn't answer, just continued to taste her. He ran his tongue down her stomach, dropping to his knees and pulling at the cotton pants she wore. They slid down her legs, catching and taking her panties along.

When she was completely nude in front of him, he pushed her hips against the door and held her there while he lowered his mouth and swiped at her folds with his tongue.

"Austin!" she called out again.

"Mine," he stated hungrily and continued. He played with her, running his tongue up and down her folds, sucking on her clit until she was lifting her hips, trying to get more. She spread her legs wider, and he helped by placing one leg over his shoulder.

He took his time, drawing small animalistic sounds from her. He added a finger alongside his tongue, opening her cunt and lavishing her sex.

"Please...more...more," she panted.

He added a second digit, thrusting his fingers in faster, then covered her clit, nibbling softly.

She screamed as her orgasm ripped through her body. Her hands held his head in place as she ground herself against his mouth.

Kiley fell back against the wall and Austin pulled her down, urging her to lie on her back. With the fingers of one hand still buried inside her pussy, he unsnapped the button of his jeans, releasing his already leaking, straining erection.

He'd only got his jeans over his hips and to his knees before he replaced his fingers with his cock. He plunged inside, holding her legs open wide to the invasion.

He rode her hard and Kiley loved it.

"Yes! Yes!" she urged.

He slammed inside her over and over, each thrust just a little faster and harder. There was no rhythm, just an intense mating between the two of them. Her nails dug into his shoulders, and she lifted her hips to accept each stroke, chanting his name.

She threw her head back and yelled as she came once again, tightening around him and pulling him over the edge with her. He snapped his hips forward, releasing his seed and claiming her once again.

When she could think again, she smiled as she looked into the happily sated eyes of her mate. With him still buried deep in her body, she knew he owned every bit of her. And more than that—she would willingly give it to him.

Chapter Seven

Jesse threw the tennis ball, laughing as the puppy, Daisy, scrambled after it. Kiley watched from her seat on the grass only a few feet away. Jesse threw the ball a dozen or so more times before she ran over and fell into Kiley's lap. Laughing, Kiley caught her. Daisy barrelled in after the little girl.

"I love my puppy!" Jesse exclaimed.

"She is a very good puppy," Kiley agreed.

Daisy nipped at the bottom of Jesse's pants then let go before doing it again, barking the entire time. Jesse giggled and tried to catch her but each time the dog backed away and barked again.

"Silly Daisy," Jesse told her new pup. She said it so seriously that Kiley couldn't hold back her grin. Jesse was such a sweet girl. The love she had for her new pet was obvious.

"Do you think Daisy can swim?" Jesse asked a minute later when Daisy had finally settled down on the grass next to them.

"Well, some dogs like water. I think I heard Labs especially do," Kiley told her. "Do you want to go in and put your swim suit on? We could find out."

"Really?" Jesse jumped up. "That would be so cool."

Jesse was hopping around on the spot, causing Daisy to bark and bounce around too. Kiley shook her head in amusement. "Okay, swimming it is."

They headed back towards the house. They were still several feet away when Daisy growled, stopping in place.

"Daisy?" Jesse asked and reached for the door.

Kiley caught her hand. "Hold on, honey."

When she turned to pick up the puppy, Daisy took off before she could reach for her.

"Daisy! Daisy!" Jesse called after her in a panic.

"It's okay, sweetheart, she won't go far," Kiley tried to calm the screaming girl.

"But she doesn't know her way home. What if she goes too far and gets lost?" Jesse asked, looking up at her with tears in her eyes.

Well damn, she couldn't let Daisy get lost. Kiley waved at one of the guards on the back porch. He walked over but kept his eyes focussed and scanning the area.

Todd was one of the younger guards and she knew he was related to Tyler in some way. It might have been by marriage—Kiley wasn't one hundred percent sure. But she did know that he wouldn't let anything happen to Jesse.

She could still hear Daisy barking and she needed to catch the dog before she got too far.

When Todd reached them, she smiled. "Would you take Jesse up to her room? Daisy got away from us and I need to go after her," Kiley explained.

"Of course I can take Jesse, but what about you?" he asked with concern.

"I want to go with you," Jesse said loudly right afterwards.

"I will be right back, Jesse. I'm sure your daddy wouldn't want you hiking through the woods right now. But you can see pretty far from your bedroom window. So why don't you watch for me from there? That way you can keep an eye out and see when I bring Daisy back," she suggested.

Jesse thought about it for several moments before shrugging a shoulder and finally agreeing. "Fine."

Kiley bent down and kissed her cheek. "Thank you. You be good now."

She was about to turn and head off when Todd spoke again. "Ms. Kiley, I really don't think that Alpha Austin would like you going by yourself either."

Kiley looked up at him in shock. Ms. Kiley? Oh hell, he must have heard that she had mated to Austin. So of course he would think she needed protection too, along with Jesse. She tried to hold in her growl but still her words came out sharper than she meant. "I'm a big girl. I'm sure Austin won't mind me going after a dog."

With that, she turned on her heel and set off in the direction Daisy had run. It wasn't difficult to follow the scent trail. The dog hadn't been in this part of the territory before, so her scent was easy to pick up without having to distinguish old from new.

She could also still hear Daisy, which was good because there was no way she was going back to the house without the dog. She glanced over her shoulder and could see Jesse at her bedroom window, waving. She waved back before returning to her mission.

She kept going north, and after a while Daisy's bark was getting closer. She wasn't too far from the house when she cut off the path and found the puppy. Daisy danced around, and Kiley growled at the little thing. "Stupid dog," she mumbled, scooping the pet up.

That's when she saw them. Several sets of footprints next to four pawprints. Kiley bent down to get a better look, making sure she had a good hold on the puppy.

The footprints were pretty fresh. She closed her eyes and concentrated on the area that surrounded her. It didn't seem likely that Tyler would have any guards out this far.

No, this was someone who had been watching the house. The imprints were deep, which made her think they had watched the house for a long time, too.

She shivered as unease travelled down her spine.

She held Daisy more tightly against her chest as she stood and slowly turned in a circle. She could feel no danger around her but still a small part of her started to panic. While she could still see the house, there was no way that she would be seen in the thick brush.

There was the lingering scent of a shifter—not one that she knew. And she had no idea when the stranger would return.

Kiley jumped when a rustle of leaves came behind her. She darted a look around. She still didn't see or sense anyone but she had had enough.

Without looking back, she took off as fast as she could towards the house. She cradled Daisy as best she could so the little dog wouldn't be jostled around too much.

She slipped down the path, scraping her leg on a rock, but it didn't slow her down. The panic remained but it was also accompanied by an urgency to get to safety. The end of the path was coming up. She jumped over a fallen tree branch and stumbled a little when she landed wrong. It didn't even hurt with the adrenaline pumping through her body. The back door opened as she hit the tree line into the yard. Austin came running at her just as fast as she was going. She launched herself the last several feet.

He caught her but her momentum knocked them both over. His arms went around her and hers were still around Daisy as she shook. "Someone is watching the house," she panted and dropped her forehead onto his chest.

Austin watched Tyler as he accepted a handshake from Lamont and then Cain. It seemed he would go public with them. He was the sixth Pack to agree. They turned to him and Lamont held his hand out.

Austin felt a little guilty but he had to do what was best for his Pack. "I'm sorry, Alpha, but…"

Lamont squeezed his hand. "There is no need to apologise. I respect your decision. This move isn't for everyone. We understand that."

Austin relaxed just a little. "Thank you, Alpha."

Lamont dipped his head. "You are an extremely good Alpha. With your mate by your side, I have no doubt that your Pack will flourish in the next few years."

Lamont released his hand and Austin couldn't hide his grin. "I believe so."

Cain, who was never one for formality, didn't shake his hand. They'd been friends for too long, both once Betas of their Packs, until Austin had taken over his and become Alpha. Cain wrapped his big arms around Austin's waist and lifted him off his feet in a strong bear hug.

"So happy for you, man," Cain said quietly.

Austin pounded on the other man's back until he was released. He knew Cain had found true happiness with his mate, Emily. Austin had yet to meet the special woman but he hoped to do so soon.

"I look forward to being as happy as you," Austin told his friend.

Cain smirked and opened his mouth to respond, when a sharp pain in Austin's chest had his breath catching. He placed a hand over his heart as his vision swam. His bond screamed at him that he needed to get to Kiley.

Without a thought for anyone else, Austin raced from the room. He heard Lamont say something about a mate but he was already in the hallway. He sped to the back door, his wolf telling him his mate was that way.

Austin scanned with all his senses for any sign of danger but he couldn't find any. Yet he could feel Kiley's fear. It was almost as if his heart beat in time with hers. He passed a couple of guards but didn't slow down. He could hear the others behind him and that made him feel a little calmer, but until he could see his mate, nothing would be okay.

She was getting closer, running to him. He thanked all the gods in heaven that he had a strong bond with Kiley, that they were true mates. He was so connected to her that when he opened the door and flew out of the house, he could feel her relief at seeing him.

He still ran at full speed, until she jumped into the air and he had to stop to catch her. He wrapped his arms around her as they fell to the ground. His back hit the ground but he cradled her and the dog she carried. His breath whooshed out of him as she panted, "Someone is watching the house."

He didn't hesitate but rolled her over onto her back and covered her body with his. The puppy she held wiggled around but there was no way he was letting his mate up until he knew she was safe.

He lifted his head as Gray, Colt, and Cain all took off in the direction Kiley had come from. The air around them swirled and he knew they had shifted.

It didn't take long before he heard the howl from Colt telling him it was safe for now.

When Austin was sure there was no immediate danger to his mate he finally took the time to look her over. Her cheeks were flushed from her run, but she was starting to calm down. However she hadn't released her hold on the dog or him.

A shadow passed over him and he looked up to see Tyler watching him. He held out a hand to help him up but Austin shook his head. He couldn't let go of Kiley just yet. He rolled off Kiley while he kept his hand on her arm and got to his feet. He pulled Kiley up with him and held her elbow to check for injuries.

"You okay?" Tyler asked her.

She nodded but allowed Austin to run his free hand over her to be sure. He was grateful. He didn't know if he could handle her independence right then, after being afraid for her.

"I'm sorry," she said, blushing, her voice cracking a little. "When I realised someone was watching the house…how close they were to Jesse, I panicked a little."

"It's okay, baby," Austin tried to soothe, running his hands over her shoulders.

"There's nothing to be embarrassed about, Kiley," Tyler added. "My daughter is the most precious thing in the world to me. I would have done the same."

"I doubt that," Kiley mumbled.

Austin ignored her comment. He would talk to her later about being so hard on herself. Right now, though, she needed to be taken care of. "You're bleeding," he told her lightly. He didn't want to make a big deal about it, but the wolf could smell her blood and he was furious. "Let's get you inside and cleaned up."

She started limping to the house.

"What the hell is wrong with your foot?" he demanded.

Kiley froze. When she glanced back at him, she was frowning. "I must have twisted my ankle. It's no big deal."

Austin almost exploded. He growled low, managing to keep most of his anger in. Tyler stepped over and took Daisy out of Kiley's arms. It was a good thing, too, because a second later Austin had her scooped up and was stalking his way through the yard.

He made sure his hold was firm but wouldn't hurt. He would get her all patched up, then they were going to talk.

The back door was still open, so he didn't pause as he entered the house. He didn't realise he was still growling until Kiley put her hand over his heart.

"Your eyes are glowing," she said quietly.

He wasn't surprised. His wolf was closer now than usual. He hadn't been this upset in a very long time. He didn't respond, just carefully took each step up the stairs. His room was the farthest down the hall. He carried her, stopping just long enough to open the door then slam it behind them.

He set her gently on the bed and turned to pace away from her. On his third pass, she tried to speak.

"Austin..."

Crissy Smith

He held up a hand, stopping her. He just needed a few minutes. Luckily she seemed to understand, since she remained silent. When he thought he had regained control, he stood in front of her, looking down.

She met his gaze for only a moment before looking away.

"Look at me," he ground out between clenched teeth. When she did, he nodded his approval. "I know it's hard for you to understand, but you are mated now."

"It's not that hard to understand," she quipped back.

Austin lifted a brow, amazed despite himself. Score one to his mate for not being afraid of him. "Apparently it is," he responded, "since you are not capable of staying out of trouble and not getting hurt."

Kiley opened her mouth, snapped it closed, then opened it again. No words came out. Austin almost laughed it was so comical.

"From now on, I'm in charge of your body, since you seem to think it's okay to abuse it," he told her sternly.

"My body?" she repeated slowly.

Austin nodded. "Yes, now take off your pants."

"Take off my pants?" she asked with a grin. "Well why didn't you ask sooner?"

Austin chuckled as she scrambled to her knees. She put her fingers on her button but paused.

"Now, are you sure you just want my pants off?" she teased.

Austin liked this part of his mate. She was flirting with him. The remaining anger drained from him. If she was in a playful mood, he would take advantage of it. In fact, he had a pretty good idea.

"You're right. You could have other injuries. Go ahead and undress completely," he agreed.

68

Chapter Eight

Kiley grinned and slowly peeled her pants down her legs. She kicked them off and stood on the bed, careful not to put too much weight on her bad ankle. She lifted the hem of her shirt and pulled it off before tossing it to the ground. She stood in just her panties and bra.

"Get rid of everything," Austin ordered.

Kiley held in a laugh. Her mate was trying to play it tough but she could see the amusement in his face. *Plus* the very large bulge in his pants, letting her know he was not unaffected by her nakedness.

She did what he'd asked until she stood before him bare.

He scratched his chin, faking deep thought. "Turn around so I can check for more injuries." Kiley sighed but did as he requested. She jumped when he ran his hands over her lower back and down. Heat followed his touch and she trembled noticeably.

"Okay, come on," he said and helped her turn to face him again. She took the hand he offered. He helped her from the bed before leading her into the attached bathroom. He lifted her and set her on the vanity before he turned and walked over to the large standing shower and turned the water on.

"Uh, Austin," she called to him.

He tested the water before coming back to her. "Now, let's see," he said and gently took her ankle in his hands.

"It's already better," she told him. As shifters, they healed very quickly.

"My body, remember?" he told her sternly. "I'll tell you when it's better."

Kiley rolled her eyes but let Austin run his hands over her ankle before he picked up a washcloth and got it wet. He cleaned her ankle, her knee, and the scrapes she'd picked up.

Kiley had never had anyone take such care of her before. She dropped her head to hide the moisture that came to her eyes. Austin's hands were gentle and he pampered her.

"There now, all better," he said, before placing a kiss on her once-hurt ankle. He lifted his head at the same time she did and their eyes locked. "I never want to see blood on your precious skin again."

She nodded, lost in his eyes.

He let go of her foot and closed the distance between them until they were flat against one another. They kissed, slowly and deeply, until she had to break away to breathe again.

"Now let me wash this body of mine," he murmured, pulling her off the counter.

Kiley let him lead her to the shower. He pushed her in and began to take off his clothes. She watched, mesmerised, as he revealed every inch to her. He stepped inside to join her and she reached out, grabbing his shoulders.

She kissed him this time. Hungrily devouring his mouth as her mind clouded. Her mate, her man, her love felt good in her arms. The wolf inside her, silent for years, began to make her presence known.

Kiley threw her head back and cried out as the lost part of her finally returned.

Her wolf had hidden deep inside her after years of being with Simon, the feeling of captivity too much for the animal to survive. Kiley had thought she'd lost that part of her until now.

"You okay?" Austin asked, concerned.

Kiley didn't even try to hide her tears of happiness. "Yes! I'm great! Better than great...with you."

Surprise flashed across Austin's face before he slammed his mouth onto hers. Kiley tasted blood—hers or Austin's, she didn't know, and it didn't matter.

She returned his kiss and ran her hands over his strong shoulders, down his back, pressing him closer against her body.

"I need to feel you. I need you inside me," she begged.

"Yes, love...yes." Austin lifted her and she wrapped her legs around his waist. Her back met the cool tile of the shower before he lined his cock up at her entrance.

Kiley sighed as he began to fill her, the feeling of completion and contentment rushing through her. Austin moved slowly, stretching as he entered her until he was buried deep. She grabbed a fistful of his hair and yanked his head back. The wolf was close to the surface now, and she didn't even try to fight it back. "You're mine now, Austin Winters. My mate."

He growled and pulled out slightly before thrusting deep. Kiley gripped his shoulders once again as he began to fuck her hard against the shower wall. The sound of flesh slapping flesh and their moans filled the room. Kiley used every muscle she had to slam herself down and meet each stroke as he rode her. Her body tingled, tightened, before she threw her head back and howled. The orgasm raced through her body, as her inner muscles clamped down onto Austin's cock, holding him prisoner, and she reached completion.

"We're not done," Austin told her through gritted teeth and started to plunge in and out again, each time faster and harder, going deep until she knew she would feel him afterwards. She wanted to—wanted to be able to remember this moment for all time.

"That's it," she encouraged her mate. "Take me…do what you want with me. Make me yours…"

She tilted her head to the side to show her submission to him.

"Fuck!" he cried out, slamming into her hard before his teeth came down on her neck and he bit.

Kiley screamed, the sound echoing in the room. Austin tore his mouth away and called her name as he fell over the edge with her.

Austin lifted his head from the pillow at the soft knock on his bedroom door. Beside him, Kiley remained sound asleep. Their lovemaking in the shower had been intense, and they had both fallen asleep as soon as their heads had hit the pillows.

Carefully he lifted up off the bed. He could smell Colt at his door as well as feel his Beta's frustration. Something else must have happened.

He opened the door but put his finger to his lips so Colt would wait. Silently, he closed the door and gestured further down the hall. Colt didn't even blink at his Alpha being naked in front of him. They shared a cabin at home, plus ran together in wolf form often, so they'd seen each other nude before. Still, some of Colt's unease left and was replaced with amusement. Austin didn't mind. He was proud of his time with his mate. It didn't bother him in the least if others knew what they had been doing.

"We found an abandoned SUV just inside the city limits. It carried the same scent as your attacker, but it's different than the one Kiley found behind the house," Colt told him.

"You think he left town?" Austin asked, although he knew the answer.

"Wouldn't make sense for him to leave. I think he wants us to think that," Colt confirmed his suspicion.

Austin nodded.

"We found a cheap motel a couple miles down the road. We think he stayed there for a couple of weeks. He would have been there before we arrived," Colt told him.

"So you don't think he is after me," Austin guessed. He was good at reading his people. And as close as he and Colt were, they could usually finish each other's sentences.

"I think he is here because of Tony. Tony said he felt he'd been followed a few times as he went from Pack to Pack. He could never pinpoint exactly where or who, just more of a feeling," Colt continued.

Austin watched his friend start to fidget, something he did rarely and probably didn't realise he was doing. "We were planning to leave tomorrow. I still have some things to work out with Kiley, but I don't think we should put it off for long. We only left a few guards at home. I would like to get back as soon as possible just to make sure everything's okay. I already gave my answer to Lamont and I know they're anxious to get Tony home."

Colt frowned. "Tony refuses to go home."

Austin was not completely surprised. "I see."

"With your permission, I could stay with Tony until we find the shifter. Tony's supposed to head to Grand Falls next. That's not far from our territory, so I would be close enough to get there pretty quick if need be."

Austin grinned. "I wouldn't want you to make a big sacrifice."

Colt's eyes snapped to his and he blushed. *Even better*, Austin thought, amused.

"Umm...I don't mind. He'll recover fast but I don't like the idea of him being out there alone with this kind of threat."

"I think it's a good idea," Austin told him. If Colt wanted to talk about his feelings for Tony, he knew Austin would listen. There were no secrets between them. He knew about Tony's preference for either sex. It didn't matter to Austin. In fact, he encouraged the members of his Pack to explore their feelings for whomever they were attracted to. Several of his members had joined his Pack when they'd been kicked out of their own for their sexual preferences.

Colt played the field... a lot. Still, Austin had never seen his friend so nervous. He'd been so wrapped up in finding his mate that he'd neglected his Pack member.

"Why don't you talk to Tony and get everything worked out? We'll discuss it further in the morning before you leave," Austin suggested.

"You're sure you'll be okay?" Colt asked, now looking even more worried. "I don't want to leave you alone either."

"Yeah, I'll be fine. We'll head home as soon as we can. I'll feel better having Kiley there. But I want to know who came after me. I know you want to know too. And I have a feeling you might need to work something else out too?"

Colt pressed his lips together before he smiled. "Thanks, Austin. I don't know how I feel but I need to know he's okay. I can't explain it... This is just something I need to do."

Austin pulled the man into a brief hug. "Any time," he said sincerely. "You know you can call if you need to talk. I'll be there for you."

"I know," Colt whispered in his ear.

They broke apart and Colt turned to head back down stairs. "You better go back to your mate," he said without turning around.

Right then, his bedroom door opened and Kiley stuck her head out. "Austin, is everything okay?" she asked softly.

Grinning like a fool, he quickly made his way to her. She wore a sheet wrapped around her body, her hair mussed, and a sleepy smile.

"Yes, baby, everything is fine," he promised.

She stepped back and he followed, closing the door quietly. "You should still be asleep."

Kiley mumbled something he couldn't hear. He grabbed her around the waist and flattened her against his body. "What was that?"

She huffed out a breath but tilted her head back to look at him. "I said I got cold without you."

Austin bent and kissed her deeply. "Well then, I should warm you back up." He picked her up.

"You gotta stop carrying me around," she complained, but was giggling as he took several long steps to the bed.

"Never," he stated and threw her on top of the bedspread.

She bounced, still laughing. "Animal!"

Austin pounced on her, holding her sweet, soft body under his. "Always," he agreed.

He kissed her hard and demandingly, thrilled when she opened for him and wrapped her arms tight around his neck.

"Austin?" she asked breathlessly when they broke apart.

"Hmm?" he purred against her neck, kissing and nibbling.

"Why were you standing in the hall naked?"

Austin looked at her in surprise. Had that been jealousy in her voice? "Because, darling, Colt knocked on the door and I didn't want to waste time having to dress then undress again to get back in bed with you."

"You could have covered up," she insisted.

Oh yeah, his mate was jealous. He loved it! "I promise next time to dress before answering the door."

"Okay," she agreed. "Austin?"

"Yes?" he was trying not to smile too widely but failing miserably.

"Get that look off your face and kiss me again," she ordered.

"Gladly." And he did kiss her again.

Chapter Nine

Kiley hugged Jesse for the millionth time in the last hour. She knew she needed to let go of the little girl but she didn't seem to be able to. She had tried so hard not to get attached to anyone there but it hadn't worked.

Jesse had yelled and argued when she'd found out that Kiley would be leaving. She'd calmed down a little when she'd learned she would be living with Austin's Pack. Apparently she spent a lot of time there visiting. With the help of Austin and Tyler, they'd even made plans for Jesse to go down there in about six weeks.

Kiley had told her she'd need help learning the territory and since Jesse had been there so much, maybe she'd be able to show her around. The girl had happily agreed.

Kiley supposed she would have things a little better controlled by then. Oh, she'd known she would be going. Austin was an Alpha and he'd told her all about his Pack, but it hadn't actually sunk in until he'd told her they needed to get home.

Home, she thought bitterly. She hadn't had one of those in so long, she'd forgotten what it felt like. As much as she'd enjoyed the apartment she'd rented, it wasn't the same as having a house, a place that was hers and her family's, a place to be comfortable and feel safe.

She'd got so used to closing herself off that she hadn't realised how much she had missed her wolf — until she'd found Austin. Now, for the first time since she'd left her family, her wolf wanted to play. Wanted to run and dance. Wanted to mate.

It was a good feeling.

But still her chest felt tight, and she could feel the panic wanting to set in. She'd sworn she would stay away from all Alpha-type men. Not only had she broken that rule, but she'd mated with an Alpha.

Now she was moving to a new territory she knew nothing about and found herself in a position of power.

Whether she wanted it or not.

Gray and Dominic stepped out of the front door and joined her and Jesse on the steps.

"We'll miss you," Dominic told her in his relaxing, deep voice. He didn't speak a lot, except to Jesse, but when he did, it was a pleasure to listen to the cadence of his voice.

"I'll miss you all too," she admitted softly. She had to fight the urge to get teary-eyed.

"You'll always be welcome, Kiley. Don't forget that," Dominic told her and bent for Jesse. "One last hug. Austin's on his way out."

The two females hugged each other. Finally Kiley pulled away and placed Jesse in his arms. "I love you, little cub," she whispered to the girl.

She turned away quickly as she heard Dominic and Jesse leave. She wiped at the tears that had fallen.

"Kiley," Gray said her name softly. She dropped her head — this was going to be just as difficult. She took a deep breath and turned back to him. The emotion in his eyes surprised her. They had spent a lot of time together and cared deeply for one another. Her heart broke a little at the look of loss on his face.

"Oh Gray," she murmured, cupping his cheek. "I'm so sorry. I have been terrible to you."

He shook his head but she wouldn't let him argue. She hadn't once stopped to think about how her finding a mate would affect him. Although they weren't in love, they'd still been close. All the other had had, at one time.

"I am so sorry, Gray. I didn't think…"

"Shh," he told her, pulling her into his arms. "It's okay. I'm just going to miss you like crazy. I can't hold your own mate against you."

His tone was kind, so Kiley believed that he didn't blame her, but that didn't make her feel any better. She vowed she would do something special for him. She'd make up for her awful behaviour one way or another.

She wrapped her arms around his waist and hugged him tightly. "I'll always love you," she said sincerely.

"I know," he told her as he released her. "I'll always wish I was your mate."

A tear slipped down her cheek. "You'll find her," she promised. "And I hope she's ten times as stubborn as you say I am."

He laughed like she'd intended. "Me too."

With two fingers under her chin, he placed a soft kiss on her lips. There was nothing sexual about it — it was a goodbye to how they once were.

They smiled into each other's eyes. That's how Tyler and Austin found them.

Kiley was pleased with Austin's reaction. While almost every other wolf she knew would have felt threatened and attacked, Austin didn't. He calmly walked down the steps. Gray dropped his hand from her face, and when Austin offered his, the two men shook.

"Best of luck in your hunting," Austin told him.

Gray nodded. "Thank you, Alpha. I won't let the threat remain any longer. No one will get to Tyler or Jesse."

Austin turned to Tyler and shook hands with the other Alpha. "I'll talk to you soon," Austin told him.

"Be careful driving," Tyler told Austin before addressing Kiley. "Just take what you want now. I'll make sure everything else in your apartment is sent in the next couple of days."

Kiley gazed up at him. She owed Tyler so much. He'd given her sanctuary in his territory without asking anything in return. He'd opened up his home and shared his family with her. She could never pay him back for everything he'd done for her over the last year.

"Tyler…"

He just grinned and spread his arms. Kiley carefully embraced him, holding back as much emotion as she could. She'd break down later—not in front of the others. She could hold on until she was alone.

Tyler hugged her and even kissed the top of her head. "We'll see you in a month or so, kiddo," he promised.

Kiley nodded, rubbing her cheek against his chest. She'd never touched him like that before but it made her feel protected. She managed to break away and, without looking at anyone, walked to her SUV.

Austin said something else behind her, then rushed up to catch her. He threw his arm around her but didn't comment on her lack of control. It seemed like her mate kept seeing her at her worst. She had no idea why he wanted her.

When he stopped at a black Explorer and opened the passenger door, she just looked up at him blankly.

"Come on, baby," he urged. "Climb in—we need to get on the road."

She started to follow his instruction before her brain connected. She stepped back. "What about my car?"

"Tyler will take care of it," Austin told her. He pressed his hand on the small of her back trying to get her to move.

"But I need it," she argued, her feet firmly planted.

"Kiley," Austin said as if he was tired. "Get in. We will get you another vehicle if you want. You can have this one. Or someone else can drive yours. I don't care."

"I need a way to get around," she tried to explain. She wasn't trying to be difficult.

"You can drive anything you want at home," he countered.

She hesitated. She didn't have much. Even her apartment was furnished. Some clothes, pictures and knick-knacks, her computer, and odds and ends. Her biggest possession was the new Tahoe. "I want to take my ride."

"Fine," Austin agreed without pause. "One of the men will drive it."

"That's silly. I can just follow behind you," she offered.

"No," he dismissed. "Now, hop up."

"No?" Kiley repeated.

Austin's grip on the door tightened. "Don't make this an issue," he said in a voice so low that he might have been talking to himself.

"Or…" She was unable to resist the challenge.

"As long as we are on the road and off territory, you are not to leave my side," he snapped.

"Excuse me?" Kiley cried.

Austin gently grabbed a handful of hair and pulled her forward. It didn't hurt but surprised her. That was a move he hadn't used before…and she kind of liked it. It made her hot when he showed his strength but didn't hurt her.

But she wasn't going to let him know that.

"Austin," she warned instead.

"For once, just listen to me. I promise that I will make sure you have a vehicle available at all times. You will not be stuck alone without a way into town or anywhere else you want to go. But right now you need to trust me. As your mate and the Alpha, you need to take me at my word that this is what is best. We need to get in the vehicles and on the road. We'll stop by your apartment and grab what you want, but standing out here, in the open, we are a target. Please get in the car."

Kiley pressed her lips together. Well, when he put it that way…

She climbed in, refusing his help.

Austin closed her door and went to the driver's side. He jumped in and locked the doors. "Put your seatbelt on," he ordered.

Kiley almost refused, just out of spite, but then she noticed his tension—something she hadn't noticed earlier.

"Austin, what's wrong?" she asked, hoping he would tell her. She didn't want him to hide anything from her. If they were going to be equal partners, it needed to start now.

"We're being watched," he told her as he started the ignition.

Kiley clicked her seatbelt into place. She needed to stop thinking about herself all the time. Her mate was the Alpha and that position came with a lot of stress. She'd agreed to move with him. She needed to stop being a problem and come up with a way to help.

She leant back in her seat and thought. She was a licensed private investigator. She would figure it out.

Kiley sat silently beside him as he drove, and Austin had almost all he could stand of her silence. They'd rushed through packing a couple of bags, her laptop, and some pictures, loaded them up and left. She'd said she had everything she needed for a few days until Tyler got the rest of her stuff sent.

Still, she hadn't said more than a dozen words to him since they'd hit the road. He was glad no one else rode with them so he could try to figure out what to say. All he'd wanted was for her to obey a simple command.

He didn't blame her for wanting her own vehicle but there hadn't been time to discuss it, and as soon as he'd realised they were being watched he'd just wanted her out of there. He'd seen Colt and Cain sneak out the back way and around the house. He knew even as he drove away that the men were chasing down the threat.

It did nothing to ease the tension he felt about his mate being in danger once again. God, how he wanted to get her back home and lock her in the bedroom for the rest of her life. Realistically he knew he couldn't, but that didn't stop him from daydreaming about it.

He glanced in his rear view mirror and saw the two cars following him. Right behind him was Kiley's SUV, and behind that was his black truck. There didn't seem to be anyone else driving down the two-lane road.

He actually jumped when Kiley's hand covered his. She was still staring out of the side window but when he turned his hand over, she laced his fingers through his.

Austin relaxed for the first time since they had started the drive home.

They stopped for gas and to go to the bathroom halfway to his territory. He let Kiley go inside alone but kept an eye on her the entire time. Once he was done filling the tank, he headed inside. They met again as she came out of the women's restroom and he was going into the men's. He pulled out his wallet and handed it to her.

"Would you get me a large coffee and some snacks?"

She smiled and as their hands touched, she sighed, "I'm sorry, Austin."

He shook his head. Really there was nothing to apologise for. He gave her a quick kiss on her lips. "I'll be quick, love."

Her eyes sparkled and she nodded.

Austin quickly took care of business and washed his hands. He couldn't wait to get Kiley home. In his heart, he knew she would love his territory.

Kiley had two coffees, bottles of water, and several snacks at the register when he joined her. He watched his men take turns watching the vehicles, using the restrooms, buying supplies, and watching his mate.

He nodded at his men, letting them know he appreciated it. He had good members in his Pack. He was proud to have them watching his mate.

He helped Kiley carry their stuff to the SUV. They climbed inside and waited until the men were loaded up in the other vehicles. It wasn't long before they were back on the road.

They had only been driving again for about twenty minutes before Colt called.

Austin answered with the hands-free device, letting the call go through the radio.

"We caught one of them," Colt told him without so much as a hello.

"Who is it?" Austin barked out with excitement. If they could take care of the problem before he got Kiley home, they would really have something to celebrate.

"Actually, we're not sure. He's not talking," Colt responded.

"Well, make him talk," Austin ordered. He tightened his grip on the steering wheel in frustration.

Colt chuckled. "Working on it, boss. Let me tell you, Cain can be a scary guy when he wants to."

Austin grinned. He knew that for a fact. "If anyone can do it, it's Cain."

Colt paused and Austin barely kept his questions in check. He knew Colt had something more to say.

"He's not a wolf."

The shock he felt matched the loud gasp from his mate.

"What is he?" Austin asked slowly.

"Not sure about that either. Except, he is…feline."

Austin's lip curled in disgust. "I shouldn't be surprised, I guess." He'd never had much love for feline shifters. Unlike wolves, or most shifters for that matter, they weren't much on family. They were mostly unruly and ran wild.

"Tony says it makes sense, though. He hasn't been able to communicate with any of the feline shifters."

"Well at least this gives us a lead," Austin agreed.

"Yeah, I just thought I'd let you know. I'll call you later when I know more."

"Good. Keep me updated."

"Will do," Colt agreed.

Austin thought over the new information. While he didn't know any feline shifters, he knew of them. The long-standing feud between the two types had been ongoing since before he was born. He wasn't even sure how it had started. But he wanted the man to talk. If he had put off leaving, taking his mate away from danger, he would have been there.

"They'll get him to talk," Kiley assured him, rubbing her hand over his thigh.

Austin bit back a moan from his mate's contact. Now was not the time to get aroused. "I just wish I could be there."

"Tyler will take care of it. You've got enough on your plate right now," Kiley told him.

Austin rolled his shoulders to relax his upper body. Kiley continued to massage his leg, and his cock hardened. He shifted to hide his reaction.

"You okay?" she asked with a teasing caress over his lap.

"You know damn well what you're doing to me right now," he accused.

She laughed. "And what would I be doing?"

Again just a faint brush over his erection. Austin grabbed her hand and pressed it fully against his prick. "Keep that up, baby, and I will pull this car over."

She closed her hand over him. "That would be a shame."

"Since we have two vehicles full of guards behind us, yes it would be."

She stiffened and looked behind her.

Austin chuckled. "Forgot about them, didn't you?"

"I seem to forget everything when I'm close to you," she muttered under her breath.

Austin was thrilled with her admission. "I know how you feel," he agreed and laced his fingers with hers.

Chapter Ten

It seemed like the drive took forever, yet at the same time it ended way too soon. As soon as Austin told her they were just outside their territory, her stomach started to jump around and the butterflies arrived.

It had been so long since she'd been with a full Pack. Every time she went to Tyler's, there were only a few members around. The way Austin talked, it sounded like his Pack was more like an extended family, dropping in whenever they could.

While the scenery that passed outside the window was indeed beautiful, it didn't take the edge off. Green grass, tall healthy trees, and plenty of open space flew by them. Kiley clenched her hands in her lap to keep herself from telling Austin to turn around.

She'd promised herself she wouldn't cause him any more difficulties. She would be the best mate she could.

She jumped when Austin's hand covered her fist.

"Relax, baby," he encouraged. "Everyone will love you."

Kiley wasn't so sure. What if they saw what Austin didn't? What if they knew—like she did—that she would never be the perfect mate? She rubbed her stomach with her free hand.

They reached a dirt road and Austin turned onto it. "Almost there."

Kiley stared out of the window as they bumped along the road. She was trying to see the Alpha house and gates. About a mile from where they'd turned off, a large cabin came into view. She didn't know who lived there and she wasn't expecting to make a stop.

She glanced at Austin, but he just smiled. Kiley took the home in as they pulled up in front. It was the most beautiful place she had ever seen. Dark, thick wooden logs made up the outside. There was a wide wrap-around porch and huge windows that would look out onto the woods just feet away. If she could have picked any house, it would have been one very similar to this.

Austin put the vehicle in park and turned off the engine. "Well, this is it."

Kiley glanced over at him, confused. "This? This is your house?"

"Our house," he corrected with a frown. "You don't like it?"

But all Kiley heard was 'our house'. She quickly unfastened her seat belt and pushed the door open. She didn't even close her door but rushed forwards. The large cabin loomed before her, warm and inviting.

She wondered how she could possibly deserve such a gorgeous home and a mate who seemed to truly care about her. Her vow to herself on the road came back to her. Austin was offering her so much and she would try her hardest to be a good mate.

Austin stepped up behind her and placed his hand on the small of her back. She closed the distance to lean her body back against his.

"So you like it then?" he asked with uncertainty in his voice.

Kiley nodded. "I think it's wonderful."

He relaxed and she was pleased her comment had been right. She had also told him the truth. The cabin was out in the middle of nowhere in perfect seclusion and the woods were so close she could smell them. The trees, the animals that lived inside, a source of water.

She felt her wolf ripple inside her. Yes, her sister wolf wanted to run and check out their new home. But there would be time for that. She would try to talk Austin into accompanying her in a run later.

"Let me show you the inside," Austin said as he started to lead her forward.

The steps were solid and when she reached the front porch she saw several wicker chairs and even a swing.

"You sit out here a lot?" she asked, hoping he did. She would like to spend time sitting with him.

"I do," Austin answered. "I like relaxing out here at night. When everything has slowed down, and I can just take the time to listen to nature."

They turned as he spoke and looked out from the porch. Wide openness filled Kiley's vision and she felt comforted by it.

"You don't have any gates?" she questioned. She had never in her life lived within a territory that didn't have security gates. Even Tyler's home had them.

"The Pack is so small, I have never seen the need for them. I don't want any of the members to feel they are not welcome in my home. We stay hidden from everyone else and haven't had any problems with other Packs. We just want to live peacefully," Austin explained.

"That's just perfect," Kiley said with a sigh. She hadn't meant to say that out loud but once the words slipped through, she wasn't sorry. Austin had a territory to be proud of.

Quietly they made their way to the front door. Austin withdrew his key and inserted it into the lock but paused to look over at her. "I want you to think of this as your home too, Kiley. If you want to change anything, then change it. If you wish to add something, then add it. It's only Colt and I here and we're pretty easy."

Kiley understood what he was telling her. And while she appreciated it, she didn't think it was going to be necessary. She was a pretty casual girl herself. Still she wondered what the cabin of two bachelors would look like on the inside.

Austin unlocked the door and pushed it open. Kiley stepped in first and her breath caught in her throat.

The front door opened to a large open area. The same dark wood that was outside lined the cabin's walls and ceilings. There were steps that led into the open room where she could see large black leather couches and chairs, a big screen TV, and a monster stereo system.

Kiley grinned and walked down the steps into the room. She looked over it with a critical eye.

She really liked the stone fireplace in the corner. There were a couple of pictures of wolves hanging on the wall and thick rugs placed throughout the room. She turned and looked into the kitchen.

Oh, that room was even better! Even though she wasn't much of a cook, obvious from the barbeque disaster at Tyler's, she still could appreciate a kitchen like the one Austin had.

"Oh wow!" she finally said.

Austin chuckled and swung his arm around her shoulders. "I take it you approve."

"Yes," she told him as she turned into his arms. "You have a lovely home."

"We. We have a lovely home," he corrected.

Kiley stretched onto her tiptoes until their mouths were just a breath apart. "We have a lovely home."

Austin closed the distance and his mouth covered hers. Kiley gripped his shoulders hard as she lost all sense of direction and let her mind drift away. The only thing she concentrated on was the feel of her mate against her.

He picked her up and she wrapped her legs around his waist. "First things first," he said against her mouth.

Kiley wasn't sure what he meant until Austin lowered her down so her back met the leather couch. His tongue was working magic and she arched up when his hand pressed over her sex.

"Austin," she panted out his name when his mouth left hers.

"Gotta have you," he said desperately. "Gotta have you now!"

They hurriedly removed her clothes and she pulled his T-shirt over his head as he nibbled and licked her neck. Kiley tilted her head to the side to give him better access.

"God! I burn for you," he confessed. She heard the zipper of his jeans come down.

Kiley used her feet to help push the fabric down his thighs. He lined his cock up at her entrance and she could feel the solid heat as he started to enter.

He slid in slowly, easily now that she was used to his body. Once fully seated, he paused and Kiley met his gaze. The emotion on his face matched what she felt in her heart.

Love, devotion, uncomplicated lust. He shared the feelings she had kept to herself. Kiley cupped his cheek and drew him down to her. "My love," she whispered against his lips.

He closed his eyes and took a deep breath. When he looked down at her once again there was just the hint of wetness. "Yes. My love," he repeated.

They kissed and he started to move inside her, each stroke slow and deep. Kiley ran her hands over his lower back, urging him on.

They made love slowly. Eyes locked together, each breath shared, as their bodies moved in rhythm. It was the single best experience of her life.

When she fell over the edge she cried out his name, tightening around him and bringing him with her.

As they calmed their beating hearts Kiley wrapped her arms around Austin and just held on. She'd gone and done it. Fallen in love with a man she barely knew, but trusted with her entire heart.

Austin shuddered above her, his face buried in her neck. It was too good a moment to let go. But the slamming of a car door broke the moment, as Kiley froze stiff while Austin jumped up.

"Who...?" she started to ask but he shook his head with a smile on his face.

"Hope you're ready, baby," he told her as he gathered her clothes and placed them in her arms. "Looks like you're about to meet the other woman in my life."

Confused and more than a little upset by his declaration, Kiley hurriedly dressed as he did the same. She'd just finished when the front door burst open.

"Austin! Colt! Are you home?" a woman called out.

She closed the door and stopped. With the open rooms, she got a look at Kiley as Kiley took the other woman in.

She was a smaller woman with short brown hair. She wore jeans and a T-shirt that said, 'Yes, I am a princess.' She was around Kiley's age and obviously felt right at home as she walked down the steps.

"Who are you?" she asked rather rudely.

Kiley frowned. "Who are you?" she retorted, crossing her arms over her chest.

"Girls," Austin drawled and they both turned to him.

He was grinning, while Kiley was just about ready to kill him. What the hell had everything they had done together, the sweet words, the love they shared meant if he had another woman at home? Because if he thought she was going to share her mate, he had another think coming.

"What's going on?" the other woman questioned him.

He motioned her forwards. She smiled and walked directly into his arms. Kiley didn't even try to bite back the growl that escaped the back of her throat. She did, however, resist ripping the woman to shreds—barely.

"Ginger! Ginger," he said lovingly. "Meet my mate."

"Your mate?" Ginger exclaimed loudly.

She turned back to Kiley who was ready to pounce if Austin didn't stop touching her.

"Kiley, this is my sister, Ginger," he introduced.

"Your sister?" Kiley snapped.

She stared at the other woman in shock. Holy Hell, she'd had no idea Austin had a sister. She was even more surprised when the other woman turned and smacked Austin in the back of the head.

"Ow! Shit! What was that for?" he complained, rubbing his hand over his head.

"She thought I was your lover, you dumbass," Ginger enlightened him.

Austin's eyes grew and he rushed over to her. "Oh no, baby! Baby, I'm so sorry."

Kiley let Austin wrap his arms around her as she watched the other woman watch her.

Ginger grinned and rocked back on the heels of her feet. "I can't believe you finally found your mate."

Kiley caught Austin's huge grin.

"Me either," he said proudly.

Austin released her and Ginger was there in a second, throwing small but strong arms around her neck. "I always wanted a sister," the other woman confessed.

Kiley relaxed against her and returned the embrace. Maybe, just maybe, she'd found someone else she'd never known she wanted…or needed.

Chapter Eleven

Austin ducked out of the kitchen into the living room with a smile on his face as his cell phone rang. After the initial shock and misunderstanding, Kiley and Ginger had become fast friends just like he'd thought.

Colt's number flashed over the caller ID and he pressed talk.

"Hey man," he greeted.

"Hey, did you get home?" Colt asked.

"Yeah, couple of hours ago."

"Good, do me a favour and stay close by the guards."

Austin's stomach dropped. "What happened?"

"The guy's still not talking much, but he did say one thing," Colt explained.

"What?" Austin asked cautiously.

Colt hesitated. "Prepare for war."

"So someone else could be after us," Austin questioned.

"I believe so. Since we didn't agree to go public, maybe they will leave us alone—if you want to take the chance?" Colt asked.

"No," Austin stated firmly. "I won't put the Pack in danger by ignoring any threat. Plus our friends will need all the help they can get."

"I think so. Tony finally spoke to the Prince of Felines. He's agreed to meet with us. He said he didn't know anything about the threat but he wasn't surprised," Colt informed him.

"I didn't know they even had a Prince."

"I guess they have a royal family. Not that they have much control over the shifters. But the Prince seemed upset about it, and we're going to meet with him when we get to Grand Falls."

"That's the shifter that's mated to the vampire and the witch right?" Austin had heard about the Alpha taking his unusual mates a while back.

Colorado was broken into three territories. His, Tyler's, and Tom's. While his Pack was small, and Tyler's consisted only of wolf shifters, Tom actually had several different animal shifters in his area. Plus vampires and other paranormal creatures.

"Yeah," Colt said, amused. "Gotta tell you, I'm curious about how an Alpha can handle those relationships."

Austin agreed. Being with his mate was already consuming every minute and thought. He couldn't imagine having to add a Master vampire to the relationship.

"Call me when you head out. I'll call Tom later and speak to him."

"Will do," Colt agreed.

"Okay. Talk to you soon."

Austin hung up and stared out of the large window to the territory surrounding the house. He'd always loved being out in the open, the freedom it provided. Now he worried that by not having the same security as other Alphas, he was making it easier for Kiley to be hurt.

Before he could think too much about it, he heard his name called from the kitchen. He joined his mate and his sister as the two women giggled about something.

His sister stood in front of the stove stirring a saucepan while Kiley sat on top of the counter watching. He strolled over to his mate, trying to convey that everything was okay. But when he kissed her cheek, she turned to him and frowned.

"What's wrong?" she asked.

Austin shook his head and offered her a smile. "Nothing, just got a lot on my mind."

She pressed her lips together but didn't call him on his lie. She also didn't believe him.

"I've got some phone calls to make. There may be some members of the Pack stopping by in the morning," he told her, trying to sound casual.

"Austin," she grabbed his arm when he tried to move away. "Tell me what's going on."

He knew he really didn't have the option of not telling her. "We have trouble with the feline shifters."

He watched as a series of emotions crossed her face until she got control. "Whatever it is, we'll handle it."

Austin cupped her face and made sure their eyes locked. "We will."

They stared at each other until Ginger broke the tension.

"Attacks? Threats? Does someone want to let me know what's going on?"

Austin stepped back. "I'll let Kiley fill you in. I really do need to make some calls." His mate nodded as Austin backed away. He headed to his office as he heard his sister speak again.

"Okay girl! Tell me whose heads I need to knock together."

Kiley laughed despite herself when Austin's sister threatened the unknown people. Sister—she still couldn't believe Austin hadn't told her ahead of time, although she liked the other woman. Ginger was loud and brash but funny, and Kiley felt comfortable being alone with her. For such a small woman, Ginger had an attitude that even the biggest guards had to fear.

She took a deep breath before filling Ginger in on everything—everything that had happened and the worry about future attacks against anyone going public. Ginger removed the soup she'd started to make from the burner and turned, giving Kiley her entire attention.

The longer Kiley spoke, the more Ginger scowled. When she was finally done, Kiley took a deep breath. Ginger just stared at her for several moments before she nodded. Then the woman turned to the fridge, opened it, and pulled out two bottles of beer.

She opened both and handed one to Kiley, before draining a third of the contents of the bottle she held.

"Well," Ginger said when she finally spoke. "That sucks."

Kiley laughed. She laughed until she had to wipe tears from her eyes. "Kind of does," she agreed when she stopped. She took a pull of her beer.

"So," Ginger looked around the kitchen. "Want to see the outside?" Kiley shrugged and jumped off the counter when Ginger motioned for her to follow.

The back door was in the living room beside the full window. Kiley stepped outside and grinned. The sun was just starting to set, the orange and red colours fading in the distance. For as far as she could see, there was nothing but green grass and trees.

"I love it here," she said out loud, not really talking to Ginger.

"Yeah," the other woman agreed. They stood in silence lost in their own thoughts for several minutes before Ginger stirred and walked to the right. "Over there." She pointed to the east set of trees. "There's a small trail that leads deeper into the wildness. That is where most of the Pack lives. Some members live in town but most of us prefer the openness here."

When Kiley looked closely enough she could see the narrow trail Ginger was talking about. It was obviously made to remain hidden unless you knew to look for it.

"Wow!" Kiley exclaimed in appreciation. "That's nice."

"When we left our birth Pack, Austin promised we would always have open space. We travelled from Minnesota until we found this place. Austin said he felt the pull of home and we searched and searched until we came here."

"This isn't your birth Pack?" Kiley asked.

"Just what have you and my brother been doing if you didn't know that?" Ginger inquired with a lifted brow and a smirk.

Kiley blushed. It seemed that with learning each other's bodies, and worrying, they really hadn't spent a lot of time talking. "Well, you know," Kiley tried to explain with a wave of her hand.

Ginger giggled like a little girl. "Yeah, I think I got it."

Kiley ignored the other woman's obvious amusement. "It's complicated."

"I'm sure it is," Ginger agreed too easily.

"Just wait!" Kiley waved a finger at her. "When you meet your mate, you'll understand."

Ginger shook her head. "I'm not worried. I have no doubt my mate will follow me around like a good man should."

Kiley snorted. "Can't wait to see that."

Ginger grew serious. "This, all of this space and the people and everything that comes with being an Alpha, Austin would give up to have his mate."

Kiley didn't respond, just stared out as the sun dipped lower and lower on the horizon.

"It would be sad. Austin is the finest man, the greatest brother, and a wonderful Alpha. It would be sad for those that neede him," Ginger continued. "But I would back him if that's what he decided to do. If that's what he *had* to do to have his mate."

Kiley frowned and turned to look at the other woman. "I'm not asking him to give anything up because of me. I don't want to take Austin away. I want to add to his life," she responded honestly.

Ginger grinned. "I'll remember that you said that. I'll remind you when things get tough. You not only got a mate but you just got yourself a sister too."

Kiley gave a mock shiver. "I hope she's sanerthan you," she teased.

Chapter Twelve

Austin found both his mate and sister on the back porch watching the sun set. He stood just out of the way and gazed at both of his loves.

Ginger had been seventeen when they'd left their home and found this one. Their parents had died in a car accident the year before and there had been too many memories for them to stay. Ginger had been depressed and Austin had been going out of his mind with worry. He knew there was a place for him, for both of them, somewhere. When he'd first seen this area, he had known he was home.

Now he felt his heart was so full it might burst.

He hadn't moved or made a sound but at that moment Kiley turned her head. Their gazes locked and she smiled.

Austin actually felt a moment of dizziness. His mate was just so wonderful. She was beautiful, and smart, and best of all—his.

He took long strides over to her chair and, ignoring his sister's smirk, leant down and took Kiley's mouth in a deep, sensual kiss.

Kiley moaned and wrapped an arm around his neck, holding him close. Austin went down on his knees and yanked her to the edge of her chair.

Their tongues tangled, duelled for control, before she gave in and tilted her head to allow him the control.

Austin liked that. Kiley could kiss—kiss him breathless—but even then, she wasn't a pushover.

"Well, I think I'm headed home," Ginger stated loudly.

Austin pulled his mouth away from Kiley's but kept her body close to his. "Make sure you're careful. Kiley told you about the threats?"

At Ginger's nod, Austin winked. "I know you can take care of yourself but if someone is around, I would like to question them instead of just burying the body."

He was only half joking. Ginger went above and beyond trying to outdo most of the men in the Pack. While it made Austin proud, it also worried him at times, and this just happened to be one of them.

"I'll be careful. I started some soup and it's on the stove if you work up a hunger," Ginger said, laughing.

Austin groaned. "Go home," he begged.

Ginger waved her hand in the air. "I'm going. I'm going."

Instead of walking back into the house, Ginger leapt over the porch railing to land gracefully on her feet.

"Show-off," Austin called and was pleased by both women's laughter.

Once his sister was far enough away to be out of hearing distance, Austin cupped Kiley's face, searching. He was thrilled when, instead of pulling away, Kiley actually leant into him.

"You okay?" she asked

He nodded. "Not actually the way I thought I would spend the first night at home with my mate," he smiled.

"And just how did you think it would go?" she teased.

Austin picked her up swiftly out of the chair and sat down with her on his lap. "I imagined trying to get my mate comfortable in every room."

"Comfortable?" she asked as she wiggled on his lap.

Austin groaned and held her still, the pressure on his erection a sweet but torturous mixture. "Can't get any more comfortable in a room than being naked and screaming."

Kiley laughed, shook her head, laughed again. Her body shook and he liked the sound. He pulled her back against his chest.

When she finally stopped laughing she wiped her eyes and twisted her head to see him. "I can't argue with you there I guess."

Austin tilted his head and faked serious. "So, my mate, where should we start?"

She lifted a shoulder in a shrug. "I haven't seen the bedroom yet."

"You haven't seen any of the upstairs."

Her nose crinkled and she tried to be serious. "What do you plan to do about it?" she questioned.

Austin rose with her still in his arms. She grunted and protested when he slung her over his shoulder.

"Austin, put me down!"

He ignored her as he made his way to the side door.

He made sure to lock it behind him and started the tour. "Okay, so this is the living room, which you should already be comfortable in."

She kicked her feet and he had to tighten his grip. "Yes, the living room. I got that."

Austin slapped her ass once and she gasped. "I'm giving you the grand tour. Work with me."

"I would work with you better if everything was not upside down," she complained.

Austin just chuckled and slapped her ass again. "Okay, over there is the laundry room." He waved his hand in the general direction. "You saw the kitchen...over there is my office. There's a study next to it but if you want to use it for your office, that would work too."

He reached the stairs. "That door leads to the bathroom down here. Usually only guests use that." He started up. "Now up here is the really good stuff."

"Austin, come on, put me down. All the blood's rushing to my head," Kiley pleaded.

"So there are four bedrooms up here. Two guest, Colt's, and our room. Ginger has stuff stashed in one of them but the other is free for any visitors. There's a bathroom down the hall but here is where you should spend most of your time."

Austin pushed his bedroom door open, brought Kiley off his shoulder, and placed her on her feet in the doorway. He hoped she liked it.

"Nice," she commented and walked in.

Austin watched her as she stalked around the room. He had a California King-size bed with a dark wood headboard and matching end tables. Off to one side was a double balcony door. The curtains were closed now but on clear nights Austin would leave the doors open when in bed. He couldn't wait to make that experience even better by getting to hold his mate.

Kiley had come to a stop in front of the bed. "My, my, what a big bed you have," she teased.

He took a few steps forward and pulled his shirt over his head. "All the better to throw you on."

Kiley smirked as she pulled her shirt off and dropped it to the ground. Austin paused long enough to open his pants and push them down.

"Oh, goodness. What a big cock you have," Kiley faked shock.

Austin stroked his already fully aroused member. "All the better to fuck you with, my dear."

Kiley threw her head back with a deep chuckle. "Well in that case..." she stated, before stripping the rest of her clothes off and climbing into the middle of the bed. "Get over here, my big bad wolf."

"Woof, woof," Austin barked, and pounced.

He landed on the soft mattress, bouncing both of them, and wrapped his arm around her waist to hold her close.

Kiley reached for him, giggling, before their lips connected. Austin didn't think he would ever get tired of kissing his mate. When Kiley kissed, she put her soul into it. She moved her body to match each thrust of her tongue.

When they pulled away they were both panting for breath.

"I can't get enough of you," she confessed in a desperate tone. "I ache to have you inside."

The admission, spoken in a soft tone, yanked at Austin's heartstrings. While Kiley was starting to open up more and more comfortably, he was growing to love her that much more deeply.

She wrapped her hand around his cock and stroked him, causing Austin to buck and groan. He meant to tell her how much he also needed her, but with one hand of hers gripping and pulling and the other cupping and massaging his balls, he was beyond speech. All he could do was grunt and whimper.

Before he lost it, Austin pulled away and pushed her shoulders down onto the bed. "Enough," he growled.

She bit her lip and smiled. Desire had brightened her eyes and she clawed at his shoulders to bring him closer.

"Please, Austin," she begged.

Austin gripped the base of his shaft and scooted between her legs. "What, no foreplay?" he teased, running the tip between her folds.

"Fuck foreplay," she mumbled as she lifted her legs off the bed and fitted them under his arms.

Well, who was he to argue with a statement like that? He plunged in, not pausing until he was buried deep.

Kiley arched and dropped her head onto the pillow. Her nails dug into his hips as she grabbed him. "Yes, yes."

Austin kept his eyes on her face as he pulled out before slamming back inside. She bucked and wiggled. The site of his mate in passion was almost enough to make him blow his load too early.

Austin lifted her hips and braced his knees. "Gonna be fast. Down and dirty," he warned.

Kiley opened her eyes and met his gaze. "Do it."

So he did. He rode his mate hard, thrusting in and out, pushing and yanking until they both screamed and climaxed. They fell into completion together. First Kiley orgasmed, her inner muscles tightening almost painfully. That was all he needed. He released his seed into her, coming in long bursts to give her everything he had.

"Perfect," she purred as they collapsed in a tangle of arms and legs, utterly exhausted, but happy.

Chapter Thirteen

Kiley stretched and rolled onto her back in the big bed she now shared with her mate. Austin's side was empty and when she ran her hand over it, she found it cold.

She frowned, until she looked at the clock. It was already past eleven in the morning. She had always been an early riser, but the night before had been intense.

Two days with Austin, in their home, and it felt like she had always been there. They made love every night before he wrapped his arms around her and they drifted to sleep. He was busy during the day but never too busy for her.

She'd find herself cornered at least once a day. She would play hard to get at first but he could always convince her to do a little exploring and a lot of loving. Each night they would run in their other form to get her used to the territory and let their wolves have fun. Afterwards they would sit in the porch swing and talk and hold each other.

She climbed out of bed and worked the kinks out of her body before heading to the attached bathroom. Austin had a large, clean, tiled restroom with a deep sunken tub, free-standing shower, and two sinks. It was almost perfect. She would have to do something about the clothes tossed in the corner, but if her mate had a little sloppy side, she wasn't sure she would mind. She felt comfortable in her own skin and in their home.

She quickly washed her face, brushed her teeth, and attempted to tame her hair.

Back inside the bedroom, she quickly pulled on a pair of jeans and a T-shirt and headed to the closed bedroom door. She paused with her hand on the knob and used her senses to find her mate.

A wave of emotion hit her first. Love, kindness, and a little bit of fear. Kiley followed the emotion through the link with her mate until she was able to feel him. He was in the kitchen, and he wasn't alone.

Guess they wouldn't get a quickie in before he had to work.

She could hear voices by the time she reached the bottom step. She took a few steps forwards and the conversation in the kitchen stopped. Kiley paused where she was.

She heard the scrape of a chair and someone murmured something.

"Hi baby," Austin greeted as he looked around the corner with a brilliant smile.

Kiley had to smile back. He looked so happy. "Morning."

He motioned her closer and she had no problem getting closer to him. His warm scent drew her to him until he wrapped both arms around her.

"You looked so peaceful sleeping, I didn't want to wake you," he whispered before kissing her softly.

"I miss you when you're not beside me," she confessed.

"Oh really, you two!" Ginger called from the kitchen. "Some of us just ate."

Both Kiley and Austin laughed and she let him lead her into the kitchen.

"You're just jealous," she accused Ginger with a smile.

Ginger waved her off but Kiley knew it was somewhat true. Since Austin had found his mate, Ginger had thought more and more about whether there was someone out there for her. Kiley patted the other woman's shoulder as she passed, heading for the coffee maker.

"So what has you up so early?" Kiley asked as she filled her cup.

"I'm trying to convince my brother that he really doesn't want to try to leave you and me behind when he takes his little trip," Ginger told her but locked gazes with her brother.

"Trip?" Kiley questioned. She hadn't known that Austin planned on going anywhere.

Austin sighed and motioned for her to join Ginger at the table. He glared at his sister before turning his attention to her.

"Colt called earlier. They never had the meeting with the Prince of Felines."

"What happened?" Kiley asked as she shot looks from brother to sister.

"The Prince was kidnapped," Austin told her quietly.

"He was kidnapped?" Kiley asked in disbelief.

Austin nodded.

"So Austin thinks he needs to go down with the search party and look," Ginger put in.

Kiley understood. "And you're going by yourself."

Austin shrugged. "I need to leave the guards here to watch over the Pack."

"And us?" Kiley questioned.

"And you," he admitted.

Kiley could tell it bothered him. He didn't want to leave her. But he was an honourable man and if he thought he should be there, she wouldn't stop him.

"I can be packed and ready to go in half an hour," she told him as she stood.

Ginger jumped up. "Me too!"

"No!" Austin barked. "You're both staying here."

The two women exchanged looks and Kiley grinned. "Not this time."

She turned and headed upstairs. She could hear Austin and Ginger arguing but she ignored them. What did one pack for a rescue mission?

She pulled a bag from the closet and started to throw jeans into it. She could hear Austin stomping up the stairs.

"You're not going," he announced as he stepped in the room.

Kiley looked up at him. He'd worry if she was there but she knew he couldn't really concentrate if he was worried about her at home either.

"I'm going and, from the sound of it, so is Ginger," she tried to calm him. "But we'll stay out of the way. I promise."

"Kiley," Austin seemed to deflate in front of her. "I don't want to leave you, but I have to go. The Prince was taken because of us."

"I know," she walked over to him and wrapped her arms around his waist. "Let us come. We'll know you're okay. You can be sure we are. We'll stay in a hotel room, I swear."

"I don't…"

"Austin, please just understand we need to do this," she pleaded.

His arms finally went around her until they held each other tight. "If anything happened to you…"

"It won't," she promised.

He dipped his head and she met his lips, sealing their mouths together.

Slowly, the passion she felt for him started to rise. She knew she would always love her mate and try to protect him. As much as he didn't want her hurt, she felt exactly the same way about him. In only a week's time, he'd become the most important person to her.

He moved, leading her to the bed, and she let him. Their clothes were removed with care until he lay over her body, poised to fill her.

"I love you," he told her, his voice strained with emotion.

She cupped his face and gazed into his eyes to let him know she was with him. "I love you too, Austin."

He entered her gently until he filled her like no one had ever done before. Carefully he made love to her. She understood what he was saying without the words.

She was precious to him. And she felt the same way.

"Mine, you're mine Austin. Until forever," she panted as she held tightly on to him.

"Forever," he agreed, with tears in his eyes.

Overwhelmed, Kiley couldn't look away. His body plunged into hers, owning her in every way. "Forever," she chanted, until her climax crested and she fell over the edge, Austin quickly joining her.

"You can come," he said quietly and Kiley held back a grin. There had really been no question.

PACK
COMMUNITY

Dedication

This book is dedicated to my husband — the love of my life and my biggest supporter. It was a difficult year but I love how much of a fighter you are. You make me proud to be your wife and I know you'll only grow stronger every day until you are fully healed.

Chapter One

Early evening heat surrounded Gray Mason as he stepped out of his Ford truck where he had pulled over to the side of the road. The sign in front of him welcomed him to Coyote Bluff, Texas. Located in the panhandle of the large state, it was a place he had never visited before. But recent signs had narrowed down to a couple of possibilities for where to find the Prince of felines—one of them being the canyons surrounding the town.

After speaking to the Alpha Council and the Pack Alpha for the west Texas area, arrangements had been made for Gray to investigate there.

He'd been hearing rumours about the town that accepted any and all shifters since he'd begun to investigate the kidnapping.

Excitement rippled through his body at the thought of the search finally going somewhere after three very long months. While the idea of an entire town full of shifters was a little unsettling to him, he would do everything in his power to finally end his journey and make his way home.

He surveyed the area directly around him, seeking any close being that might be a threat. Sensing he was alone, he pulled out his cell phone and called his Alpha.

"Hey, Gray, I was starting to wonder," Tyler greeted him.

Gray had to smile. Tyler would worry whether Gray called in or not, but Gray liked knowing that someone would at least notice if he was missing.

"Yeah, sorry about that, boss," Gray answered and he leaned against his tailgate. "Crappy reception down here."

"Just be careful. I contacted the sheriff there to let him know you would be stopping by in a day or so. He seems like an okay guy, but remember we don't have any ties there," Tyler warned.

"So he's not family?" Gray enquired, asking his Alpha if the man was a wolf shifter.

"I don't think so. The town is supposed to be full of other shifters but I just can't tell over the phone."

Gray grunted. It wasn't that he didn't like the others—he just hadn't met many. Most of his dealings were with the felines, and those experiences had not been good.

"I'll check into the hotel tonight, get a run in, and see what I can nose out before I meet with him tomorrow," Gray informed the other man.

"Just be careful. There is no wolf Pack there, but that doesn't mean that there are no wolves. You don't want to trespass against them before you know who you are dealing with. Especially without back-up."

"No problem. I'll stay away from any marked spots," he promised.

"Then call me tomorrow and get some rest," Tyler ordered.

"Will do." Gray hung up the phone, still grinning. He had been away from his Pack for so long he was starting to feel the loneliness more and more each day. While some wolf shifters had no problem going rogue, the true, deep comfort he found with his Pack mates was fading and it made him edgy. And an agitated wolf was never a good thing. He needed his family. He needed to get home soon.

Normally, he only shifted a few nights a month to let his animal out. The longer he was away from family, the more agitated both he and the wolf became. Running late at night seemed to be the only way he could calm himself, and even that was not working like it had.

"Coyote Bluff," he mumbled under his breath as he climbed back in his truck. "Out of all the animals…"

Pulling back onto the main road, he followed directions on signs until he saw what he'd been looking for. The hotel looked like an old cabin from the pioneer days. He parked in front of the door and got out, pleasantly surprised to see that, while it might look old, it was a sturdy building. The railing spreading from the entrance to both sides was composed of thick pieces of wood with delicate carvings.

A closer look revealed that the carvings were of several different animals. The detail—each species practically came to life—was amazing. There seemed to be more to this town than he'd first thought. He hefted his bag over his shoulder and pushed open the large oak door.

What greeted him first was the scent of fresh, hot home cooking. He'd been living out of convenience stores and on fast food for so long that his mouth watered as he thought about a home-cooked meal. His stomach rumbled in agreement.

"I guess that means the first order of business will be getting you something to eat," a tall, slender woman said, coming to his side, laughing.

Gray smiled at the pretty middle-aged woman. "Didn't realise I was so hungry until I smelt whatever you have cooking."

The woman laughed again, throwing her head back. "Oh no, Claude does all the cooking. But I will tell him you said that. I'm guessing you are Mr Mason?" she asked and guided him to the small, neat reception desk he hadn't noticed. "I'm Dorothy. Claude and I own this place, so if you need anything you just give me a holler."

"Yes, ma'am. Gray Mason here to check in and check out dinner."

"Oh, I am going to like you, Mr Gray Mason," she told him, patting his hand. "Just sign this registration form. We will charge your credit card when you check out. The dining room is open from five in the morning to eight at night. But if you want anything when it's not open, you just let me know and I will show you around the kitchen. It is open to all our guests. We get a lot of business in the dining room from the town folk so don't you worry about what time you eat. We've got plenty to feed everyone."

Gray nodded and signed the paper she'd given him.

"There are places to grab food in town also. We have a café, a coffee shop, a bakery, the pizza joint, and even a steak house on the other side of town heading out. All good food, although no one cooks like my Claude."

"Now, Dorothy, I think you may be a little biased." Gray turned as a heavyset man joined them. He was smiling and looked friendly, but it was the power behind his eyes that told Gray so much about him.

This was a shifter. Not wolf or feline, but something just as powerful. Gray stiffened and turned to face the man directly. He had hoped to avoid any display of dominance.

The smile fell from the other man's lips as he held out his hand. "Claude Gentry."

"Gray Mason, and Dorothy is correct. It smells amazing," Gray told the other man as they shook. While his wolf might be straining to get out, Gray was professional enough to control his instincts. Being a detective in a very human world had tested him enough.

As soon as the words left his lips, he felt the change in the other man. Instead of a mood to match the cautious handshake, the man returned to his joyful self. "Well, thank you, son. Let Dorothy get you checked in so we can feed you," he told Gray with a friendly slap on his back.

Gray turned back to the woman in time to see her send Claude a worried glance before smiling at him once more. Gray breathed in deeply, trying to place any familiar scents. The woman was surely human, although she smelt like Claude. But he just couldn't place the other man. The scent was more fresh air and fields than the wild and woodsy scent of wolves.

He couldn't come right out and ask without sounding rude, so he just pushed it to the back of his mind as he accepted his room key and listened to the directions to his room.

Passing through the cabin—he no longer thought of it as a hotel—he appreciated the beauty and comfort of the décor and feel. He liked the little place already.

* * * *

Dinner had been fantastic. With a full belly and after a couple of bottles of good domestic beer, Gray was starting to relax. As he stepped out onto the back porch, he glanced around, taking in the sights.

Despite the name, Coyote Bluff was a gorgeous town. He always felt better being surrounded by the woods and forests of home, but the canyons that surrounded him now had their own charm. He couldn't wait until later when he would be able to change forms and run.

But for now, as he waited for the evening to pass, he took a seat in one of the many chairs on the porch and kicked back. The restlessness that he had felt since before he'd arrived calmed, and peace settled deep inside him until his eyes started to droop and he let himself drift.

It was the light sound of footsteps that kicked his instincts into gear and had him popping his lids back open. Just off to the side at the porch steps stood a little boy, about five or six, staring at him.

Gray dropped his feet onto the deck and nodded in the kid's direction.

Taking that as an invitation, the little boy scrambled up the steps to hover over him. "I'm Toby, I live next door, my aunt said I could come over and get some cookies from Claude, he makes really good cookies and he always saves me some."

The words flew so fast and with such a heavy southern accent that Gray actually had to think about what had been said. Once he put it all together, he grinned. His Alpha had a young daughter, so he'd had some dealings with small children. "I haven't had the cookies yet but I hope you'll save me one."

The boy started to nod immediately. "I will. I promise."

Before Gray could respond, the boy scrunched up his face and sniffed. He knew the child was scenting him, and, while it would have been rude from an adult, he had a feeling the young boy he had just met didn't worry about things like that. Discreetly, he breathed in the boy's scent also.

He was shocked to smell cat.

"You smell funny!" Toby told him, leaning closer.

Gray couldn't hold in a laugh at the boy's exclamation and puzzled face. Once he quieted down, he knew that, no matter what species Toby was, the kid was all right. "I don't think I smell that bad. I took a shower earlier," he teased.

This caused Toby to shake his head so quickly he almost fell over. "No, you don't smell bad—just funny."

So he hadn't smelt another wolf before. That was interesting.

"Well, I'm a wolf so maybe that's it," Gray offered.

And found himself with a lap full of kid.

"You're a wolf!" Toby squealed. "A wolf! That is so cool! I always wanted to meet a wolf. Jim says that when I'm bigger I'll be able to meet everyone, but right now it's not safe."

Gray took in the boy's pout and pleading eyes and patted his back reassuringly. "You should listen to Jim—he seems like a smart guy. And right now it may not be safe but hopefully when you are bigger it will be."

"But you're a good wolf, right? You won't eat me or anything?"

Gray forced back another chuckle. "No, I promise I won't eat you."

The child relaxed in his lap. "That's cool then. What's your name? Did you tell me already? I don't remember you telling me, but sometimes I don't listen too well."

"I think I might have forgotten to tell you. My name is Gray."

"Gray?" Toby chewed on his lip. "I like that. Is it because in your other form you are grey?"

It was a good question and kind of made Gray proud of the boy, which surprised him because the child was still a complete stranger. A feline. Oh well, he could puzzle over that later. Right now he was enjoying his new friend.

"Actually, I am not grey at all as a wolf."

"Huh?" Toby thought about that.

"Well, little man? What are you?" Gray finally asked.

"Oh!" Toby jumped down so fast he almost toppled them both. But then he balled his hands on his hips and stuck his chest out. "I'm a bobcat!"

"Really?" Gray wouldn't have guessed that. Maybe that was why Toby's scent was a little different from the other felines he had met. He had never met a bobcat before. Lions and one tiger, but Toby was his first bobcat, so Gray told him that.

"Really!" the kid was squealing again. "That's so totally awesome!"

"Toby Jameson Williams!"

The boy and Gray both startled as a woman rushed up the steps.

"I am so sorry, mister. I didn't know he was out here pestering you. He was supposed to run into the kitchen and be right back," she hurriedly told him, pulling Toby to her side.

Gray stood and was almost knocked back by the woman's beauty. She was probably in her early thirties, with bright green eyes and reddish blonde hair. She was quite a bit shorter than him, and with her curvy body and ample breasts he was embarrassed to find himself getting hard.

She stood in front of him in nothing fancier than old jeans and a tank top and he wanted to pounce on her. He took a step back just to be safe. It had been so long since he'd been so attracted to anyone.

"It's fine, really. I was enjoying visiting with Toby," he told her sincerely.

She smiled then, relaxing just a touch, and it took his breath away. The fact that the female in front of him had the scent of a cat didn't seem to bother his body or his wolf, who was scratching to get out and play.

"Aunt Beth! Gray is a good wolf! He promised not to eat me," Toby told his aunt with all the innocence that could only come with one so small.

"Oh my! He didn't!" she exclaimed, hand going to her mouth.

Gray chuckled to show her he wasn't offended. "Yes, I did promise that and I always keep my promises, buddy."

Toby grinned back and finally the woman laughed.

"You'll have to excuse us. We haven't dealt with...with your...kind much," she stumbled to excuse.

Gray waved her off. "I understand. This is new for me, too. Toby is my first bobcat."

"Aunt Beth is a bobcat, too!" Toby added helpfully.

Gray had figured that but was glad to have it confirmed to him. That way he could get his head around the fact that, while she might be the sweetest-looking thing, she was still a cat and therefore still suspect.

"I thought I heard voices out here," Claude said, joining them on the porch. He carried a small plastic bag with him. "Beth called over to send Toby back, but I hadn't seen him. I take it you both have met our new guest?"

"Yes, Claude! And he's a wolf. But a nice wolf. He won't eat me."

Claude glanced over at Gray, who just nodded in agreement. Okay, it had been funny but now he was starting to worry about all the wolf talk. He hoped it wasn't the same around town or he would never be able to get anything useful from the residents.

And he needed to find something there. They needed a lead.

Chapter Two

Beth led Toby back to their house, still thinking about the wolf shifter. It had scared her to death when she had spotted her nephew right in front of the man. Every protective instinct she had in her had wanted to jump in front of the boy until the threat was gone.

Instead, she had been stunned at how open and friendly he had been. Not to mention handsome. Even as she'd crossed the yard, desire had battled her fear.

But she couldn't afford to think like that. While her community might be built on tolerance of human and inter-species relationships, she was still a cat and he a wolf. Sometimes it wasn't meant to be, and, attracted or not, this was one of those times.

Well, maybe she could still think about those gorgeous eyes that had practically set her on fire. His built body and height didn't hurt either. No one had to know, did they? If he had been a cat, or any other species, she would have thought he'd make the perfect mate.

She inwardly sighed as she followed Toby up the stairs to his room while he went on and on about the wolf next door. She would have to warn her brother that Toby was completely taken with the stranger. When Toby's natural curious nature came out and he got this way, only time would divert his attention.

Together the two of them followed Toby's nightly ritual of brushing teeth and getting ready for bed. Once her nephew was tucked in, she kissed his forehead. "Daddy will be home soon and in to check on you," she told him.

"Cool! I will tell him all about my new friend!"

She smiled down at him, although she had every intention of beating him to it. That way, at least her brother would be a little more prepared than she had been.

Back downstairs, she made herself a glass of iced sweet tea and went to sit on the front porch swing. Her body was still humming happily after the encounter with the wolf shifter and although she couldn't act on it, she thought she might as well enjoy it while she could.

Few wolves ever ventured into Coyote Bluff. Wolves tended to keep with their Packs and in their territory. The ones that had come by usually didn't last long. They were too dominating to leave things alone around town, and while the people might be tolerant of one another, they were also protective.

Their ways worked for them. And no one was going to let a rogue wolf come in and take over. A few had tried, but they were almost always quickly run out of town.

With the exception of one wolf, none had ever stayed. Mark was a special case, though. The wolf was so tormented and afraid that he jumped at his own shadow. Even after a year of living in town, the wolf hardly ever left his house and, as far as she knew, never shifted.

She wasn't completely sure what had happened to him and she never pressed. They had become friends, but she knew she was one of only a few. Toby himself had never met him.

The story about the feline Prince being taken had reached them when it had happened. The town wasn't into the politics of the felines and others, but given the number of felines in town, they were asked to keep an eye out for anything suspicious. The rumour of the wolves helping search for him seemed to be true, if the reason for Gray's visit was really with the hopes of helping.

The sheriff, Jim, had told them some of the searchers might be coming down, but Beth hadn't really thought any other shifter species would care about the Prince.

Half of her *own* species didn't care. Cats were solitary creatures, and while they did have a royal line that governed the big laws, most felines lived their own lives and didn't get involved in each other's business.

It wasn't like that here. That was what she liked about her home. She could live close to her family and wasn't expected to fend for herself. Very un-cat-like.

Her brother Dawson and Toby were the only close family members she had. Their parents had left them right after they had become adults. The oldest sibling—her and Dawson's brother, Casey—had joined the military and they hadn't seen him since. That had been twenty years ago.

The headlights from her brother's patrol car bathed her in a spotlight as he parked. She scooted over on the swing as he stomped the dust off his boots then took a seat next to her.

"It's a nice night. I thought the heat would never break," he greeted.

It had been unusually hot for May. Already hitting in the hundreds and summer wasn't even upon them yet.

She handed over her tea to share and nudged his shoulder. "Toby made a new friend."

Relaxing back into the wood swing, Dawson chuckled. "What is it this time? A fish in the pond or maybe a rat from the barn?"

Toby was forever making friends with anything that moved. Shifter or regular animal, it didn't matter.

"Wolf shifter," she said quietly.

Dawson stiffened and out of the corner of her eye she could see him thinking about his words before he spoke.

"So he made it to town? Jim wasn't sure what day, but had thought within three."

She nodded. "Came in tonight. I didn't know he had arrived yet and Toby wanted some of Claude's cookies."

"And instead found a wolf?" Dawson guessed.

"Yep. When he didn't come right back, I went looking for him and found him on the porch of the inn."

She could see Dawson straining himself to keep calm. She should probably stop teasing him, but what were sisters for?

"Damn it, Beth." His patience was finally up. "Do I need to kick a wolf's ass or not?"

Giggling, she slapped her brother's leg. "Nah, he promised not to eat Toby."

Dawson groaned. "Please tell me he didn't use those exact words."

"Oh, he sure did."

"Damn it," he groused. "I never would have said that if I had known Toby would take it so literally."

She snorted, unable to hold back her amusement. "Well, Gray seemed pretty cool about it if that helps."

Shaking his head, he stood. "If he is here for more than a few days, I can only imagine what else will be said. But I guess I'll find out tomorrow. Jim wants me to show Gray some of the trails. We don't think anyone has been past the barriers into the unused parts of the canyon, but really it's too big to know for sure. The park rangers are covering the public entrances."

"Is that why they're here? They think someone might be hiding in the canyon?" she asked. Usually her brother kept work to himself, but if he was willing to talk, she wanted to know. She had the same curious nature as her nephew.

"It's nothing to worry about," Dawson told her, switching back to 'big brother'. "If anyone is here, we will find them for sure. It's been a long hot day. I'm going to work out before I shower."

"Okay. Now that it's cooled down, I might go for a run."

"Just be careful. Especially with a strange wolf in town."

"I promise not to be eaten by the big bad wolf, either," she teased.

Dawson rolled his eyes but went into the house without another word. It was a good thing, because once she caught her own words, she blushed, thinking about one way she wouldn't mind being eaten by the wolf.

She sighed and set her tea down on the table. A run was a good idea. She could burn off some energy and hopefully not be up all night thinking about the sexy man next door.

Trails to the canyon area were all over town. It gave the residents easy access to let their animal sides loose. The public access to the canyon was on the other side of the area, with hundreds of acres in between. Even if they were spotted as animals, no one would be the wiser. And she could smell the humans before they would ever see her. Plus, the park rangers kept all bridges and roads to their area closed off. It helped that most of the rangers were shifters or related to one somehow.

That was how the community worked. They looked out for one another. Humans had the police. The shifters only had each other.

It was a short ten-minute walk to the clearing where she could shift. She climbed up and into the cave she and Dawson used, quickly shedding her clothes before becoming a bobcat.

She stretched, enjoying the pull on her muscles. Even though it had been less than a week since she'd shifted, it felt like it had been so much longer. She rubbed against the walls of the cave, giving in to the instinct to mark her territory. There were no other bobcats in the community other than her brother—and when he finally shifted, her nephew—but it still felt good to her cat to follow tradition.

Since she didn't actually like to run, but was more of a climber, she decided to head up to the top of the canyon so she could lie around under the moon. There was a small creek close by too.

She started up, leaping and jumping as much as she could. Her curious nephew always asked how she felt when she got to shift, and as hard as she tried, she could never find the right words. It felt freeing, like she was finally completely herself.

The thick foliage covered her as she stalked around, wishing for a playmate to pounce on. Sometimes her brother would come with her, but most of the time she was alone. Even other cats in town preferred to be by themselves. Her cat seemed to be missing that part of its personality.

A low tree branch offered her more fun as she climbed and chewed on it. As she started to scratch, she heard the yowl of a lone wolf not too far from where she was playing.

Planning on just getting a look at the wolf, she leapt from the branch and prowled towards the sound. It was less than five minutes before she caught a woodsy scent ahead of her. Crouching, she started crawling forward.

There at the creek she had planned on visiting herself stood a fully grown wolf. Her senses told her it was also a shifter, but she would have guessed that even without them since she knew how rare that type of wolf was. The red wolves were an endangered species reported to total less than one hundred in America.

Looking at the animal, she was awed.

She squatted low to the ground to keep her hiding place as he dipped his head to drink from the clear creek. *What a beautiful creature*, she mused as he stretched his neck back and howled again. Even though she was a cat, she still felt the loneliness that call conveyed. An answering rumble gathered in her throat and she had to hold herself back.

In the wild they were natural enemies. Even while human, she had never met a wolf who didn't think he was better than her.

With a heavy sigh, she laid her head down on the ground. She must have been louder than she'd thought because his head snapped in her direction. She was downwind so she knew he hadn't picked up her scent.

She tried to make herself as small as possible, belatedly realising that spying on a wolf she didn't know wasn't the brightest idea she'd ever had.

To his credit, he didn't charge her. Instead, he tilted his head to the side and lowered himself much the same way she had.

She watched as he slowly crawled closer to her. When their gazes met, he stopped.

The same pull she had felt earlier returned and her muscles bunched as she waited.

He started towards her again, just as slowly and carefully, and she also scooted closer. They had started several yards away, but all too soon—and yet not soon enough—they were in the open with just a few feet separating them.

The wolf rolled to his side and pawed the ground. If she could have, she would have laughed. Instead the sound that came out of her was more of a small purr.

The wolf's ears perked up before he did it again.

So, as he'd asked, she moved to rest next to him. They didn't touch—just breathed in each other and shared the night. Side by side they stayed as the stars over them twinkled and the canyon sounds sang for them.

It was nice—peaceful, even—and she relaxed enough to close her eyes.

A whisper of a hot breath passed over her as the wolf bumped her chin with his head. She nuzzled into him without thinking.

The zing of awareness that shot through her body shocked her. He must have felt something too because he jerked before nudging her again.

If they were in human form, she had no doubt they would be kissing. But as animals...

She jerked away. Damn it, she was a bobcat. There was no way she could have these feelings for a wolf. As carefully as she could, she inched away from him. He turned back onto his stomach, watching her.

As he moved towards her, she swiped at him with her claws still sheathed. She didn't want to hurt him but she had to get away.

What in the world had she been thinking? They hadn't just been playing—they were flirting, practically making out.

Once she had enough room to flee, she turned and took off. She didn't look behind her. Didn't dare. She just ran away.

She scrambled down the canyon cliffs, not slowing until she got to her cave. Just as she reached her spot, she heard the heart-breaking sound of that howl.

Didn't matter, she told herself. They were from two different worlds.

Chapter Three

Gray wasn't in the best mood when he woke the next morning. The interaction with the bobcat had kept him tossing and turning all night. He hadn't meant to scare her away. He hadn't meant for anything to happen at all.

But when he had heard a small rustle in the wind and had turned and seen her, his brain had gone and he had been left running on emotion. It had been so long since he'd been able to run with his Pack. The loneliness had got to him and he'd sent his call out to the wild. To find Beth in her other form there when he was so low had seemed like fate.

But he had pressed too hard and too fast. She didn't even know him and yet he had wanted to cover her with his scent and have hers all over him — to make a claim.

He quickly ran though his morning routine, not even taking the time to relieve his morning wood. His hand had lost all appeal over the last few months, anyway.

He perked up a little at the wonderful smells from the kitchen once he got to the dining room.

"There you are!" Dorothy greeted him as he entered. She ushered him to a table with a window view. "Best seat in the house."

It was—a nice view of the canyon with the sunrise coming up.

"I was worried you would miss the magical moment," Dorothy told him. She poured a cup of coffee from a tray and set it in front of him.

"Magical?" he enquired politely.

"You just watch. You'll see," she promised and patted his shoulder. "I'll go get your breakfast."

He opened his mouth to remind her that he hadn't ordered yet but she was already headed in the direction of the kitchen. Shrugging, he looked back out of the window.

That was when he saw it—the blending of colours as the sun hit the canyon surface. He leant forward to try to catch every inch possible. Yellows, oranges, reds— all mixed together until the world before him came alive.

A bald eagle flew into sight and dipped low as if greeting the morning.

"It's pretty amazing, huh?" A deep voice interrupted his admiration.

Gray hated to pull his attention away but turned to greet his company. "It really is," he agreed.

The striking man in front of him wore a deputy's uniform. He was also a cat, and an older version of young Toby.

Gray stood and held out a hand. The man looked shocked for a second but quickly schooled his face.

"Gray Mason," he introduced.

"Dawson Wilson." They shook and Dawson motioned back to the window. "Not a lot of people get to witness Mother Nature coming alive. You should count yourself lucky."

Gray understood the underlined meaning of the words. He shouldn't wear out his welcome. "I do," he assured the other man.

"Sheriff Manor told us about your visit yesterday and asked if I would be willing to show you some of the unmarked trails that might be worth investigating. Since I was here, I thought we could discuss exactly what you are looking for while we enjoy some of Claude's cooking," Dawson suggested.

"Well then, please join me. Dorothy said she was bringing me some food…"

"She saw me come in. I eat here every morning so she'll take care of me," Dawson explained. "But before we get down to business, I would like to get one thing out of the way."

Gray tried not to tense. After what had happened the night before with Beth, he had no doubt her brother would tell him to stay away. The man had every right, too. They didn't know Gray. From what he gathered about the other wolves who visited, they had every right to wonder about his intentions. Hell, even *he* didn't know what his intentions were.

"I understand you met my son last night."

Gray nodded cautiously. "Toby."

Dawson surprised him by sighing. "He's a good kid. Curious and loves adventure, but I know he can be a little much. I would just appreciate it if he starts to bug you that you tell Dorothy, Claude, or my sister Beth. They can keep him out of your hair."

"Honestly, I wasn't put out in any way last night. My Alpha has a daughter a few years older than him and, with my being gone so long from the Pack, Toby was actually a very welcome sight. You're right, though—he is a great kid."

Dawson seemed to relax. "Thanks, man."

Dorothy came back with two plates of food and a cup of coffee for Dawson. Once she'd refilled Gray's cup and was on her way to help someone else, Gray got a good look at the food. Eggs, bacon, sausage, biscuits and gravy, and hash browns covered every inch of the large plate. And the smell... He could have died and gone to heaven.

"Luckily, they're used to serving shifters so every plate is always packed full to fill us up," Dawson told him with amusement.

"I've got to tell you, I don't eat this good at home," Gray shared.

The two men dug into their breakfasts. A comfortable silence settled over the table. Dorothy topped off the coffee as she walked by but never interrupted.

Once he'd stuffed his face and had mopped up the last of the juices with a bit of biscuit, Gray patted his stomach and leant back. "Damn, that was good."

Dawson grinned over his own empty plate. "Yep. Now you know why I'm here every morning."

Gray smiled back and picked up his cup. He already liked the other man. With Dawson's help, maybe he would finally be able to make some headway in the investigation. Dawson seemed like the kind of man Gray would enjoy working with also. He just got the feeling that Dawson was a straight shooter who protected his family and his community.

"So, Jim—the sheriff—said you had reason to believe that the ones who took the Prince may have travelled through here, or might even still be here?"

"Yeah, there hasn't been enough evidence to really point out who they are, but we've come up on a couple of their hideouts. We always seem to be missing them by a week or less, so some of the Alphas are worried we have a leak warning them before we get there."

Dawson nodded for him to continue.

"This last time we tried to keep it as quiet as possible. But somehow they must have been tipped off because they were gone when we got to the camp in Oklahoma. They had only been gone a couple of hours, and while they'd tried to burn all of their papers and stuff, they didn't get to it all before they took off. We were able to dig out some half-burned papers and there were maps. One of the locations was the canyon."

"And the others?" Dawson asked.

"Some caves in New Mexico, and a location down in the swamp near New Orleans. We split up and I came here. It might be nothing but we have to check it out."

"Let me ask you this," Dawson said, lowering his voice. "Why do you care? What do the wolf Packs have to gain in finding him?"

It was a fair question and Gray would have been surprised not to have been asked. "That's tricky. Yes, the Prince had agreed to meet with our wolf representative to discuss him joining some of our Packs who will be going public. Just to meet—he had not said one way or the other if he would consider joining. That's tied into my motivation to help. By all accounts, the Prince was taken because he'd even agreed to meet. If we caused him to be taken because of that, it is our responsibility to help get him back."

Gray paused and glanced back out of the window. "This is nice. The town, this community you all have here, protecting one another. It's like a Pack. But not everyone has that. We have several rogue wolves that don't have Packs, cats that are solitary and live alone, even other shifters that have no family at all. Little by little, they're being hunted down like their lives mean nothing. There is no one to protect those shifters. By becoming known to the world, we will be able to bring awareness to those who would hunt us."

"You have strong feelings about this," Dawson noted.

"The natural wolves that share my breed are almost extinct. And, while they are trying to reintroduce some into these parts, it will never be the same. I also lost a good friend of mine about ten years ago. He was a grey wolf and was out hunting in protected lands. Two hunters killed him. They were busted and all they got was a slap on the wrist. They killed a *man*. Yes, he was a shifter, but he should have been protected there."

"I understand, but, without hunting, some animals will take over," Dawson argued.

"Yes, but if we have protected land to run in and the penalties are stiffer, then it's a start," Gray volleyed back.

Dawson sat back and held up his hands. "I agree with you, man. And I think it's a good idea but I wonder how it will work. What would keep people from kidnapping a shifter to try to become one themselves? We know that can't happen. You can't be bitten by a wolf or scratched by a cat and become a shifter. How do we prove that?"

Gray shook his head. "I don't know. Tony, the wolf who is the representative for the shifters and the government, says it's all about education. The government, or a select group of them, knows about us. Hell, some *are* us. He says that once we come out everyone will be surprised by how high the support goes."

"Huh. Well, we aren't going to figure it out today. I brought an extra pack for you, so if you're about ready to head out, we can get started. Leaving this early, at least it isn't a hundred degrees."

Gray stood along with him. "I'm ready." He had dressed in jeans and a T-shirt, his hiking boots were old and worn in, and his ball cap was stuffed in his back pocket.

The two headed for the door.

"I pulled my SUV in front this morning—" Dawson started.

"Daddy! Wolf!" Toby ran to the two men and threw himself into his father's arms.

"Toby, his name is Gray, not Wolf," Dawson gently corrected the youngster.

"Sorry, Daddy. Hi, Gray!" Toby greeted, waving his arms frantically.

"Hey there, little man," he told the boy, patting his head, and Dawson put him down. He turned to the woman hovering in the back ground. "Good morning, ma'am."

Beth smiled and blushed a little, but thankfully seemed okay with him. "Good morning, Gray."

She was just as stunning as yesterday. Every feeling of rightness he'd had being in her presence returned. He stepped closer to her and was thrilled when she did the same. That was when he caught what the other two members of her family were talking about.

"Not today, son—Gray and I have to work. But we will be home for dinner. Why don't the four of us have dinner here tonight?"

"Really? Cool!" Toby was already excited.

Dawson glanced at Gray and he nodded. He wouldn't mind spending some time with the family. He really wanted to talk with Beth, too.

"All right, then we better get going and you go have breakfast," Dawson told his son.

"Maybe after dinner you wouldn't mind taking a walk with me?" Gray asked Beth softly.

She darted a look at her brother but nodded. "I think I would like that."

Elated, Gray grinned.

"See you later, Toby," he told the boy, walking past him.

"Bye, wolf Gray! See you tonight!" he hollered back happily.

Beth hushed him as she led him back the way they had come, and the two men headed outside. The heat was already starting to rise as they reached the patrol vehicle.

Gray pulled on his cap and sunglasses from where they'd been hanging on his shirt, and climbed in.

"There's an old ranger station about a half mile down an old road. If they didn't want to come through town or the public entrance, that would be the best bet. It's overgrown but, if they were determined enough, they could get into the canyon that way."

As they drove, Gray got the first look at the town in daylight. Cute cobblestone streets covered the downtown area, with old-style black lamp posts on the corners and no traffic lights.

"Up ahead is the station. There is the sheriff, Jim Manor, and two deputies—me and a human named Stan Davis."

"Human?" Gray asked, surprised.

"Most of the town is either shifters or their families. All know about us so it's safe. Stan's brother is a mechanic. He's married to Tammie, who runs a hair salon named Foxy Ladies. She's a fox shifter."

"A fox?" Gray leaned closer to the side window as they passed first the station then three buildings later the salon. "I have to be honest—other than wolves and a few felines, I have never met any other shifters."

"I don't imagine you have. Most wolves stay within their territory and with their own kind."

Gray was about to defend his species but Dawson cut him off. "And there is nothing wrong with that. Wolves stay together. It's one of the traits I admire most. The only family I have besides Toby is my sister. Everyone else has taken off to be on their own. Even Toby's mom left after a year."

"Oh man, I'm sorry to hear that," Gray replied honestly. If he were lucky enough to have kids, he couldn't see himself ever leaving them.

"It's our way. I can't fault them, but I also don't agree. We are human also—I like to think more human than animal. So leaving your child, your family... I just don't..."

Gray let him trail off without pushing. The comfort he felt with the bobcat family was unusual. It also felt instinctual and he would just have to trust it.

"Anyway, we moved here so Toby could grow up with other shifters and never have to worry about being picked on for being a small cat. The bigger species can be brutal about that."

There was a story there but Gray let that pass also.

"I don't know why I am telling you all this. I just really want you to understand how important this town is to me. This is a safe haven. Your comment about it being like a Pack was dead on. If the people you are after are here, I want to help you catch them. Help you get the Prince back. But I don't want anything to hurt the town or its residents. My friends."

Gray glanced over at the other man. Every emotion showed on his face. "I promise to do my best to protect the town and everyone in it. I've been on the road for three months now. This is the first time I wanted to stop and just rest without pushing twenty-four hours. There is just something about this place, or maybe the people, that just calms me."

Dawson laughed, tossing his head back. "Careful, man, we might just keep you."

Gray smiled but was somewhat troubled. That was what was starting to worry him—the settled feelings that had been with him since he'd arrived.

Back at home, things had changed. The Pack was growing. Some of the wolves in Colorado were moving around, as his Alpha had decided to go public, while another Alpha—Austin, the mate of a good friend—had chosen to stay hidden.

Austin had made the best decision for his Pack and his family, and Tyler, Gray's Alpha, the best for them. But with Austin and Kiley mating and her moving away, Tyler's daughter Jessie growing up, and himself getting older, Gray had started to feel like life was passing him by.

He enjoyed working as a detective and with his Pack. But there was more to an existence than work.

He just needed to finish his current mission before he could decide on the rest of his.

Chapter Four

The old ranger station was indeed run-down, with overgrown foliage covering the building and drive. As Dawson parked, Gray looked out of the window, trying to see if anything had been disturbed.

"It's been about a week since the last rain," Dawson informed him as they exited the vehicle.

"We're only about three days behind them, so if they came through here, there might be some trail." Gray shared his hope.

"The building still looks secure," Dawson observed. "But let's check it out."

As they searched around the outside, Gray tried to breathe in and remember every scent for future use. Most of the smells were old, but a few — three separate ones — were stronger than the others and seemed to be newer.

"They didn't get inside, but I can smell strangers. Maybe up to five days old? Not sure, but I don't recognise them."

Gray nodded. Back behind the building was some broken and stomped-down vegetation. "You see that?" he asked, tilting his head.

Dawson followed his line of sight, backing away from the window he'd been trying to look in. "Let's go."

Slowly and soundlessly, they started the search. It wasn't a clear path—whoever had been through had been careful—but they were still able to get a mile from the station before they had to make a decision on which way to go. It helped that Dawson knew the area well.

"If it was me, I would head east to the caves. If they go too far west, they could run into tourists and the rangers. They might be able to blend in there, so it's still a possibility, but I just don't think they would risk it if they were trying to hide someone," Dawson offered his opinion.

"I trust your instincts. Let's head west then," Gray agreed.

The trek up the canyon and closer to the caves was hard-going. They stopped after an hour and thirty minutes at the first of a series of caves to grab a drink and eat energy bars while they discussed a game plan.

"What do you think about shifting when we get closer? It would be easier to search, we can cover more ground, and use our animal instincts to see if anyone has been through," Dawson enquired.

Gray took a swig from his water bottle. "That will work for me."

"I, uh… I have shifted with others from town so I don't think my cat will have any issues, but will your wolf…?" Dawson asked, finishing with a wave from his hand.

Gray remembered the night before and smiled. "I think it will be okay."

"Good." Dawson stood from where he had been sitting against a rock. "Let's get back to it then."

They gathered the wrappers and bottles and stuffed them in their packs. They climbed for another fifteen minutes before they came to a small group of trees with cover to hide their things.

"Let's start at the first cave and go from there. Once we get to where the paths intercept, we should get an idea if anyone has been through."

Gray nodded in agreement and they started to strip. Gray ran often with his Pack so he had no problem stripping in front of the other man. They separated a little when it came time to shift.

Only minutes later, he waited in his bigger wolf form for the bobcat.

Dawson jumped onto one of the large rocks and stretched. Gray shook his body, feeling the muscles move and pull. He loved his other form. Enjoyed the freedom.

Dawson vaulted down and joined him and the two of them took off in a slow run. They didn't want to use up energy they might need later. They'd had to leave the radio Dawson had carried with their clothes. No cell phone reception, so that wouldn't be able to help, either.

The day was more for recon than anything else. If they came up on anyone, they would have to handle it with just the two of them. With enough time, if the Prince wasn't in immediate danger, or they had too big of an area, they could call in backup.

They reached the first cave and Dawson went first. While he nosed around the opening, Gray watched his

back, keeping every one of his senses open to any danger around them.

Dawson looked back at him and Gray nudged him to go ahead. He didn't smell any others around so it should be pretty safe.

Gray stayed outside while Dawson searched the cave. After the bobcat came out and shook himself, they moved along to the next one.

It was another hour of searching, the two of them growing more and more frustrated, before they picked up a scent that should not have been there.

Gray smelt another wolf.

He lowered himself to the ground and growled low in the back of his throat. Dawson turned to him and followed his direction.

This was what they'd been looking for—a sign that someone had been up there. It could have just been a lone wolf, but Gray didn't want to take a chance.

Gray stood watch as Dawson moved farther up the canyon, which was becoming steeper until even Dawson had a little trouble with his footing. Gray stayed close, though, giving Dawson room but still offering the security he would need to concentrate on any scents.

The two of them followed the faint trail for another half an hour before Dawson stopped and rested. Gray sat close by, on watch. When he felt a nudge and Dawson dipped his head, he understood the message to change back to human.

Once both men had gone from animal to human, they shared a troubled look.

"Wolf and feline," Gray shared.

"Yes, the farther up we go it gets stronger." Dawson shook his head. "The beginning of the trail was a lot harder to find. Now that we're getting closer, it's like they're waving around their scents. I don't know whether they got careless or if they don't care if we find them."

"A trap then?" Gray asked, as he'd had the same thought.

"I don't know," Dawson admitted. "But I have a bad feeling."

Gray nodded. "So do we turn around and get help or should we go further?"

They stood thinking for several minutes before Dawson spoke again. "There's something else. One of the scents. I know it."

"From town?"

"No..." Dawson started but was interrupted by a low menacing growl.

Gray moved without even having to think about it. He jumped in front of Dawson, shifted, and blocked the other man from the wolf slowly approaching from a ledge just overhead.

The dark wolf was bigger than Gray, but he had no doubt he could handle him. That was until another growl reached him from behind. He felt the disturbance in the wind as Dawson shifted into his feline form, and the two of them backed up against each other.

Gray watched as they were stalked. The muscles in his legs flexed as he prepared to defend. He was less than ten feet from the wolf. He couldn't tell how close the other one was but the stiffness from Dawson's body told him it wasn't far.

Gray took a deep breath. The other wolf watched him and, just as Gray prepared to jump, the larger wolf launched itself off the ledge.

Gray caught the wolf in mid-air and they went down hard. The wolf could fight, that was for sure.

Gray was in good shape from being a cop and as protection for his Alpha, but the wolf he fought was good—very good.

They nipped and bit as they rolled around. He couldn't take his eyes off his opponent but he hoped the commotion from the side was Dawson faring better than him.

Gray just managed to stop himself from being pinned by teeth around his neck. He pushed off the other wolf, dragging his claws against the underbelly of the enemy. The black wolf snarled at him and went for him again when the small body of a bobcat knocked into the wolf.

Dawson had come to his aid. Gray rose from the ground as Dawson backed the wolf up. Gray was just ducking in for another attack when he stopped at the loud and vicious roar of a cat.

They froze and glanced up at the feline above them. A bobcat, similar to Dawson but just a little bigger, was within striking distance.

The cat roared again before he started to shift.

"Stop!" the now naked man ordered. "Shift."

Gray glanced at Dawson but his attention was frozen, staring up at the stranger. He nudged his partner, asking what they should do. Did he know the other shifters?

He nudged Dawson harder and finally Dawson shook himself and nodded. They stepped back together to get more distance from the strangers before they started their shifts.

The two they had fought were back to human just as Gray and Dawson finished.

Gray looked over the others warily. The wolf he'd fought was a big guy—huge and muscular with tattoos down both arms, his chest and abdomen. The big Semper Fi tat over his heart was testament to where he had received his training. The one that Dawson had taken on was about Gray's size, clean-cut, and looked like a typical soldier. Then he took in the man still on the ledge above them. He was tall but thinner than his partners, though still muscular, and his demeanour screamed leader.

"Dawson," the man greeted and jumped down, landing gracefully on his feet.

Dawson had once again gone tense beside Gray. "Casey."

Gray watched the interaction. Casey moved slowly towards them and Gray didn't like the way Dawson started to shake.

He shuffled his feet and tried to make himself bigger and block Dawson.

The man coming towards them put up his hands. "Dawson…"

Gray was unprepared for Dawson to come around him and punch the man. His head snapped back. Before he recovered, Dawson hit him again. Gray grabbed Dawson's arms and pulled him back as the other two men started forward. But the man he'd assaulted held up a hand.

"It's okay."

Dawson didn't even try to break free of Gray's hold. Instead he stood there, breathing hard, and glaring daggers at the other man.

"I know what you must think…"

"Save it, Case," Dawson snapped. "I'm all right, Gray. You can let go."

Gray still wasn't sure but he dropped his hold anyway. Maybe they could get some answers.

Dawson straightened. "You all have just assaulted an officer of this county and his consultant. I would like an explanation before I haul all your asses in to jail."

The two wolves bristled before they were waved off. "RJ, Mike—please meet my brother, Dawson." Then he walked towards Gray and held out a hand. "Casey Williams."

Gray cut his eyes to Dawson, who barely nodded his confirmation. Gray shook hands, noticing the power of the cat close to the surface. "Gray Mason."

"Ah, the Wolf Council's representative," Casey said with a smile. "Didn't think you'd get here so quick."

Gray stiffened but Casey just grinned.

"Follow us. I think we have some explaining to do."

Casey led the way back up into the canyon. Dawson and Gray walked side by side, with the two wolves bringing up the rear. Gray didn't like strange wolves at his back and he stayed on alert. He needed to know what was going on. They obviously knew who he was.

The path was well hidden. He and Dawson probably would have found it but only in shifted form and by scent. Casey called out as they approached a cave entrance. A small but sturdy man edged out.

Dawson and Gray both took fighting stance and prepared to shift.

"Stop." The power behind that voice had everyone freezing. "We are not enemies."

Gray gasped when the person belonging to the voice walked out of the darkness. After months of searching, he now stood face to face with Prince Zachary, the leader of the felines.

"What the hell!" Gray growled. He had been away from home for months in hopes that they would be able to rescue the Prince and stop a war between the two species.

"Grayson." Prince Zachary bowed his head in respect. "We have much to speak about. Please come sit with us."

Gray's feet started to move before he had even realised it. It was a shock just how much pull the Prince had. He felt a little better with Dawson at his back.

The Prince motioned them to the pallets of bedding on the cave floor. Gray sat warily and noted the Prince eyeing Dawson. "Dawson Williams." He held out a hand.

Dawson looked uncomfortable but grasped the Prince's hand. He let out a small unmanly squeak when he was pulled into the arms of the Prince.

"I have wanted to meet you for so long. Your brother has told me stories of this canyon and your family for many years. Forgive me, but I feel like I already know you."

Dawson cut his gaze to his brother. Casey shifted a little on his feet. It was interesting, this family dynamic, but Gray was getting impatient. He wanted to know what was going on and he wanted to know *why*.

Prince Zachary released Dawson, who sat down quickly next to Gray. Gray gripped his shoulder to show support while the others nodded. Dawson nodded back in thanks.

"Before you is RJ Cross, Mike Jackson"—he motioned to the two wolves—"and Jesse Grimes." He waved his hand at the small feline shifter who was still eyeing them.

"Also let me convey my great appreciation to the Wolf Council for everything they have done for me and my people over the last few months," Prince Zachary started.

Gray bit back mentioning just how much they had done only to have the Prince found just fine.

"Until last week I was under imprisonment by a few of my trusted advisors," Prince Zachary told them. "They would discuss the wolves' involvement in the search. Even had pictures of all of you. That was how I knew who you were."

"We were tracking Zach also and almost ran into one of your other teams. It seemed like we were getting much of the same information," Casey added.

"If you were going after the Prince, why didn't you let the team you saw know? Don't you think that would have helped with the search instead of everyone covering the same ground?" Dawson questioned.

Casey shook his head. "We didn't know who to trust. We kept getting close but they would pull out and move before we got there."

Gray could understand that—he really could—but that didn't help him feel less frustrated. "So instead of letting us know you had the Prince safe, you continued to run and lead us here?"

"We weren't trying to draw you in. When we went in for Zach, there were only a few guards. We want everyone responsible."

"Okay." Gray agreed with that strategy. "Why tell us now?"

"You're good," Casey complimented. "And I know I can trust Dawson."

Dawson snorted. "You don't know anything about me, Case. You left. We haven't heard from you in years."

Casey frowned and scooted closer to his brother. "I've kept an eye on you and Beth as best I could. My unit does a lot of work out of the country, and the rest of the time we protect Zach. I had people watching."

"Oh, that makes me feel so much better," Dawson drawled bitterly. "You've had people spying on me."

Casey tried to respond but the Prince cut him off. "It's one of the reasons we're here. Anyone who knows I've been rescued will have no doubt your brother was involved. He wanted to make sure you and your sister were safe—that they didn't try to get me through you."

"Why would anyone come after us?" Dawson asked suspiciously.

Casey linked his fingers with the Prince's. "Because we're mates."

Chapter Five

Gray knew he was staring but he couldn't help it. Dawson's brother was mates with the feline Prince. He hadn't seen that one coming.

"You've got to be kidding me!" Dawson jumped to his feet.

Casey rose and crossed his arms over his chest. "He's my mate."

Dawson shook his head and looked over at Gray. "This is nuts."

Gray climbed up. "Makes sense, though." He glanced over at Casey. "That's why you kept getting close. You could feel him through your bond."

Casey nodded. "I was on a mission when he was taken. Only a few people knew that we"—he waved indicating the group around him—"weren't in the residence. I knew it had to be someone we trusted behind the kidnapping."

"Who was it?"

It was the Prince that answered. "My cousin Raphael. He was one of my advisors."

157

"Dawson, come on, man. We need to hear the rest of this." Gray tugged Dawson back to sitting down. He noticed, when Casey sat, it was closer to the Prince.

"I mean no disrespect to you, Prince Zachary, but this is just a lot to take in. If you're mated to Casey that means my sister and son really are in danger."

"They are being protected. I have an old major that used to be in the unit looking out for them," Casey assured his brother.

"What...? Who?"

Casey smiled. "Claude."

"From the inn?" Gray had to ask. He'd felt the power and strength from the man. "He's not a wolf or a feline." He glanced at Dawson for confirmation.

The tattooed wolf, who had until then remained quiet, chuckled.

Gray glared at him.

"Hey, it's okay, man. I never could figure it out. Finally, right before our last tour together, I asked him."

"Well...?" Gray prompted when the man didn't continue. He found both he and Dawson were leaning forward.

RJ smiled in return.

"RJ!" Casey snapped.

The wolf RJ laughed again. "He's a hawk shifter."

"Hawk, like a bird?" Dawson scoffed. "No way."

RJ nodded. "I swear."

"Huh, that's interesting," Dawson noted but waved a hand at his brother. "But it's still beside the point. You put your family in danger. It might not matter to *you*, but *I* do have Beth and Toby to protect, whether you sent someone to watch over them or not."

"I care. I've always cared," Casey told him quietly.

Dawson obviously wasn't buying it.

"If I followed your trail here, what's to say the others won't? Why not just come out in the open and tell everyone what happened?" Gray questioned, trying to get them back on track. Maybe it was a good thing he'd never had any siblings.

"You were closer to finding Zach than anyone else. We left the maps, hoping someone on our side would pick up on them. But we didn't want it to be so obvious. Just didn't think you'd be so damn quick," Casey told them.

"We've been keeping watch. We think the cats will come in through the canyon," RJ added.

"That means they have to go through the tourists and park rangers." Dawson shook his head. "That would be stupid."

"The alternative is going through Coyote Bluff where you are. And if they are following the wolves, they know Grayson is there, too," Prince Zachary reasoned.

Gray thought about it. They really were right. Anyone going back after the Prince would fare better going through humans than an entire town of shifters. "What's the plan?"

The smaller man that had been guarding the Prince grinned. "Lay in wait."

"That's it?" Dawson practically yelled. "That's your great plan?"

"This is the best military unit in the world. Every one of us is a shifter and specialises in some kind of warfare. I'm pretty sure we can take care of a few untrained cats," RJ snapped.

All of the felines around the cave growled.

"You know what I mean!" RJ insisted but Gray noticed he leaned away from them all.

"An entire unit of shifters?" Gray asked, curious. "Was that done on purpose?"

The men all shared a meaningful look before Casey answered, "Yes. You know the Alpha Council and the Prince's advisors have spoken to government officials about the shifters going public?"

Gray and Dawson nodded.

"They had to have found out about us some way. Shifters have been serving in the military for hundreds of years. It doesn't take much brainpower to figure out some of us are harder to kill."

"Yeah, but..." Gray had a thousand questions. He wondered if his Alpha or their friends knew.

"There were many bad years back fifty years or so. Shifter soldiers were taken and experimented on. Zach's family was a huge part of stopping that," Casey told them proudly. "Instead, the royal family worked out a deal with the government. The shifters would continue to join the military, with the government guaranteeing their identities would remain secret. They would be able to take on missions that were not safe for the regular humans. Ones that were guaranteed to kill humans, the shifters could take and survive. The government recruited specific species with the approval of the royal family."

Gray sat in shocked silence, trying to take it all in. "If they already know all about us, then why are we even planning on going public?" Gray questioned.

"While the governments, here and in many other countries, are aware of our existence, that does not protect shifters from those who don't know about us. We can have laws to control hunting, but I still lose thousands of my species a year. In some states, if you see a cougar or even a bobcat, it is lawful to shoot right away. There must be something done about this.

I'm losing too many children all too often," Prince Zachary informed him.

Gray nodded. It was the same thing Tony had always told him. Before he had become their Alpha, Tyler had lost his best friend back in college to hunters.

"So if you're already involved with the government and okay with being in the public, why did your cousin kidnap you?" Dawson wondered.

"When this all comes out, there is a good chance that the military missions will also be exposed. The credit to end the torture of the shifters will go to the royal family," Prince Zachary informed them. "My cousin wants that credit."

"You don't?" Dawson asked with a raised brow in disbelief.

"No." The Prince stroked a hand down Casey's back. "I would prefer to keep the military missions a secret. To protect the ones I love."

Dawson looked away from the Prince and his brother, but Gray kind of thought it was nice. Man or woman, a mate was a mate. Wolves mated for life, so it was very sacred for them. He knew not all felines did the same, but he could almost feel it in his bones that Prince Zachary and Casey would be together for life.

"What can we do to help? I'm sorry, but I do need to tell my Alpha and the other teams to stop looking. They are away from their Pack and families. It is starting to take a toll on everyone."

"I understand but I have to ask you to tell only your Alpha for now, if you are sure you can trust him," Prince Zachary requested. "I believe he can be trusted, but my cousin is working with some wolves. We need to capture them all this time."

Gray nodded. "I can do that. As long as I can speak with Tyler about it, I agree to keep all of this under wraps."

"What about the sheriff?" Dawson enquired.

"One of the reasons I picked the canyon was because of Jim. If this went wrong, I was going to contact him," Casey admitted.

"I think we should bring in the sheriff," Dawson told his brother. "In the long run it will be better to have his support. I know you all think you can handle this but just being able to get to the Prince speaks volumes on how organised these guys are."

The military men all exchanged looks before they eventually nodded.

"We'll head into town and talk with Jim. See if we can get any reports from the rangers," Dawson said.

"We have no way to communicate with you, though," Gray mentioned.

RJ stood and walked over to his backpack. He pulled out a handheld radio and passed it over to Gray. "Use channel eight. It's as secure as we can make it with the technology we brought with us."

Gray accepted the radio and nodded. "We'll head back into town and meet with the sheriff. Find out what we can. We won't contact you unless we encounter any problems. But how about we take a run tonight and meet back up about midnight?"

RJ nodded. "Two wolves won't cause too much suspicion even if we are being watched."

Gray stood. "Then we have a busy night ahead of us."

The other men dipped their heads in goodbye as Casey stood to walk them to the front of the cave.

"I'll give you a minute," Gray told Dawson, clipping him on the shoulder.

He strolled back into the sunlight, glad to get out in the open. He didn't like the closed-in feeling. Natural wolves might make a den in a cave like that, but he preferred the freedom to be able to run.

Dawson and Casey spoke in low but urgent tones and Gray did his best to ignore them. Not easy with his sharpened senses so he ambled farther away, humming low to himself.

Dawson followed behind him a couple of minutes later. He was shaking his head and mumbling.

"You okay?" Gray asked his new friend.

Dawson glanced up and offered a small smile. "On one hand, I'm relieved to see him again. I know Beth will be thrilled beyond words. But, on the other hand, he was close by and didn't contact me, put my family in danger, and has a whole other life I know nothing about. I'm angry...and just a little impressed by him."

"I bet that punch felt good, though."

Dawson laughed like Gray had intended. "It did. Really good. But he better watch out—Beth has quite a left hook herself."

The mention of the pretty feline had Gray's body responding. He hadn't got over the strong feeling from the night before or even the quick appearance she'd made at the inn. He wasn't sure what to do about his feelings. He knew what he *wanted* to do but the entire situation was complicated.

"You want to talk about it?" Dawson enquired as they jumped down an opening in the canyon.

"About?" Gray asked, distracted by his thoughts of Beth.

"Look, Gray." Dawson stopped walking. "I know my sister. That little display of nerves this morning at the inn is not like her. She's confident, smart, and at ease with everyone. Something about you made her nervous."

Gray exhaled. "She makes me nervous too."

Dawson threw his head back and cackled.

"Not funny," Gray grumbled and started to walk again.

Dawson caught up with him and threw an arm over his shoulder. "Come on, man, it's funny. The big bad detective wolf is nervous about the little bobcat?"

"It's not her animal that makes me uneasy and you know it. One of my best friends just found her mate. I didn't think Kiley would ever mate with anyone. We'd... We'd spent some time together but it just never felt destined..." Gray tried to explain.

"You couldn't force it because it just wasn't there. There was someone else for her," Dawson finished.

Gray shrugged. "Pretty much. But it had me wondering if there was someone waiting for me too. I thought about it a lot while I was on my own these last few months. Now I'm not sure if these feelings I have..." Gray hesitated. "If I just want it so bad, I'm reading more into the attraction than I should. And it's weird discussing this with her brother."

Dawson pulled him to a stop. "Just be honest with her. Like I said, Beth is smart. I have to believe it will work out. One way or the other. Just take things slow and see. I don't want her hurt. It would kill me." Dawson glared. "Remember that. But I want her happy."

Gray patted his shoulder. "We have time to figure it out."

"Good." Dawson motioned ahead. "Then let's hit the road. I think you have a date tonight. With two chaperones."

Gray groaned good-naturedly but trailed after the other man.

Chapter Six

Beth watched Toby as he played in the front yard. She'd seen her brother and Gray pull up earlier. The wolf shifter had waved before heading into the den. She'd asked how it had gone when Dawson had passed her going into the house, but he'd shaken his head and told her it was complicated.

She wasn't sure what that meant but she hoped the two men had got along. She'd spent the day thinking about what had happened the night before. She could admit that the strong feelings she'd had for Gray from the beginning meant something. And she was determined to see where they might lead. Gray might only be there for a little while, but they owed it to themselves to explore what was going on between them.

"Don't climb on the dog house," she called to Toby.

The little boy grinned and waved, heading towards the swing set Dawson had built.

"I swear, he's a monkey instead of a bobcat," Dawson voiced behind her.

She chuckled. "I agree." She felt him come up beside her and leaned a little into him.

"There is something I need to talk to you about," her brother announced softly.

Beth turned to give him her attention.

He motioned to the porch and they both sat on the swing. "We found more today than we thought."

"About the Prince?"

Dawson took her hand in his. "We *found* the Prince."

Beth gasped. "That's wonderful!"

"Yes and no. He'd already been rescued. The trail they left was supposed to bring the kidnappers into a trap. Gray just beat them there."

"You don't think Gray's involved, do you?" She didn't want to think that way about the other man.

"No, no way," Dawson said adamantly. "But, with them hiding in the canyon, I'm worried about the repercussions for the town."

Beth could see where he was coming from.

"But more. You and Toby are in danger."

"Us? I doubt anyone will bother us," Beth tried to assure her brother.

"They might if they know a member of the rescue team is your brother," Dawson told her quietly.

Beth frowned. "How would...?"

"Crap, Beth! Casey was there!" he finally blurted out.

She inhaled sharply. "Casey is here?"

"Yeah." Dawson wrapped an arm around her shoulder. "He said he's been keeping an eye on us."

Beth bit her lip, not sure exactly what she was feeling. "Maybe you should start from the beginning."

* * * *

Thirty minutes later Beth stepped into the inn dining room ahead of Dawson and Toby, still reeling from what her brother had told her. Military units, kidnapping, mates... It was all so much to take in.

She spotted Gray already seated at a table set for four. He noticed her and stood, smiling. She gulped. Wow, he was an attractive man.

Everything she had learnt about him spoke to how dedicated he'd been to finding the Prince. Not many people would have done that for a stranger. She didn't know any other shifters who would have sacrificed so much for another species.

"Wolf!" Toby cried and raced around her.

Gray laughed as he hefted Toby up in the air.

Dawson was shaking his head as they reached Gray and Toby. "Toby, what have I told you about not calling people by their name?"

Toby stuck his lip out. "Sorry, Dad."

All the adults were smiling as they sat at the table. Beth found her gaze trapped in Gray's as he took his seat next to her. He leaned in and her breath caught.

"I'm glad you came," he whispered.

Her head bobbed up and down.

"Maybe after dinner we can take that walk," he offered.

"Su...sure."

"Why are you whispering?" Toby asked loudly from Gray's other side.

He straightened and winked at her. "I'm sorry, Toby. Whispering is rude. And what did you do today, young man?"

Toby grinned widely and launched into a story about how he and his best buddy Jimmy had wanted to learn how to fly. But Aunt Beth wouldn't let them borrow sheets for a parachute.

Dorothy came over to take their orders and everyone chose the night's special of meat loaf and mashed potatoes, except for Toby, who wanted Claude's chicken fingers—the 'best chicken fingers in the world'.

"Did you call your Alpha?" Dawson enquired across the table.

Gray cut his eyes to Beth and Toby.

Dawson just nodded.

"Yeah, Tyler agreed to keep it under wraps but wants to call in a couple more wolves for protection. He doesn't want it to come down on the community here."

Beth smiled. She liked that everyone was worried about the residents. She still couldn't believe that her older brother was so close after all the years.

"I told him I wanted to stay here and see this through." Gray glanced at her. "That I had a few things I needed to see to." Gray blushed as he said it.

Beth bit back a giggle. It was quite cute. "Good," she approved, nudging his foot under the table.

Gray beamed and leant back in his chair.

The rest of dinner went smoothly. Beth found herself leaning in and losing herself in the conversation about Gray's Pack and friends. But even though he laughed and told stories, she could catch the impression that Gray wasn't one hundred per cent happy.

The stories were always about others in his Pack. What he had witnessed. And a longing in his voice told her he was missing something. She wondered if he even realised it.

The dinner dishes were cleared away and Toby got a plate full of cookies with a glass of milk while the adults decided on coffee. Claude walked into the dining room and waved at them.

"Will you excuse me for a minute?" Dawson asked, pushing away from the table.

Dawson motioned to the outer room and Claude nodded.

"I wonder what that's about?" Beth wondered out loud.

Gray didn't answer, just picked up his coffee. She got the feeling he knew, though. She would ask Dawson later.

"You haven't been downtown, have you? We have a beautiful pond and garden," she mentioned to Gray, wanting to share it with him.

"No, not yet."

Dawson interrupted, coming back to the table. "Toby, you ready to go home? It's almost bedtime."

Toby groaned dramatically but jumped up into his dad's arms when offered.

Dawson looked over to her. "Coming, Beth?" He smirked at her.

She didn't know how her brother knew, but the look on his face said he didn't expect her to follow. "Actually, I'm going to show Gray around a little."

Gray stood and held out a hand. "I'll call you later."

They shook and her brother peeked over at her. "Be careful."

She watched her brother and nephew leave the dining room before turning back to Gray. "You ready?"

They walked silently through the inn until they were outside. Beth took a deep breath once outside in the warm air. She loved the Texas nights. Still warm enough to do anything without having to worry about a lot of rain or bad weather. Even in winter the lowest lows were only forty degrees.

"You love it here," Gray observed from beside her.

Beth hadn't realised she'd closed her eyes but opened them and looked up. "I really do. Let me show you why."

They walked side by side down the drive onto the main road. "The canyons give us the privacy to shift and with so many different species we have enough space to keep everyone happy."

"I've almost always shifted in forests," Gray admitted. "Since I've been on the road it's been hard to find places, but I have to admit the canyon holds its own beauty."

She sighed happily and wrapped her arm around his, glad that he saw a little of what she did.

She pointed out all the attractions the community had to offer as she led him to the middle of town. Gray asked questions and commented as they slowly made their way.

When they were just outside the gardens, Gray paused. "Wow!"

Beth had to agree. She loved this area. You could smell the flowers for miles with shifter-heightened senses. On a night like this with the soft breeze it was probably even further.

She took Gray's hand and pulled him under the arch into the circle. His eyes were everywhere and he continued to take deep breaths. She let him just enjoy the sight and smells for a while.

Finally he rotated around and cupped her face. "Thank you for sharing this with me."

He leaned in slowly as if to give her time to pull away. She didn't want to, though. Instead, she rose to her toes and closed the distance.

Gray's lips were moist and the kiss strong without being forceful. She tilted her head and opened to give him access. He moved his hands from her face and wrapped his arms around her waist.

She moaned at the solid embrace, loving the way he surrounded her.

"Beth," he panted out as they paused to catch their breath.

"Yes," she hissed, taking his mouth again.

Pure heat this time. While the first kiss had been sweet and romantic, now she attacked his mouth, pouring all the passion she felt into him. He groaned and she swallowed the sound. Wrapping her legs around his waist when he lifted her up, she pressed intimately against him.

"God, Beth," he murmured against her skin, mouthing down her neck. She arched, pressing her pussy harder into his cock.

He was rock hard and she wanted to feel him. "I want you," she told him, starting to rock. It felt so good. He was solid against her and if she didn't get him inside her, she felt like she would explode.

"Can't... We can't here," he disputed even as he continued to explore her, his hand under her shirt kneading her breast.

Oh, they could and would. "This way! Come here." She dropped her legs to the ground and grabbed his hand.

She tugged him further into the garden around where she knew was a private stretch of grass. Once she knew they were hidden by the bushes, she pushed him back.

He dropped to the ground, pulling her with him to sit on his lap. She wrapped her arms around his neck and kissed him again. Both of his hands were under her shirt now, pushing it up and off. The warm night air still caused goosebumps to break out on her.

"From the moment I saw you I couldn't believe how beautiful you are." Gray spoke while cupping her breasts. She arched her back, pushing into his hands. "I need to taste you."

"Yes..." she moaned while he laid her back. The grass was damp but she didn't mind. Especially when he pushed aside the cotton bra she wore and closed his lips over her taut nipple.

She whimpered, it felt so good. Too good.

"God, your skin," he marvelled, moving to her other breast and nipple. He teased, tormented and lavished attention upon her while she cried out in ecstasy.

"Please... Please," she begged, needing more.

His fingers caught the opening of her jeans while he stimulated her with his mouth as he moved down her body. She grabbed at the back of his head, holding onto him as best she could.

He unsnapped her jeans and lowered the zipper, and she lifted her hips to help push them down.

His eyes met hers and she could see the heat and passion. "Tell me you want this, Beth. That it's okay. I'll stop now but I want to taste you."

She had to take deep breaths to calm herself.

"Tell me this is more than just lust. That you won't regret that I'm a wolf in the morning."

It was on the tip of her tongue to tease him but, when she saw the flash of insecurity in his eyes, she stopped in time. She caressed his head before cupping his jaw. "I know who you are, Grayson. I want you."

He nodded. "Thank God!"

She shrieked when he yanked her pants the rest of the way down and closed his mouth over the thin cotton of her panties. Even with the thin barrier, his mouth was hot. She dug her heels into the dirt under her.

"Your smell…" He groaned. "Got to taste."

He snapped the edges of her panties easily and inhaled deeply. The first lick was just a tease.

"Gray… Gray…"

He growled and held her hips. "Mine."

She actually screamed when he opened her and started to feast. "Oh my…"

He used his tongue to push inside her, his lips to suck her clit, and his fingers to tease everywhere.

"More… Please more," she pleaded.

He gave it to her, slurping and nibbling as he brought her closer to the edge. Hands under her ass, he tilted her hips and ate at her. Finally it grew to be too much. She wanted to hold out, to wait until he was buried inside her, but she couldn't. She raked her nails into the ground and shook as she finally climaxed.

Gray licked her clean even as she started to pull at his shoulders to move him up. He lifted his head and grinned the perfect big-bad-wolf grin.

She drew him up into her arms so they could kiss. She could taste herself on his tongue, but more, she felt his erection bulging. She cupped him through his jeans and he bucked while moaning.

She worked his jeans open and down before wrapping a hand around his hard shaft. She pumped him a few times while he rocked against her hold. As good as he felt in her hand, she wanted to feel him stretching her.

"Make love to me," she demanded, giving him some rough pulls.

He grunted and kissed her hard. She knew she had him.

"I want to see you," he commanded, settling between her legs. "Keep your eyes open, watch me, and feel me."

She tried her best as he gently began to push in. He'd already used his tongue and fingers to open her so, while he fitted snugly, she had to close her eyes on just how right it felt.

"Beth," he coaxed, pulling out and sliding back inside.

She lifted her head and their eyes locked. He thrust back in harder and deeper. She remained entranced, until he let go of his control. Breaking eye contact, he threw his head back and started to plough into her, each masterful stroke deep and claiming, letting her know that he owned every inch of her. She lifted her hips and met each frenzied plunge as they drove to the edge of desire.

Before she even realised she was ready, she felt the tingle inside. Her back bowed and she called his name as he pushed her into her second orgasm of the night. She clutched at him as he rode her through her climax until he finally cried out and pumped his seed inside her.

Ragged breaths mixed as he leaned his forehead against hers.

That was no question the best sexual encounter she'd had in her life. She wrapped her arms around his neck to hold him to her. He mumbled something so she loosened her grip. "What?"

He laughed breathlessly, still not fully recovered. "I said you have to come back to my room with me. We have to do that again."

Dropping her head back, she snickered. "That's the best idea I've heard in years."

Chapter Seven

Gray didn't want to leave Beth—she felt so good tucked close to his side, her hair fanned out against the white pillowcase. He pressed a soft kiss to the side of her neck. He hadn't planned for the night to go quite like it had.

He'd been hoping for a nice quiet walk and maybe to be able to sneak a kiss or two. He wanted to woo Beth like she deserved. The walk had been wonderful but when he'd seen her in the garden, moonlight behind her, he just hadn't been able to control himself. The first kiss had done him in.

He had no doubt he wasn't reading deeper into his feelings. Beth Williams was the woman for him.

Now the real issues would start.

He didn't care that she was a feline. He'd questioned her earlier, making sure she understood what he was. But now would come the backlash of what everyone else thought. He'd never heard of mating across species.

He slipped out of bed as quietly as he could. He had just enough time to shift and meet the other wolf. He pulled on a pair of jeans and a T-shirt before grabbing his shoes. The door clicked softly as he closed it behind him, and he had to fight the feeling to go back and kiss her one more time.

Shaking his head at himself, he made his way through the inn, remaining silent so he wouldn't wake anyone else up. He used the back door to leave and immediately caught the feline scent. He crouched, dropped his shoes, a growl rumbling in his throat. Danger too close to his future mate had his wolf disturbed.

"Easy, wolf." Casey Williams stepped out of the shadows.

Gray straightened and crossed his arms over his chest. "What are you doing here?"

Casey shrugged and walked up the steps. "I wanted to… I had to see for myself they were okay. I didn't want to bring trouble to them."

Gray relaxed. He could smell the sincerity from the bobcat.

Casey nodded to the porch furniture. Gray took a seat first. Casey passed by him to lean against the rail before stiffening. He took a deep breath and hissed. "You've been with my sister," he accused.

Shit, he really should have showered but he hadn't wanted to leave Beth. Besides, he'd thought he was meeting RJ and hadn't thought Beth's scent would be an issue. Gray held up both hands. "It's not what you think."

But Casey wasn't listening. He snarled and took a step towards Gray. Gray had jumped to his feet to defend himself when the back door slammed closed.

"Casey Williams, don't you touch him!"

Both men froze as Beth stepped away from the door.

"Beth," Casey murmured her name.

She smiled, her entire face lighting up, and held out her arms. "Hello, big brother."

Casey moved quickly, pulling her into a tight embrace and rocking her back and forth. Gray felt like an intruder witnessing such an emotional display. But he was happy for both of them too.

Casey drew back and cupped her cheeks. "You are so beautiful."

She laughed. "You're not too bad yourself."

He hugged her again before letting her go and glancing over at Gray. "Maybe we can talk later. I need to discuss something with Gray."

She shook her head and patted his chest. "Nice try. You and Gray can talk about what's going on with the Prince in front of me. However, you will not discuss my relationship with Gray."

"Your 'relationship'? He's been here two days and you have a relationship?" Casey asked sarcastically.

Casey's tone agitated Gray enough that he started to growl. Beth pulled him back to the furniture. "Down, boys. Casey, you don't get to question anything I do with Gray or anyone else for that matter. You weren't here before and, while I'm glad you're back, I am an adult."

Gray had started to grin at her show of independence to her brother until she'd mentioned someone else. Was there someone else? He hadn't thought to ask before. They'd just met and...

Beth slapped his chest. "Knock it off. There is no one else."

Gray blushed at being caught.

Casey moved back to lean against the rail again. "Sorry, but you are still my sister. Family has to look out for one another."

"Great!" Beth said cheerfully. "I'd love to meet the Prince and ask him why, if he knew about us, he never came to see us. I mean, even if you were out of the country he still could have called or let us know you were still alive."

Casey had the grace to drop his head. "I am sorry about that. I kept meaning to get hold of you all. But every time I came close, something would happen and I felt...knew it would be safer if you didn't have any contact from me."

Beth snorted. "You keep thinking that, Case. In the meantime, you have no say about me and Gray."

Casey nodded while he frowned. Gray didn't think this would be the end of the subject, though.

"Now, if you guys would like to discuss what dragged Gray out of bed at almost midnight, I'm all ears."

Obviously Casey wasn't going to be able to keep her out of the discussion any more than Gray was. With a heavy sigh, Casey waved his hand at Gray to start.

"Jim wasn't happy that you didn't let him know what was going on. I think he'll have a few words with you when he sees you," Gray told him, just a little amused. "But he agreed that he needed to add support to make sure no one got away and nothing was left to chance."

"We can handle this," Casey argued. "We have been doing this kind of stuff for years."

"But he has to protect his community, too."

Casey ran his hands roughly over his face. "I know. I just didn't think it would be so complicated."

"Someone kidnapped the Prince. That's pretty damned complicated already," Beth piped up.

Both men glared at her. She ducked her head, smirking,

"Anyway," Casey restarted, "I really thought they would come after Zach and it would be done. Over fifty people entered the canyon today. Seven of those stayed to camp and didn't leave. I don't know if they took the bait or not."

"Maybe they decided to come in like we did," Gray suggested.

"Claude's had some guys watching the town limits. No one except you entered that he didn't know."

"So we don't know any more than this morning?" Gray questioned even though he knew the answer.

"It's frustrating," Casey shared. "I just want this over with. We decided our last mission was it. We're ready to get out. I want to spend time with my family. RJ's brother just accepted a position as Alpha and has asked him to come home. Jesse will stay with the Prince as his personal guard after all of this. And Mike... I'm not sure what Mike's plans are but he says he's tired of fighting for everyone else."

Gray could understand. The men had lost a lot of time serving.

"There are other members of the team but us four started together and want to finish together. I trust those men with my life...with my mate's life."

"Everyone needs help. I might not have ever served in the military, but no matter how good you all are there are still people who can take some of the pressure off. That way you can spend time with your family," Gray offered.

Beth took his hand and squeezed it gently. "Let us help you, Casey."

"Yes, I know," he conceded. "I'm just not used to having civilians involved. Or sisters."

Beth just beamed at him.

Gray chuckled.

"RJ and Mike are doing a sweep of the canyon tonight. Trying to pick up any scents that don't belong."

"The sheriff wants to head up to talk to you and the Prince first thing," Gray added.

"I'll let the others know," Casey said before pushing away from the porch.

Gray stood, bringing Beth up with him.

Gray and Casey shook hands before he pulled Beth in again. "It's good to see you, sis."

She hugged him tight. "Glad you're home."

Casey turned and stepped down the porch. He disappeared back into the shadows.

Beth pivoted to Gray. "Now, why don't we discuss you leaving me in the middle of the night to meet with strange felines?"

"Now, darling," Gray drawled as best he could. "You know you're the only feline for me."

She threw her arms around his neck. "Good, now take me back to bed. I need my beauty sleep."

Gray hauled her up into his arms. "I'll take you back to bed, but I don't promise you'll get much sleep."

She attached her lips to his neck as he strode across the porch and in through the back door. She didn't let up on her assault even when he stumbled a couple of times.

"Don't drop me," she taunted, running her tongue into his ear.

He shivered, making his way to his room as quickly as he could while trying to not drop her for real.

Once he reached his door he pushed it open, slipped inside, and closed it by pressing her back to it. She laughed and threw her head back.

He covered her mouth with his, thrusting his tongue inside and swallowing her moan. He was already hard as he rubbed against her. His body had never responded so quickly or surely before. Just another sign that she was meant for him.

She gripped his cock through his jeans and squeezed. His knees went weak and he fell forward, knocking her further against the door.

"It's my turn," she said with promise in her voice before dropping slowly to her knees.

He gasped when she ran her hands up the inside seam of his pants.

"I get to taste you now," she told him, rubbing her cheek against his erection. "Tease and pleasure you."

"You don't have to..." he tried to tell her but almost swallowed his tongue when she mouthed his cock through his jeans.

"I don't have to do anything but taste you," she agreed.

She deftly unsnapped his jeans with her slender fingers before pulling them down.

"Mmm. No underwear," she purred, nudging his erect shaft with her nose. "I like."

"Damn!" he yelled when she wrapped one hand around the base of his dick and licked the head.

She moaned around the tip of his cock and it was all he could do not to thrust into the warm, moist haven of her mouth. "Beth, please, I'm..."

She popped off and gave him a sexy grin. "You're going to enjoy this," she assured him.

Yes, he was, but he didn't know if he would survive it. Her lips wrapped around his shaft and she swallowed him all the way down her throat. The way she used her tongue on the vein under his cock head almost had his eyes rolling to the back of his head.

"Baby... Baby..." He fisted his hands to keep him from grabbing her head and just pounding into her mouth. It was sweet torture what she was doing to him.

She pulled back, hollowing her cheeks and sucking.

"Jeez, oh God," he pleaded with her.

She moved her head up and down his shaft, gripping his hip with her free hand to encourage him to move. And, God help him, he had to move. He thrust shallowly at first, trying not to hurt her, but eventually he snapped and cried out, plunging his hips in time with her moving on his cock.

All too sudden the tingling started and he knew he was going to come. He slid his fingers through her hair.

"Baby... Beth..."

She hummed and he took that as permission. Three more thrusts and he slammed his head forward into the door, biting back a howl as he released.

She swallowed him down and kept sucking when he didn't go completely soft. He pulled her off his half-hard dick and up into his arms. He tasted his seed mixed with her unique taste as he plundered her mouth.

Holding her tight, he stumbled his way to the bed, still unmade from earlier. He dropped down, covering her body with his. He yanked his shirt off that they hadn't managed to remove, before attacking her clothes. She was naked and bared for him in seconds.

"You're the most amazing woman I've ever met," he told her, fingering her clit before slipping two fingers through her slick folds and opening her up.

She clawed at his back. "In me... In me..."

He growled and flipped her over. "Hands and knees! Come on, baby," he encouraged.

She hurried to comply, arching her back in invitation. He nipped her right ass cheek and she squeaked.

He ran his tongue over the small hurt. "Perfect. So perfect, honey."

She pushed back into him. He lined his cock up to her entrance and pressed in. She opened for him, pulling his cock in and squeezing.

"So good," he praised, pulling out and slamming back in.

It was going to be quick. Even though he had just come, he was so out of control for this woman. He set a hard, steady pace pounding into her tight, wet pussy. His wolf was close to the surface demanding he claim their mate. His eyes began to shift and his teeth elongated. He held the animal back and continued to hammer inside.

She pushed back, met each crazed stroke, urging him on. Screaming, she started to climax, the walls of her cunt clamped down, and he came, spilling his seed inside.

She collapsed on the bed. He couldn't hold himself up any longer and fell on top of her.

"You're trying to kill me," he murmured.

She laughed breathlessly. "But what a way to go."

Chapter Eight

Morning came too early. Gray groaned at the sunlight sneaking its way into his room. He pulled his bed partner closer and buried his face in the back of her neck.

Beth hummed softly, snuggling back into him. He cupped her breast and started to kiss down her shoulder. She rolled over and their lips met.

"Good morning." He smiled at her when they pulled away.

"Mmm, morning." She snuggled deeper into his arms. "I could get used to waking like this."

So could he. And he wasn't sure what to do about it yet, so he kissed in her response. She responded beautifully, opening to him and allowing him to roll on top. She ran her hands down his back while he nibbled on her neck.

"Beth." He loved to say her name.

The pounding on the bedroom door startled them both. Gray glanced at the clock and noticed he was already late. "Damn it."

He kissed Beth one more time before picking up his jeans and hopping into them. More pounding. "All right, all right—keep your pants on."

He opened the door to an amused-looking Claude. "The sheriff is already downstairs and Dawson is on his way. Wanted me to make sure you were out of bed."

He could hear Beth laugh behind him. He nodded to the older man. "I'll be right down. Thanks."

Claude nodded and headed back down the hall. Gray closed the door and pointed his finger towards the bed. "I'm late. You keep your sexy ass there while I shower. No more distracting me."

She licked her lips, causing his cock to twitch again. "Want me to wash your back?"

"No!" he growled at her. "I have to leave the room before noon."

Her happy voice followed him into the bathroom. "I'll just entertain myself then."

He thumped his dick, trying to get himself under control, and jumped in a lukewarm shower. It was the best he could do under the time constraint.

Less than ten minutes later he was back, dressing while Beth smirked at him from the bed. He loved her playful attitude and really could see them sharing mornings like this together.

Once he was ready for the day ahead, he leaned over the bed and kissed her as chastely as he could. "Please be careful today. We don't think anyone is in town, but you never know."

Thankfully, she nodded. "Toby is probably already downstairs. We'll stay either here or at the house. We'll even stay out of town."

She must have read the relief on his face.

"Hey, I won't do anything to put Toby at risk," she promised.

"Or yourself?" he added.

She smiled shyly. "Or myself. I promise."

He kissed her again, this one deeper and a lot dirtier. His cock, which had finally settled, perked right back up.

"Trouble," he grumbled at her, pulling away and adjusting himself.

"See you later," she called and blew him a kiss.

He smiled the entire way down the stairs to the front entrance. There he met the sheriff, Dawson and Claude. Dorothy handed him a travel mug of coffee and a foil-wrapped package.

"For the road," she told him with a fond smile.

He dipped his head in thanks. "Appreciate it."

"You and Gray head out the same way as you did yesterday. Go the direct route. Claude and I will follow and make sure no one else is tailing you," the sheriff ordered.

"Claude?" Gray asked, becoming uneasy. He didn't want to leave the inn unprotected.

"I have my deputy stationed here and Claude has a few friends close by. Everyone here will be safe," Jim answered his unspoken question.

Gray nodded and followed the other men out.

Gray drank his coffee and chowed down on the best breakfast burrito he'd ever had. "I got to tell you, I could move here just for the food," he told Dawson.

"Are you thinking about it?" Dawson asked quietly.

Gray glanced over at him, not realising before that he had been silent so far. "Thinking about what?"

"Moving here," Dawson clarified.

Gray crumpled up the foil and took a drink of his rich coffee to give him time. He knew he was stalling. So did Dawson by the frown he gave him.

"I've thought about it," he admitted, not looking at the other man.

"Look, Gray, I won't pressure you. Beth is a big girl and she knows what she's doing. Like I said yesterday, just be honest with her. I'm not going to go all big brother on you."

"Yeah, one of you is enough," Gray muttered.

Dawson cut his eyes to him so Gray filled him in on Casey's visit the night before. Dawson got a big kick out of what Beth had said about meeting Prince Zachary.

"I can just imagine what she'll have to say to him," Dawson shared with a grin.

They sat in comfortable silence for a few minutes before Gray spoke up. "Can I ask you a question?"

Dawson shrugged. "Sure."

"Does it bother you?" Gray questioned. "Your brother taking a male mate?"

Dawson blew out a breath and looked like he was choosing his words carefully. "It doesn't bother me that his mate is male. It bothers me that he kept that part to himself."

Gray relaxed back in his seat.

"The three of us were always close. It hurt when he left. You know most felines stay solitary but his leaving… It felt like he put his animal nature before his family."

"Beth said something similar the other night," Gray told him.

Dawson smiled. "Beth and I have always felt the same. Family is the most important thing. We are humans first. Our parents were never there for us.

188

Even when they were here, they always wanted to be somewhere else. I don't know if it moulded our outlook, but I know I will never leave my son."

"Toby is a great kid," Gray assured him.

"Yeah. When I met his mom I thought we both wanted the same thing. And I think she did in the beginning, but it turned out she just couldn't stay. I still can't forgive her for leaving him."

Gray took in everything that was said. Would Beth change her mind like Toby's mom? He didn't even know if they could have kids or what the result would be if they did.

"Have you ever heard of two different species mating?" he asked.

Dawson tilted his head in thought. "I know a few who have mated with humans. Claude and Dorothy, as matter of fact. Plus Casey is a bobcat and Prince Zachary is a lion, but as for a wolf and a bobcat, I just don't know."

That was what Gray had figured.

"I guess you will have to decide how far you want to take it," Dawson suggested just as the ranger station came into view.

They repeated the same steps as yesterday, looking into the closed station before walking around to the trail that was barely there. Gray didn't get any sense of being followed, not even by Jim and Claude. So either the other two shifters were still pretty far behind or they were better at hiding their scent than he'd thought.

Gray and Dawson had a better idea of where they were going this time but still took the time to cover their tracks and double back to make sure they didn't lead anyone to the Prince's hideout.

They stayed in human form, so the trip up the canyon took longer than it had the day before. Several times they had to help each other up embankments where their animals had easily jumped.

They took two breaks to drink water and eat a granola bar before they finally made it to where they had run into the wolves and Casey. Just as he'd suspected, as they reached the area, RJ Cross was waiting there for them.

He jumped down, landing gracefully on his feet. "There you are."

Gray leaned against a rock and glared at the other man. Gray was in good shape but the late night and second day of hiking up the steep canyon were taking its toll on him. His back muscles protested and his legs were starting to cramp.

Meanwhile, RJ seemed full of energy. "Where's the sheriff? Casey said he was coming with you."

Gray motioned behind them. "He's heading up with Claude. We split up so we could keep an eye out for if anyone was following."

"Cool!" RJ hopped back up on the ledge. "We need to get started before I die of boredom. Here comes Mike."

The other wolf stalked down in his animal form. He moved quietly, glancing behind him a few times. He shifted and seconds later a naked man stood in front of them all.

"I think they're here," he announced, accepting the bottle of water RJ handed him.

"About damn time," RJ muttered. "Time we finished this."

Gray exchanged looks with Dawson, not sure how he felt about the upcoming conflict.

"They came through this morning as soon as the gates opened. They didn't take a map or ask about any of the trails. The ranger had the feeling they knew where they were headed."

"Are you sure it's them?" Gray had to ask.

Mike scowled at him. "Yeah, I sniffed around their vehicle. They're shifters and I recognised their scent from the cabin we took Zach from."

"So it's on." RJ clapped his hands together. "We need to tell Casey."

The other men nodded and they followed them to the cave they'd been to before. Jim and Claude would just have to catch up.

Casey greeted his brother with a hug and Gray with a handshake. Prince Zachary looked tired but offered them a small smile as they entered the cave. The other feline stood at the far cave wall, rifle on his shoulder.

Mike explained to the rest of them what he had seen and found out.

"So it's time," Prince Zachary acknowledged, although he seemed more resigned than RJ and Mike had been.

Casey rubbed his shoulder. "We capture these guys then at least we know, when he goes back to get your cousin, there will be fewer complications. It has to be done."

"I just don't want anyone else hurt on my account," he told his mate, shaking his head sadly.

Casey wrapped an arm around his shoulders and pulled him off to the side of the cave.

"How long to do you think it will take them to get up here?" Gray asked Mike and RJ.

"I figure about two or three hours, tops. It's one thing to map out the canyon and know where to go, but a whole other thing to do it when you're on foot. I knew where all the shortcuts were, and luckily they didn't or they would have beaten me here. I expect they will come shifted. There are a couple of wolves, two cats, and something else," Mike informed them.

"Something else?" RJ questioned his buddy.

Mike shook his head. "Couldn't get a good read."

"Jim and Claude should be here by then also. So five of them and nine of us—pretty damn good odds," Dawson stated.

"Seven of us," RJ corrected. "Jesse stays with Zach to guard him. No one will get their hands on him again."

"I can take care of myself," Prince Zachary interrupted, coming back over. "You need Jesse with you."

"Not gonna happen," Casey voiced, narrowing his eyes at his mate. "Above and beyond all else, you are the Prince of our people. Jesse will guard you."

"I am also one of the most powerful cats in the world," he argued back.

"No," Casey snapped. "You stay here."

"I'm sorry to get in the middle, Prince Zachary, but I have to agree with Casey. We need to finish this, capture these men, and get you to safety. I have a son and sister who are dying to meet you. And you don't want to disappoint those two," Dawson added respectfully.

The Prince opened his mouth and closed it again. Finally, he nodded. "Nicely played," he grumbled. "You take after your brother more than you think."

Casey beamed and Gray hid his own smile. He could see the family dynamic coming together. It made him feel warm inside that Beth would have these men in her life. Would he be part of the family too? He just didn't know.

He shook the question from his head. He had to concentrate on the task before him.

"We should split up and take our positions. It might be a few hours but we can't take any chances," Casey suggested.

The others all agreed. "Gray and RJ will take point. They'll take the furthest position," Casey directed. "Dawson and Mike will go south — block anyone from sneaking up on us that way. I'll wait for the sheriff and Claude. They'll cover the high ground."

"What about you?" Dawson enquired with a lift of his brow.

Casey grinned. "I'm bait. I'll lead them to us."

Zachary and Dawson started to protest but Casey held up a hand to cut them off.

"My show, my call."

"Sounds good to me." RJ grabbed a pack and threw it over to Gray. He caught it easily and looked down at it. "Water and some beef jerky," RJ clarified. "Should hold us over till we get some action."

Gray shook his head at the other man but hefted the pack to his shoulder.

"I can't tell you how much I am looking forward to a hot shower and a nice home-cooked meal," his partner told him as he motioned towards the mouth of the cave. Gray didn't blame the man. Hadn't he just had the same thoughts?

Gray caught Dawson's eye and gave a slight nod of his head. He clasped the other man's shoulder and followed the young wolf out. He hoped everything went according to plan.

Chapter Nine

While the canyon was truly a beautiful environment, the waiting was driving him crazy. It'd been two and a half hours since he and RJ had left the cave and still there was no sign of anyone else.

"So you're retiring after this?" Gray asked the other man.

"Yeah, my older brother accepted an Alpha position in a Pack in New Mexico. Our Pack has so many strong dominants—and our Alpha has several sons who will take over the Pack—that my brother's name was mentioned as a replacement for the New Mexico Pack."

"You'll move with him then?"

"Yeah." RJ was crouched down flexing his fingers. "Dylan and our younger brother Ben are going to head there in a couple of weeks. I'll meet them there."

"What are you planning on doing?"

"Ben's set up a storefront in town for me. I'll have the first tattoo shop there."

"Cool," Gray noted. RJ had enough ink to show that he enjoyed it. "Did you do all of the unit's tattoos?"

"Yeah, but my favourites are the two custom pieces I did for Zach and Casey. I'd like to do that more. Give mates something to show off."

Gray could imagine having a picture of Beth's sexy little bobcat on his body. "That's awesome, actually."

RJ chuckled. "Glad you think so. I'll give you a good price when you mate."

Gray bowed his head in thanks. "Appreciate it."

Of course, all the talk about mates made him think of Beth. He knew she was the woman meant for him. Even his wolf agreed that she was the perfect mate. He wanted kids, didn't care if they were wolf or feline, but he wanted a future with Beth.

He also knew that future would not be in his Pack. Even if he could get the other wolves to accept a bobcat into the Pack it would mean taking Beth away from her family, and he didn't want to do that either.

But he would be giving up a lot. His position in his Pack—even having a Pack—his job, and his friends who were his family…

"Sounds like some heavy thoughts over there," RJ commented.

"Yeah," Gray admitted. "Some decisions to make once this is all over with."

"*Alpha red to alpha black,*" squeaked from the radio.

"Alpha black," RJ answered.

"*Headed your way.*"

RJ and Gray both stood and started to strip. In just moments, they were shifted into two big wolves, crouched, and waiting.

Movement below them and then a bobcat broke through the brush, hightailing it over fallen rocks. A squeal from ahead showed a large flying bird.

RJ growled and jumped from his hiding place. Gray followed, barely landing before having to duck to avoid the large swoop the bird made.

He managed to stay on his feet right before a hard knock into his side had him sliding over the canyon ground.

"Alpha red, alpha black," the radio went off again. *"Three more coming in from the south."*

Gray wasn't sure who that was but he didn't have time to find out as he picked himself off the ground and faced the wolf that had run into him. He snarled at the animal.

Bigger than him, the wolf was from the grey breed, but Gray would fight to the death if need be. He caught the wolf as he launched himself at Gray again. He got a piece of his leg and bit down, getting a huge paw to his head.

They scrambled around, each trying to gain the upper hand over the other. He could hear the sound of fighting around him. He wasn't sure who was there or even how many. He kept his eye on his attacker even when he heard the loud roar of a cat. He ignored everything around him and lunged.

He caught the wolf in the side, but he managed to kick and get away. Gray stalked him and went after him again. He was pushing him towards the edge of the cliff. Gray didn't know how far it went down but it was his only option right then.

One last jump and he managed to roll the other wolf over. He heard the hit and looked down. The twenty-five-foot drop wouldn't kill him but he would be out of the fight for a little while.

Gray had turned to go back to the battle when a large feline landed on his back. He dropped down, rolled, and fought to get back to his feet, knowing he had a pretty good gash on his shoulder. An angry cougar crouched across from him.

Gray was used to being smaller than other wolf breeds but this cat was huge. He growled and faked an attack. The cougar moved left just how Gray wanted. He went in low, taking the cat's back legs out. He fell but swiped at Gray's side.

Caught by just the edge of the claws, he hissed in pain. But, while the other shifter might be bigger, Gray was faster. In a series of quick moves, he went after the cougar again and again, backing him up the same way he had done with the wolf. The cat was smarter, though, and swung around to avoid going over the cliff.

A growl behind him, then a big black wolf was rolling into the legs of the cat. Gray took the advantage and landed on the cougar's chest, taking him down. He closed his jaws around the cat's jugular and bit down.

He was clawed at but the black wolf butted the cat until the cat finally relented. Gray shook his head in warning before he let go. It was only then that he realised the sounds of fighting had ended.

Next to him the wolf—RJ—shifted to human form and straightened. "Damn, man—who thought a little wolf like you could fight like that?"

Gray glared at the other man but didn't really mean it. He was just thankful for the help. RJ grabbed the cat around the neck. "Shift," he ordered.

Gray took in the wreckage around him, noting four men on the ground with Casey standing over them. RJ hauled the cougar, now in human form, up.

"There's one more down there," Gray told him.

RJ laughed. "I don't think he's going anywhere for a while but I'll get him."

He shoved his prisoner at Gray, and he led him to the others. Casey was already on the radio.

"Good job, alpha blue. We'll come to you."

"There were more and they split up. These six, then another six who ran into Jim, Claude, Mike and Dawson. No one got to Zach," Casey told him.

"They okay?" Gray enquired.

"Minor injuries." Casey gestured to him. "You okay?"

Gray's shoulder was screaming at him but he would heal. "Yeah, fine."

Casey cut his eyes to where RJ was hauling the wolf over his shoulder. "Let's move."

The trek down the canyon took a while with their prisoners' hands tied but they made it. RJ would push at them occasionally but it was more for dominance than to hurt anyone else.

The sheriff had his gun out, holding it on his own tied-up prisoners.

"Steve," Casey spat at one of the men Mike was covering.

Steve scowled at him but didn't say anything.

"I see your dad didn't make the trip with you," Casey noted, crouching down in front of him. "Too much of a coward to get his own hands dirty?"

The man lunged at Casey but Mike caught his shoulder and threw him back down.

"That's what I thought," Casey said in disgust, standing again.

"Where is your father?" Prince Zachary joined them as he stepped down from the ledge above with Jesse right behind him.

The man glared but didn't say anything.

"No worries. We'll get him," Zachary told the young man, grabbing hold of his chin. "While you and your friends here will be processed for kidnapping, torture and treason, I'll deal with your father."

Gray watched the scene closely. It looked like he was the Prince's nephew. The family resemblance was close enough.

"The rangers are on their way," Jim told them, closing his phone.

Gray collapsed against a rock. He needed to shift again but wanted to wait until the prisoners were gone.

"You okay?" Dawson asked coming up beside him with a noticeable limp.

"Good, you?"

"Fine." Dawson waved his hand. "Little shit had sharp teeth."

Gray chuckled, relieved that the whole mess was finally finished. His part of it, anyway. The wolves had promised to find and rescue the Prince of felines. He'd completed that mission. Of course, the felines still had to round up everyone else who was involved but that would be up to them how they handled it. The wolves were done. He could go home now if he wanted. He just wished he knew what it was he *did* want.

"Who's got the beer?" RJ asked, falling in on the other side of him.

"First round's on me," Gray told him with a nudge.

"I got the second," Dawson said tiredly from Gray's right.

"Damn, sounds good," RJ muttered, letting his head fall back and closing his eyes. "Sounds fucking fantastic."

Chapter Ten

Beth knew the men were back. It was early evening and the talk of the town was all about the twelve men the rangers had taken to the jail for the sheriff. Dawson had gone home to shower while Gray had headed up the stairs ten minutes before.

"Why don't you go see if the wolf needs a little help?" Dorothy told her, passing over a room key. "I'll keep an eye on Toby."

She'd been sitting on one of the chairs in the great room watching Toby colour on the coffee table. She accepted the key with a smile. Toby's attention was still on his artwork so she quietly left the room and headed up the stairs.

She hadn't noticed any lingering injuries on either man but shifters healed fast so that didn't mean it hadn't been a tough fight.

Gray's room was empty when she entered. She could hear the shower running in the attached bathroom. She left the key on the dresser and padded across the room.

The bathroom door was silent as she pushed it open. The room was filled with steam but she could still make out Gray's naked body through the glass.

Shit, he had a fine body. She stripped and quietly opened the stall door.

"Damn, baby," he murmured. "I was just wishing you were in here with me."

She pressed against his back. There were several large scratches that had started to heal. It hurt her heart to see him injured. She carefully kissed the wounds. "I didn't get to wash your back last time. I thought I would volunteer my services again," she told him, wrapping her arms around to slide over his stomach.

He chuckled and grasped her hand she was moving lower. "It's not my back that needs attention."

She smiled against his shoulder and stroked his hard cock. He moaned, his hips thrusting forward. He felt good in her hand. She liked that just the thought of her had him raring and ready to go.

She glided around to his front to face him, keeping a hold of his shaft.

He cupped her face and bent to run his lips over hers. "It was just a day but I missed you," he confessed quietly.

She rose to her toes. "I worried about you."

He kissed her sweetly, wrapping his arms around her to hold her close. Beth opened for him, let their tongues twirl and tease. As expected, the kiss quickly turned to passion and she gasped into his mouth as he ran his hands down her back to cup her ass.

She rocked up, letting go of his shaft and hanging on to his shoulder.

"Hold tight," he ordered, picking her up and pressing her back against the wet shower stall. He nibbled down her neck to her collarbone as she arched for him.

His hard cock poked at her entrance.

She wiggled, letting him know that she wanted him inside her.

He slipped in slowly, helping her wrap her legs around his waist so he could thrust deeply into her.

Hot and solid, deep inside her. She gripped his shoulders hard, accepting him as he continued to gently enter her.

"You feel so good, baby," he whispered against her flesh.

"Yours," she told him. "I'm yours."

She had to say the words. She knew he would be leaving her soon. She hoped he planned on coming back, but she knew that soon she would have to let him go. She tightened her grip even more. "Yours, Gray."

He slammed inside her and stopped. "Open your eyes," he demanded.

She hadn't even realised they were closed. She complied with his request and her breath caught at the emotion she saw on his face.

"Do you mean that?" he asked hoarsely. "Will you be mine?"

"Yes, Gray, I want you forever. I know I have to let you go, but I wish I could hold onto you," she confessed.

"Beth..." He moaned her name like he was in pain.

He started to move again, to pound deep inside, filling her like no one else, pushing her to the edge.

"My Beth!" he called out, plunging his hips faster and harder.

She tightened her legs and met him stroke for stroke. "Yes, yours," she egged him on.

God, no one ever... It was so good... She needed more... "Gray!" She screamed his name as she climaxed.

"Mine, mine, mine," he chanted, pounding into her over and over. "Mine!" he growled out and exploded inside her.

She hung on as he filled her with his seed, wishing she could keep it inside her for the rest of the night. He shook while he came down, moving his hips slowly once again, never pulling out.

"Not done," he told her and smacked off the water. He hefted her up higher in his arms and pushed open the stall door.

They only made it as far as the bathroom rug before he laid her back and, still hard inside her, started to thrust once again.

"Look at me. Show me," he demanded.

She locked her gaze with his, grabbed his lower arms, and gave herself over completely. His eyes glowed and she could feel the power pouring off him.

"Yes, yes, yes," she chanted.

He snarled, threw his head back, teeth elongated as his wolf pushed to the surface. "Mine."

"Yes!" she yelled as she came once again.

He growled and slammed into her once, twice, then one last time before releasing again himself. He collapsed on top of her, his panting matching hers and filling the small room.

"Don't let me go," he breathed out.

"No, no, I won't," she promised, hugging him close.

Beth didn't know how long they lay on the floor but finally she started to shiver and Gray lifted his head.

"That was intense," he said, looking a little sheepish.

She giggled. "That was awesome."

He dipped his head and kissed her gently. "You are amazing."

She hummed, kissing him back. As long as he thought so, she was happy. Once they had broken their lip lock, he stood, lifting her with him and towelling her off before drying himself.

She loved the attention he paid to her, making her feel so cared for. He was a strong man. A wolf who could have come in and tried to take over the town like the others. Instead he had worked with her family and other shifters for a Prince who wasn't even his species. She was so proud that he had chosen her. But she was still scared that he would have to leave—that what had been said in the shower had been all passion and not reality. She had known before she'd even joined him in the shower that he was it for her. She was in love with him.

Once dressed, they sat on the bed together while he held her hand, both not sure what to say.

"Beth..." he started but paused, pressing his lips together.

"It's okay, Gray," she assured him. She didn't want to hear him say that he had to leave.

He shook his head. "I have to call my Alpha. Give him an update on what happened and have him pull the other wolves from the search."

"Oh," she said, confused. Not what she had thought he was trying to say.

He squeezed her hand. "When I call him, I want to tell him I'm not coming back right away. That I might not come back at all."

He didn't look at her when he made the announcement. She dropped down in front of him to make sure she was really hearing the words.

"Say that again," she asked, holding onto his knees.

He blinked and met her eyes. "I want to stay here. I know it's only been a couple of days, so I can give you time. Stay here at the inn and maybe take you on a couple of dates. To get to know you better and let you get to know me."

"You want to stay? You want to date me?" she repeated.

He snorted. "Well, actually I want to mate you and make you mine. Become a family with you—your mate, a nephew to Toby, a brother-in-law to Dawson and Casey, and someday a parent with you."

Tears filled her eyes but she held them back...barely. "Mate me?"

He nodded, never looking away. "Twice almost did already. Last night and again just now. I would never do that without your permission, but yes, in the long run I want to be your mate."

"Gray," she cried, her tears spilling down her cheeks.

"I have no idea how it would work. If we can even mate being two different species. But you told me that we were more human than animal. I have to believe you. And the thing is, both the human part of me and the wolf want you. You and your bobcat."

"Oh God!" she sobbed. It was everything she wanted. More than she had allowed herself to hope for.

"I don't know what is going to happen but I know I want you," he told her, sliding down the bed and kneeling just as she was.

"Yes, please, Gray. I will love you forever. I'll be the best mate. Stay with me!" she begged, so happy that her words tumbled out without thought. "I love you."

He yanked her to him, hugging her hard. "Thank God," he said over and over into her ear. "Thank God."

The shrill sound of a cell phone interrupted their moment.

"That's Tyler," he told her, letting go. "Stay with me?"

She nodded and moved into his lap, and he reached for the phone on the nightstand.

He held her tight as he answered. "Hey, Tyler."

"Gray, are you okay?" his Alpha asked.

Beth rested her head against his chest, hearing both sides of the conversation easily.

"I'm good, man. You can let the others know that it's over for us. We captured twelve men. Casey Williams said they would be leaving soon to gather up the other men that were involved."

"Good, good," Tyler said over the line. "I called the sheriff's office and spoke to Jim already. I thought you would be there but he said you headed back to your room to clean up. You weren't hurt, were you?"

Gray grimaced so Beth stroked his chest. "No, no—I've already healed. Just wanted to shower before I called in."

"Grayson." Tyler's voice took on a stern tone. "What is really going on?"

Gray sighed and gripped her hand hard. "There's something I need to talk to you about."

"Okay," Tyler encouraged. "You know, whatever it is, I'll support you."

Gray blew out a breath but didn't continue.

Tyler waited a few minutes then a heavy sigh came over the line. "You're not coming back, are you?" the Alpha asked.

"No, I'm not," Gray admitted.

Tyler's voice was sad. "I see. Tell me about her."

Gray smiled and started talking to his friend, not his Alpha. Beth could tell the difference immediately. The dynamic between the two men was something more like brothers than Alpha and Pack member.

Gray sang her praises and Beth blushed a little, glad the Alpha couldn't see her.

"She sounds great, I can't wait to meet her," Tyler told him sincerely. Beth grinned. She couldn't wait to meet the other man either.

"But what else? You had to know I would support you taking a mate, what else is going on?" Tyler dug deeper.

Gray was running his thumb over the pulse in her wrist. "She's not a wolf."

She jerked and glanced to him. Did it matter that much to him?

"Okay, that is not unheard of—" Tyler started.

"She's a bobcat," Gray finished.

Tyler was silent on the other end. Beth even pressed closer just to make sure she didn't miss his reaction. When it came it surprised her. The low chuckle slowly turned into a loud belly laugh.

Gray actually took the phone away from his ear to glare down at it before putting it back up. "Tyler!" he snapped.

"Sorry! Sorry!" Tyler sniggered just a little. "But I can just see you obsessing over the fact that you were in love with a feline and what were you going to do."

"It's not funny!" Gray exclaimed. "I don't want to hurt her. What if we have kids?"

That set Tyler off all over again. Gray rolled his eyes and frowned.

"Oh, don't pout, Gray!" Tyler teased. Beth didn't know how the Alpha knew that was what Gray was doing but she found it funny. She started to giggle herself.

Gray threw the hand upward that wasn't holding the phone as he scowled at her. It just made her snicker more.

"Gray, listen to me," Tyler demanded, serious even though his voice still held amusement. "You can mate a bobcat. You can even have children. You found your mate."

Gray was nodding, relief filling his face.

"Now go celebrate. I'm leaving tomorrow to come down there. When I get there we can talk about this more. I'll give you the numbers of a few couples that I think can answer some of your questions."

"You don't have to do that," Gray stammered.

"Grayson, I will see you in a few days. Now hang up the phone, go eat dinner, and love on your mate," Tyler ordered.

"Yes, Alpha," Gray answered, smiling, and hung up the phone.

He looked down at Beth and she wrapped her arms around his neck. Before she could start on the *loving on the mate* part, Gray's stomach growled.

"I guess that's my cue to feed you," she teased, standing and offering her hand.

Gray grumbled—he could have used a little bit of loving—but followed Beth easily out of his room and down to the dining room. He was starving. He'd shifted four times during the day and each shift, plus healing his shoulder, had taken a lot out of him. He'd been exhausted standing in the shower wishing he'd dragged Beth with him upstairs. But when she'd stepped into the shower stall with him, it was like she'd shared her energy with him and all he had wanted was to claim her.

And so much had happened since he'd stepped into the shower. God, was that only an hour ago?

Inside the dining room, they saw RJ, Mike and Jesse at a large table.

RJ waved them over. "Dude, they have homemade chicken pot pie, mashed potatoes, and rolls from scratch."

Gray took the seat next to him, pulling Beth down beside him. The way the men were shoving the food in, he had better order before they ate it all.

Dorothy waved at them, sending Toby to his aunt, and motioning she would bring them plates.

"I drew you a picture!" Toby came rushing over.

Gray accepted the picture and looked down at the drawing of three cats and a wolf.

"That's me, Daddy, Aunt Beth, and you," Toby told him proudly.

Gray lifted the boy into his lap. "It's wonderful! I love it, Toby."

"Really?" The young boy sounded so excited.

"Really," he promised.

"Into your seat, Toby, so everyone can eat," Dorothy ordered the boy while she held a large tray of plates of food.

"Okay." Toby scrambled around to sit next to Beth while Dorothy started to fill the empty space in front of them with plates. RJ was right—the plates were filled with the best food he'd ever smelt.

"Told you!" RJ said smugly, leaning over and snatching one of Gray's rolls.

"Hey!" he protested with a laugh.

"Homemade, dude!" RJ taunted, waving the roll at him.

Dorothy smacked the back of his head. "You behave, RJ Cross, or I'll be giving your brother a call."

"Yes, ma'am," RJ said, dropping his head. Gray noticed he kept the roll tucked in close, though.

Dorothy shook her head and smiled. "I'll bring you boys a beer."

"Yay!" RJ cheered, digging back into his food.

Everyone laughed and Gray picked up Beth's hand, placing a kiss in her palm before he started on his own plate, feeling true happiness for the first time in what felt like forever.

Chapter Eleven

Casey Williams pulled out his Desert Eagle and met RJ's eyes. He nodded and waited while the other man held up a hand to the other members of their unit behind him.

Five seconds. He watched RJ's fingers come down one at a time until he held up a fist. Once the countdown was up, they moved into action. Casey kicked in the front door and heard the other part of the team break down the back door. They ran into the old house, weapons drawn and ready.

There in the centre of the living room with a rifle in his hand was the man responsible for the kidnapping of his mate.

Casey raised his own gun. "Please try," he encouraged. "Please."

One twitch and his team would fill the man with dozens of rounds of bullets. The man's eyes darted around before he threw the rifle down.

"Damn it," RJ groused. "I really wanted to shoot someone."

Casey watched as Mike and Jesse secured Zach's cousin, making sure it was done properly. He pulled out his cell phone and hit the first speed dial button.

"Got him," he told Zach when his mate picked up the other line.

"Bring him to me," he was ordered.

Casey walked over to their prisoner. "Your presence is requested by the Prince," he said with a nasty smile.

The man's eyes widened and Casey felt a deep satisfaction in getting to him. "Get him out of here," he told his men.

He turned to see a grinning RJ leaning against the wall.

Casey nodded to the other man. "Let's get out of here. I have a mating ceremony to attend and you need to get to your brothers."

They walked out side by side. Their last mission had been a success.

* * * *

Gray glanced around the inn's backyard, looking for his mate. He found her lounging in the grass with Toby, his good friend Kiley, and his Alpha's daughter Jessie.

"Great party," Tyler told him, coming up and handing him a beer.

Gray grinned at him. "I'm glad everyone could make the trip." Not only had his Alpha driven down, but Kiley and her mate Austin, almost every member of his Pack, plus most of his friends he'd made from the other Packs had as well. Even Prince Zachary, Casey, Jesse and Mike had arrived the day before. The small ceremony he and Beth had thought they were having had ended up being over one hundred shifters.

One of the greatest things was that everyone who had arrived in town had simply fallen in love with the community and the people. Even the town folks had come out and opened up to the wolf and his friends. And no one had eaten Toby, either.

He chuckled at the memory of Toby's face when all of the wolves had started showing up. But, as children would do, Toby made instant friends with everyone. Jesse, Tyler's daughter, had declared him the most awesome cat ever. He couldn't wait to see what would happen once those two were actually able to shift.

The event had proven that mixing the different species and coming together could be accomplished. They had not run into any negativity about the cross-species mating. It gave him hope for the future when in just a few months they would be announced to the world.

"We wouldn't have missed it for anything," Tyler said, throwing an arm around his neck.

Casey and the Prince joined them, both giving Gray a hug and congratulations. Gray thanked them when they welcomed him to the family. Tyler looked on proudly.

"RJ sends his well wishes also, though he couldn't be here. His brother's ceremony is coming up and there have been some issues," Casey informed him.

"Everything okay? Anything we can do?" Gray offered.

Casey waved it off. "He says it's just grumbling for now. I'm sending Mike over to check on things tomorrow. He'll let us know."

Gray nodded. "If you need me just say the word."

Casey slapped his back. "Oh, don't worry, we will. That's what families are for. So remember that when I want to borrow a lawnmower or something."

Gray lifted a brow in question.

"Zach and I bought a house here. We're going to split our time between here and his home."

"Awesome! Beth will be so happy."

"Congratulations, guys," Tyler told them.

They made small talk for a while before wandering off to grab some food.

"You look happy," Tyler pointed out.

Gray looked around. "I am. I really am."

"I was going to tell you that you would always be a member of the Pack. Always welcome, both you and Beth. Then I got here and realised I didn't need to."

Gray turned and looked at him. "No?"

"I can see your Pack is here now," Tyler pronounced with a smile at the crowd and hugged Gray close.

"You'll still always be my family," Gray whispered to his best friend.

Tyler slapped him on the back. "Oh, I know—you'll not get rid of us that easy."

Gray knew he was lucky as he watched his Alpha walk away. After what had seemed like forever, he'd finally found his mate and a new home. Jim had offered him a job with the sheriff's office, which Gray had gladly accepted but only after he took Beth on their honeymoon trip. They were going to spend some time visiting different attractions in the country. First stop would be the Grand Canyon in Arizona. He thought Beth, who had never left her community, would get a big kick out of the canyon. He couldn't wait to shift with her there while they explored.

"You have a sappy smile on your face," Beth teased, coming up behind him and wrapping her arms around his waist.

"I can't help it. You turned me into a sappy, smiling man," he joked back.

"I thought I just turned you on," she taunted, slipping her hand lower.

"Why, Beth!" he exclaimed with a smile, turning in her arms. "I'm shocked you would try to seduce me at our mating party."

She threw her head back and laughed. "Oh, I'm not trying."

She tugged forward towards the kitchen.

"Where are we…?"

She opened the tall, walk-in closet door and shoved him inside.

"The closet, babe?" he chuckled.

"Oh shut up!" she ordered with a smirk, opening his jeans and finding him already hard. "Or I'll have to shut you up."

She didn't manage to shut him up completely, though. As her hot mouth wrapped around his cock, he cursed, pleaded and begged.

"Please, baby… Please," he chanted, needing so bad.

"Mmm…" She used her beautiful mouth to push him over the edge.

"Love you," he told her over and over. "Love you so much."

And he did.

PACK MATES

Dedication

For the fans, who have waited — and begged — for the Were Chronicles to continue.

Chapter One

Late March and it was already ninety degrees in south-east New Mexico. Nikki Stratton groaned as the air conditioner in her old Jeep barely managed to cool the interior of the vehicle.

Thirty-two years old and she'd been called home like a teenager. She resented the fact that she had let her older brothers demand her appearance and was still disgusted with herself for not putting up a fight.

She continued to speed down the interstate towards her home town. Both dread and anxiety sat in her stomach. A new Alpha had been named for her Pack. Since she still maintained Pack status, she had been beckoned home to welcome him and the new members he had brought to join their family. That was what she supposed, anyway. It wasn't like Brandon had actually *told* her why he wanted her home. He'd just stated she needed to leave the next day. Justin hadn't given any hint either—had just told her the new Alpha would take over this week and she needed to come home.

It wasn't even that she didn't want to be there. She had planned to take a vacation and spend some time with her siblings soon, but being ordered home left her feeling like a cub again. She loved her brothers but sometimes it was more about the Pack than their immediate family.

Her oldest brother Brandon was town Sheriff and enforcer of the Pack. Her other brother Justin was a teacher, both in public and in Pack life. Their wants and needs had been built around being able to serve their fellow wolves. Nikki just wasn't born that way. She liked to be free, to travel and be on her own. Unusual for a wolf, yes, but not unheard of. Away from home, she had not only met other wolves who felt like she did, but other shifters, too—felines, birds, and even a very nice shifter bear family. Nikki felt more at home with them sometimes than with her old Pack.

Her family had never understood her independence but at least they'd always supported her. She really couldn't bitch too much about it. And she was starting to feel guilty and just a little childish about her feelings. Except...she liked her life. Now she worried that her carefully constructed way of life was about to change. Why else would she have to come home? With no choice in the matter? They'd never asked that before.

The exit sign for their town came up and Nikki had to fight the urge to keep driving. She slowed to make the curved side road that would take her straight into downtown Midessa, a small, private cotton and farming community close to the Texas panhandle.

Little had changed in the year and a half she'd been away. She'd gone to the big city of Houston, Texas, to attend college and had never moved back. Oh sure, she'd made certain that she returned every few years or so, but she wasn't ready to settle down quite yet. And living in Midessa would ensure that would happen.

The welcome sign on the county line drew a sigh from her. She felt like a different person when she was there. Always having to defend her nomadic ways and trying to explain why she wasn't ready for a mate or children yet.

Yet, if she was completely honest, it felt good to know she always had a place to come back to. Yes, even if she never said it out loud, sometimes she missed her family.

She let up off the gas pedal even more to drive in at the posted thirty-five miles per hour. She wouldn't put it past Brandon to pull her over and ticket her if he caught her speeding. She chuckled to herself—it had, in fact, happened before.

The library was closed already, reminding her that at six on a Sunday night she wouldn't have to worry about running into too many people. The café was open and had a half-full parking lot. But the other buildings—post office, salon, thrift store—were dark and locked up tight. Lights blazed to the right. Of course the Sheriff's office was open. Like the café, it was an all-day-and-night business. Not that there was a lot of crime, but put a group of secretive wolf shifters in a community and you were bound to have several paranoid people. She happened to be related to one.

As if her thoughts had brought him out, she watched as the front door of the Sheriff's office opened and Brandon stepped out.

His dark brown hair looked to be several weeks past a trim and reached over his ears. His strong muscular shoulders and arms bulged from his khaki uniform shirt, while his long legs ate up the ground as he made his way to the street. He turned and his green eyes flashed as he spotted her vehicle. The grin he sent her was so much better than the pictures she carried, she couldn't help but smile back.

He wrenched the door to her Jeep open before she'd even parked. She slammed it into the P and turned the key right before he pulled her out and into his arms.

"Hey, sister," he greeted her, squeezing tight.

"Bran!" she managed to squeak out.

He chuckled and set her on her feet. "Let me look at you." He did the customary check she went through every time she came home. He ran his hands over her head, down her hair to her face, finally resting on her shoulders.

He nodded. "You need to eat more but you look good."

She rolled her eyes. She hadn't expected him to say anything different.

He grinned and threw an arm around her neck, yanking her close once again. "I was just headed to meet Justin for a bite. Now you can join me."

She groaned. After driving for a day and a half she really wanted to rest.

"Oh, don't complain. You need to eat. Then Justin can grab a ride home with you instead of waiting on me."

He slammed her vehicle door closed before he led her away. It didn't escape her notice that he didn't lock it up—something she could never do back in Houston.

She let herself be dragged down the street heading back to the café she'd passed on her way into town. She let her eyes roam over the stores as she passed and noticed a new flower shop, tattoo parlour, and dry cleaners.

"New businesses?" There hadn't been any new shops in the entire time she'd grown up there.

"Cameron started working with the new Alpha to bring his Pack members here before he stepped down. He wanted us to be comfortable and see the plus side of adding to the Pack," Brandon explained.

"How many did we add?"

"Over fifty."

She gasped. That was almost how many the Pack had had before. In a matter of a few months, the pack number had doubled.

"It's a good thing," Brandon responded to her reaction.

She noticed he'd said that with more feeling than normal. Either he was still trying to convince himself or there were already problems. She'd have to talk to Justin about it later.

Justin didn't usually try to keep her out of what was happening, thinking he was protecting her like Brandon always did. Not all the time anyway.

She knew her brothers couldn't help it. Brandon had raised his two younger siblings since he'd been barely an adult. Their father had left them as soon as he felt they were old enough to be on their own. The loss of his mate had been just too much for him to live with.

She wanted to remember good times with her parents but as she got older, she found it harder and harder to bring up those memories.

Just as they reached the door to the café, she was greeted with a shriek and an armful of woman. Chuckling and glad she still remembered the scent of her best childhood friend Sabrina, she grinned.

"Nik!" Sabrina held her close.

"Hey there, honey." She hugged her friend back.

"I can't believe you're back. I was just saying the other day that you haven't come to visit in forever. You haven't even meet little Julian yet."

Since she was still being squashed, she gently tried to extract herself from her friend. Sabrina didn't seem to want to let go.

"Baby, give her room to breathe or you're gonna make her pass out," Sabrina's mate Max said, coming to her rescue and pulling her friend from her.

Sabrina laughed. "All right."

Nikki smiled and looked over her friend. Sabrina had grown to be such a lovely woman. Short-cropped blonde hair, styled and sassy, fit her petite frame and her quirky personality.

But it was the glow in Sabrina that warmed her heart. She looked so happy.

"We have to catch up. Oh, we have so much to talk about," Sabrina said as she grabbed Nikki's hands.

"Oh yes, and I'll finally get to meet baby Julian and see Jesse and Jeremy," she agreed. She still talked to her oldest friend as much as she could, but with two busy lives, work, family and everything else, it had been too long. "Why don't you bring the kids over for breakfast in the morning?"

"A breakfast cooked by someone else?" Sabrina asked with a smile. "We are so there."

Nikki nodded and pulled her friend in for another hug. "Eight o'clock—don't be late."

Sabrina agreed then let her mate lead her across the parking lot.

"She looks so great," Nikki told her brother.

"She's happy," he answered simply. "But I want to know why you're not making your favourite brother breakfast?"

She slapped his stomach as she pulled the door open. "Justin can eat if he wants to."

Brandon growled and reached for her. She laughed and jumped out of the way, bumping into someone.

"Oh sorry," she murmured as she looked up. She actually had to tilt her head back to see the man in front of her.

"Oh, no problem at all," he responded with a deep rumble that vibrated the air around her.

Her breath caught as she stared up at the man. Dark, almost black hair hung over his dark eyes. His lips tilted up at the edges in a small smile as he moved to the side.

She didn't even realise she had moved closer until Brandon touched her lower back, breaking her attention on the stranger.

"RJ." Brandon greeted the stranger. Nikki didn't miss the tension in her brother's body or his tone.

"Good evening, Sheriff." The man nodded. "Ma'am."

Nikki snorted. "Ma'am?"

Amusement shone in the stranger's gaze. "Well, if I knew your name…"

"It's Nikki Stratton," she replied, holding out her hand.

He took it and winked. "RJ Cross."

Electricity sizzled from her fingertips up her arm. She was locked into that dark gaze and her body tingled with need. His dark eyes sparkled back at her.

"Now that everyone's met, can we go eat?" Brandon snapped from beside her.

She sighed and removed her hand from RJ's hold. "Well, I guess I'll be seeing you around town," she told the handsome stranger. She really, *really* wanted to see him again.

"Oh, I can almost guarantee it."

Nikki didn't want to leave his presence—there was just something about the man that called to her. But with her brother tugging at her arm, she allowed herself to be manhandled into the café.

She could feel RJ's eyes on her as she was forced away from him.

Chapter Two

RJ Cross watched the young woman until she disappeared to the back of the café. The smile fell from his face once she was out of sight. Without question, she was one of the most intriguing women he'd ever laid eyes on.

Her long dark hair was streaked with blonde, which added an attractive touch. Her green eyes had sparkled and her slender body was just to his liking. But being a Stratton was an added complication.

He and Brandon Stratton hadn't started on the best of terms. He shook his head and started back down the street to his shop. Instead of going inside, he walked to the back where he had his Harley parked.

He was glad he had decided to stop at the café before going home. Running into Nikki Stratton was a pleasant twist to the already long day.

He climbed on his bike and started it up. The rumble and vibration under him felt good and he took off towards the main street.

The small community he'd moved to with his Pack was a pretty piece of America. The Pack had come from the mountains of Colorado, and he'd worried that his family and Pack members wouldn't adjust well. The last eight years spent in the military had kept him from having a place. His older brother had asked for him to come home, and RJ had known it had been time. He'd met some great people along the way, but he wanted to settle down. To be a part of something else. So it was great that, so far, most loved the town they had found, including him.

The quick ride to the house he was staying at with his brothers ended, and he thought about riding around for a little longer. He enjoyed driving the long, empty roads throughout the territory but he had business to take care of.

He parked under the carport between the two trucks that had beaten him home. The lights were on in the front windows as he made his way across the wood porch. He let himself in and was greeted by the coolness of the air and the sound of a ball game on the television in the den.

He followed the noise to the doorway where he found his two brothers. His eldest brother was lounging in one of the leather chairs, legs spread as he slouched, drinking a beer.

RJ's younger brother had his head buried in a book as he sat on one side of the large couch. He ruffled his 'little' brother's hair as he stepped beside him and dropped down next to him.

"Hey!" Ben grumbled, not looking up from his book.

RJ grinned as he met Dylan's gaze.

Dylan smiled and shook his head. "How was work?"

RJ just shrugged. Opening a tattoo shop in a small town might not work out but he enjoyed his art and didn't really need to work anyway. "Had a couple people drop by, but no new customers. I think they wanted to check out the new Alpha's brother more than any art."

Dylan nodded. "Give them time. The town will open up to us."

RJ hoped he was right but that wasn't his biggest concern. "I stopped by the café tonight."

Dylan must have caught something in his tone because he switched the game to mute and sat up straighter.

"I overhead two men talking about the ceremony," RJ told him.

Beside him, Ben put his book down and shifted towards him. Now he had both their attentions.

"They suggested there might be a challenge after the ceremony."

Dylan sat back, and RJ let the man think. The rumours about a challenge had started to build in the last few weeks. Now just days before the ceremony, they had picked up even more. It had always been a possibility when Cameron King had asked Dylan to take over as Alpha that a challenge would come from someone who wanted the top position.

There were only two ways to become an Alpha of a Pack—to be appointed or to challenge the standing Alpha. Cameron King was an honest, kind, and well-respected Alpha. Dylan was new to the territory. An unknown.

"Any idea who?" Dylan asked quietly.

RJ ran his hands roughly over his face. This was the tricky part. He didn't want to add to the gossip but he had to protect his brother. "Talk is Brandon Stratton."

Dylan didn't look surprised. "I thought it would be. He is the closest wolf to matching my strength. Cameron did tell me he spoke with Brandon when he started to think about stepping down. Let him know about me." RJ waited for his brother to continue. "At the time Brandon didn't want the position. Said he wasn't born to lead and knew it."

"Doesn't mean he didn't change his mind," Ben spoke up for the first time.

Smaller than his two brothers, Ben Cross was the quiet and peaceful one. He'd been born with the ability to calm those around him. It was what made him such a good diplomat for the Pack.

"Yeah, it's one thing to not want to be Alpha and another to have someone else come in and take over," Dylan agreed.

"The thing is," RJ interrupted, "Brandon might not like it, but I don't get the feeling he's planning on challenging you. He hasn't exactly welcomed me, but he doesn't go out of his way to make up conflict. Other than the argument when I first reached town, he has been somewhat civil."

All three of them sat in silence, thinking their own thoughts for several minutes, before Dylan spoke again.

"Well, there is nothing we can do until the challenge is issued. Just keep an ear out."

RJ tilted his head in agreement. They had to wait. Nothing more to do. He might not like it, but it was Dylan's call. "I'm going to head up to shower."

Ben picked his book back up and sent him a wave of his hand but Dylan still stared at him. "Is that all?" he asked quietly.

RJ didn't know how he did it. His older brother was always able to tell when something was going on with one of them. He thought about telling him about Nikki but didn't want to add to his brother's worries.

And maybe he wanted to keep her a secret just a little bit longer.

He could still smell the citrus from her shampoo, feel the softness of her hand in his, and wanted to enjoy the moment before he had to deal with the tension between the two families.

"For now," he answered his brother vaguely.

"I'm here if you need me," Dylan told him before reaching for the remote again.

RJ headed up the stairs to the first room down the hall. He liked being closest to the stairs in case of problems during the night. He had served as an Enforcer in his Pack as well as the Pack in the military, which was actually a shifter unit. There had been a mixture of species but they had been run like a Pack. He still thought of them that way.

But after his latest mission to protect the feline Prince and the battle once he'd been rescued, RJ had needed some time off. Dylan's call that he needed him home had come right when he was looking for an excuse.

Everyone could tell that Dylan had been born a natural leader, and when their Alpha had heard Cameron King wanted to retire, he had suggested a meet between the two men.

Their Alpha Craig was a good man and had several sons who would be able to lead their Pack into the future. Dylan would never have challenged them if they ran the Pack fairly, and Craig knew it. Craig had been offered a position on the Alpha council and as any good leader would, had suggested some changes before he'd left. One of them had been for Dylan and Cameron to meet, Craig believing that Dylan should get the chance to lead his own Pack.

So Craig had urged Dylan to meet with Cameron and had even talked several others into joining the Pack Dylan would lead. More had come than any of them had thought. Craig had understood and encouraged them all. He wanted his Pack members to flourish but with over two hundred shifters under his command, he knew there were some wolves who couldn't reach their potential in such a large group.

Moving to the new territory was a great opportunity for them all.

His room was dark and cool as he pushed the door open. He'd brought his furniture from the childhood home they'd lived in all their lives. He missed the old house and was glad he had something to remind him of home. He had a small apartment above his shop in town but he had yet to do more than move in a couch, futon, and odds and ends. It was convenient if he worked late or needed to grab a shower, but he liked being home with his brothers. Plus, until he knew all threat to Dylan had passed, he would stick close.

He tried to picture Nikki there with him in his bedroom. Would she find it too masculine, or would she see the beauty of the stained wood the way he did?

The large four-poster bed dominated most of the north wall. He was a tall man at six–foot-five. He liked to have plenty of room to sprawl out.

But thoughts of having Nikki on every inch of the bed had his cock coming to attention and throbbing.

He could just see her spread out in the middle of the bed. Legs open and inviting, arms stretched above her head, her body arching in need.

He pulled his black T-shirt over his head and dropped it to the floor he sat on the edge of the bed and pulled off his boots and socks. The desire he had clearly read when he'd locked gazes with her had tempted his control. And just the one touch they'd briefly shared had sent his blood boiling.

He wanted her hands on him as he caressed that sweet skin.

He stood but couldn't resist dropping his hand low to play with the zipper on his jeans. He wanted more than just her hands, though. Her mouth, with her easy smile, had been made for pleasuring a man.

He groaned as he pictured her on her knees in front of him. Oh yeah, he could almost feel the warm, wet tongue tracing his balls before sucking him in.

He manoeuvred out of his jeans quickly until he stood stark naked, panting with need. He licked his palm then started to stroke himself, each rough tug drawing him closer to completion. It had just been his hand for too long, and now that he'd found a woman who called to both the man and wolf, he was quickly ready to explode.

He concentrated on each detail of Nikki Stratton as he urgently played with himself. Oh, he couldn't wait to mark her with his mouth, his teeth and his cum. Bend her over the bed and pound into her just as he sank his canines into the back of her neck.

It was the last fantasy that sent him over the edge. His seed shot out as he pumped his cock and almost collapsed at the intensity of his orgasm.

He dropped back on the bed and smiled.

Complications be damned. Nikki Stratton would be his.

Chapter Three

Nikki had enjoyed dinner with her two brothers. Justin had delighted her with stories of both his second-grade class and the pre-teen wolves he taught. Brandon had remained quiet throughout most of the meal.

She bided her time until Brandon was headed back to the station and Justin sat in the passenger seat of her Jeep.

"What's going on?" she asked her brother as she turned south off the main street to where their small home was. It was obvious that she had been brought home for a reason. Brandon had always been the adult, but the tension in him was new. Something big was going on.

Justin sighed and looked out of the window. "The ceremony in a few days is getting people worked up."

She darted a look at him but he still faced away. "It's not like we didn't know it was going to happen." Brandon had called and told her Cameron was stepping down. He had explained about the new Alpha coming and how their community would grow.

"Yeah, but knowing and it actually happening are two different things," Justin told her.

Nikki guessed she could understand that. "Have you met the new Alpha?"

"Once. He seemed like a good enough guy," Justin admitted. "But he's not from here."

"Well, Cameron has already picked the Alpha and it was agreed upon by the council," she reminded him. "What is there to do?"

"The new Alpha could be challenged right after the ceremony," Justin informed her quietly.

Her hands jerked and the vehicle swerved. She righted the steering wheel. "Shit, a challenge?"

She'd never seen a challenge but knew enough about them to know that a challenge for the position for Alpha would be major. Some of her friends had told her stories about the Pack being taken over. The Alpha who was beaten never lived.

"Who would be stupid enough to challenge the Alpha?" she asked.

When Justin just turned and met her stare she knew. "Oh, good God! He can't!"

Justin just shrugged. "I don't think he even wants to. But he's getting a lot of pressure right now."

And suddenly she understood. She wasn't home just to welcome the new Alpha. She might be saying goodbye to her own brother.

Tears pricked her eyes as she peered out of the windshield. The sights that surrounded her were so familiar, but they didn't soothe her like they normally did. Now they made her feel sick.

They'd lived there since her grandfather had joined the small community and had brought his young mate back home. Her grandmother's family had been part of the territory for several decades.

The wide open space that expanded for miles and miles was home. But home also meant family. Her family was just Brandon and Justin.

"We can't let him," she practically yelled in the small, quiet confines of the vehicle.

"We don't have a choice. If he decides to do it, we have to support him," Justin murmured.

She couldn't believe her ears. Could Justin really believe that any good to come out of the challenge? She pressed her lips together and glared over at him. The pain on his face brought her up short. If he knew, how could he back Brandon?

"Justin?"

He held up a hand stopping her. "Talk to Brandon. He knows how I feel already and he needs to know your thoughts also. But no matter what he decides, we will stand behind him."

Nikki didn't say anything, unsure what could actually be said. She turned down the gravel road that led to their cabin. It was only a half mile to the house and the entire time her mind ran though several possibilities. All ended with her losing so much.

She pulled up to the front of the house and heard the barking. The sound brought a smile to her face. Faced with so much new information, it was good to know some things didn't change.

She opened the driver's door without waiting on Justin. She braced her feet shoulder-width apart and waited as the barking came closer.

A black streak raced from around her house before she suddenly had a full-blooded sixty-pound black Lab on her.

"Hey, Bear." She rubbed the dog from his large front paws on her shoulders down his back. She received several wet kisses as welcome.

Justin's deep laugh came from in front of the house. "Guess he missed you."

She glanced over and her heart swelled. It was obvious the dog wasn't the only one. She wanted Justin to wrap his arms around her and tell her it would be okay. Instead, she let him turn away.

"Justin?" she called out before he could make it up the steps.

He turned and raised an eyebrow in question.

"What's the new Alpha's name?"

"Dylan Cross."

She didn't hear him walk into the house, couldn't hear anything over the pounding in her ears. She pushed the dog off her and sat down heavily on the bottom step.

"Christ. Cross?" she whispered to the night.

Bear lay at her feet and licked her hand. She had no idea what that meant.

Obviously her brother hadn't liked the man she'd met at the café. The hostility had been easy enough to read. But was it because he was related to the new Alpha or something more? She normally wouldn't have thought anything about getting involved with someone her brother didn't approve of. In fact, that had been how she had picked her high-school boyfriends. But this was something else entirely. Not only was her body practically vibrating at the thought of him, her wolf—who typically stayed mostly silent—was scratching and clawing at her to go find him.

She could almost taste the strength that had come from the stranger. He might not have been Alpha material, but he had been dominant. And if he was related to the Alpha that didn't speak well for any challenger.

Brandon had always been quick, strong and smart. But she was scared to death it wouldn't be enough this time.

She buried her hands in Bear's thick fur. "What in the world are we going to do?" she asked. Of course, the dog didn't answer.

The wind picked up, forcing her to go back to her Jeep and grab her bag. Bear stayed with her and she was glad for the company. She walked in the front door and the feeling of being home hit her at once. Her eyes blurred from the memories that assaulted her. The living room still had the old worn furniture that had once belonged to her grandparents.

The light was off in the dining room and further back to the kitchen but she knew no changes had been made there either.

The stairs still creaked as she made her way up. She smiled, jumping over the seventh step—the loudest—that had given her away more than once when she'd tried to sneak out as a teen.

She passed Brandon's and Justin's rooms on the way to her own. Justin's light shone under his door, but she wanted a little time alone to think things through before she spoke with him again. There had to be something she could do to help Brandon.

Her room hadn't changed a bit in her absence, and that was both comforting and sad. Would it really hurt her to come back more than once every couple of years? While she had been travelling and working, her brothers were trying to figure out the future of the Pack.

She really felt terrible that she hadn't wanted to come back. Brandon and Justin had obviously needed her.

Hoping a hot shower would clear the exhaustion from travel and help her think more clearly, she dumped her bag on the bed and grab her shower case from it. She had the master bedroom with the bath inside, while Brandon and Justin shared the other bath in the hall. She had told one of them to take her room so they could have the private bath, but Brandon had ignored her and Justin had said as soon as she was mated he would.

She'd answered in that case it would still be hers for a while.

She turned the hot water on and began to strip. Stepping inside the stall, she sighed and let the steam and heat relax her. Starting to wash her hair, she thought about the man she had met earlier. RJ was the kind of man that you would notice from down the street—his dark good looks, height and build, and tattooed arms.

She hummed to herself thinking how damn good-looking he was. Just the kind of guy she usually found herself attracted to.

Oh, not normally as attracted as this, but it had been a long while since she had been with another shifter. She craved the dominance male wolves had in them, but in the people she surrounded herself with she rarely found what she longed for.

She filled her hands with body wash and ran her hands down her neck to her chest. Her breasts felt heavy and she wished there was someone in the shower with her. Of course that made her think about RJ again. His large hands would be able to cup her perfectly and his wide smooth lips would feel fantastic against her skin.

Crissy Smith

She moved her hands lower until she skimmed against her mound. She slipped a finger lower, rubbing her clit hard.

Spreading her legs, she leaned against the wall of the shower. The stall was too small for two people, but she could still imagine RJ on his knees in front of her licking her folds.

Her imagination and own fingers brought her to the fevered edge she craved. "Oh God," she murmured, sliding two fingers deep inside her pussy. Pumping in and out, she trembled…almost right…there…

A flash of RJ holding her against the wall, his deep voice telling her to come, had her finally falling over the edge.

Spent and warm, she turned off the water and wrapped a towel around her body. She had a lot to think about. Maybe she would catch a little nap before Brandon came home.

Chapter Four

Dylan was already gone by the time that RJ made it down the stairs the next morning, but Ben was dressed in his suit drinking a cup of coffee.

"'Bout time," his younger brother complained. "I've got to get to work."

RJ frowned as he reached for a clean coffee cup. "So what's stopping you?"

It wasn't like he usually got up with his brothers. He liked to work late and had never been an early riser. He enjoyed having his own business so he could set his own hours.

"Because I wanted to talk to you," Ben told him as he stood and rinsed out his coffee mug. RJ moved to the kitchen table his brother had just left and took a seat, waving his hand so Ben would get on with it.

"One of the women I work with said that the Stratton sister was coming to town," Ben informed him.

RJ froze. He wasn't sure where his brother was going with this.

"From what I understand, she keeps Pack status but hasn't been home in over a year."

As casually as he could, RJ leant back in his chair. "And?"

"You don't think it's funny that the ceremony and maybe challenge are only days away and she is suddenly back here?"

Now that he thought about it, yes, it was a little strange, but he didn't want to admit it to his brother. "What? You think she's part of the challenge?"

Ben shook his head. "No, of course not, but it doesn't mean they're not up to something."

RJ thought about it, but really, what could the young woman do? Besides she had flirted with him the night before. Plus she hadn't even blinked at his name when he had told her he was a Cross. He would almost guarantee she hadn't a clue about his family.

Almost guarantee. He was pretty good at reading people but he had been distracted by her.

"I'll see what I can find out," he promised. He had already planned on it.

Ben's shoulders relaxed and he felt guilt turn his stomach. He should tell Ben about meeting Nikki Stratton. But instead he watched his brother pick up his briefcase and waved goodbye.

"Where to start?" he asked the empty room. He would treat it like any other investigation as an Enforcer. He picked up his coffee cup, topped it off and made his way to his laptop. He would run some basic searches on Nikki Stratton.

He would know where to go from there once he knew more about the woman. Stepping into his bedroom, he couldn't help but remember the fantasies he'd had about her. He'd woken hard and needing and had had to jerk off again before he'd gone in search of his morning caffeine.

One way or another, he needed to decide what to do about her. He couldn't keep her from his family for much longer.

* * * *

Nikki had slept like the dead. She'd meant to be awake when Brandon had got off shift but she hadn't heard a thing once she'd passed out in bed. Upon waking, she had been thrown for a minute before she could place where she was. Then the memory of the trouble they could be in had her stomach in knots as she had dressed for the day.

She looked forward to seeing her friend again but she now wished she hadn't invited her to breakfast. She needed to have a conversation with her brother.

She moved quietly around the house, starting the coffee pot and turning on the television before she started breakfast.

She was just placing the cinnamon rolls in the oven when Brandon appeared in the doorway. She poured him a cup and set it on the bar between them.

He grunted his thanks and took a seat.

Gently placing the spatula she was holding onto the counter, she leaned against the bar.

Brandon drank half the coffee before he glanced up at her.

"Justin told you?"

Nikki nodded. Guess it was going to happen now. "How could you even consider it?" she asked softly.

He looked down and rubbed the side of his mug. "I hadn't really. Some of the older members approached me and I figured they were just upset and would get over it."

"But they didn't," she guessed.

"No, as the ceremony gets closer they are getting more desperate. Word is that Dylan Cross will fill his inner circle with his own wolves. Cameron had discussed that some of our Pack would be involved, but I guess Dylan is backing out on that. So we would be losing the Pack and that scares people. Especially if the shifters do go public soon as planned. If I don't do it, then someone else will."

"Someone not as strong as you," she filled in.

He didn't answer so she just watched him, the man who had been her mother and father for the last twenty years.

"Do you even want to be Alpha?" she asked when he remained silent.

He looked up and she read the answer in his eyes. He didn't but he felt trapped.

She walked around the counter and wrapped an arm around his neck. "I don't want to lose you," she whispered into his ear.

He hugged her tight and they just held each other. Nikki couldn't believe this was happening. She had to find a way to save them all.

"We'll figure it out," she promised.

He gave her one last squeeze before letting her go and standing. "In two days? I've been trying to come up with another way for months now. And I don't want you to get involved. I just wanted you home. I wanted to have some time with you."

She bit her lip at the lost look on his face. She had never understood before how much responsibility her brother carried.

"I love you."

He smiled, just the corners of his lips curving up. "I love you too. I gotta get ready for work. Just yell when breakfast is ready."

She watched him go. There had to be something she could do.

She didn't have long to think about it before the back door open and the whirlwind of her best friend entered. Hands full of bags and children, Sabrina swept in, distracting her from her problems.

Breakfast was a noisy but wonderful event. The kids had woken Justin up, so he'd made it down right behind Brandon. They shared a look of worry but both remained quiet.

Both men eventually left for work, leaving the women and kids. Sabrina ushered the two older kids into the den to watch television as Nikki sat with another cup of coffee at the table holding baby Julian.

Sabrina topped off the mugs before sitting down beside her.

"How are things around here?" her friend asked.

Nikki was glad she had brought it up. She didn't want to confide too much but she needed to talk to someone. "As well as can be expected."

Sabrina sent her a sympathetic look. "I know a lot of the other members of the Pack are worried, but I don't know that a challenge is the way to go. Cameron is giving his blessing for the new Alpha. He has been working on the transition being as smooth as possible. I think it was a great idea of Dylan Cross to bring the Pack members in before he took over so everyone could merge together."

Nikki was glad her friend agreed. "How's it been around here since the new members came? Any problems?"

"No, as far as I've heard, they've brought in more money, businesses, and are a pretty good bunch."

"Then why all this talk about the challenge?"

Sabrina shrugged. "It's mostly the older generation. You know how they are about change. And this is a big one."

"Yeah, but Cameron wouldn't bring someone in he didn't trust. It couldn't have been easy to decide. He even consulted the Alpha council."

"I know. But you know how it is. So much has happened within the shifter world in the last few months. Talking about going public, the feline Prince being kidnapped, and now a new leader here. They are just trying to control something."

Nikki thought about the new information. "Does Cameron know? He should be able to do something."

"I don't think so. He wouldn't want a challenge. He would for sure try to talk to Brandon. But what can you say? I haven't actually heard if Brandon is going to challenge. Just the rumour that he should."

"Someone has to tell Cameron," Nikki insisted.

"And if Brandon doesn't challenge it could put him in jeopardy. What would you do in his position? He can't act on a rumour."

"What do you know about the new Alpha?"

"Just that he was an Enforcer at his old Pack. He showed all the signs of being a great leader but their Pack had several wolves descended from the Alpha who would want the position. To be an Alpha, he had to go somewhere else."

She had to ask, Nikki knew, but she dreaded bringing up the name. "What do you know about his brother, RJ Cross?"

Sabrina grinned. "Good-looking, smart, but a little rough around the edges. He owns the tattoo parlour in town, drives a Harley, and has every woman in town lusting after him."

"Hmm," Nikki murmured, not exactly happy that the thought of every woman in town making eyes at the stranger made her feel extremely jealous. Damn, she'd just met the guy.

"He has another brother, too," Sabrina informed her.

"Really?"

"Younger than Dylan and RJ. He works at the paper with Max. Max says he's quiet and keeps to himself. Nice and wicked smart."

"So both the brothers already work in town?" That was good information. If she wanted to protect her brother, she needed as much information as she could find on them.

"Yep, why? What are you going to do?" Sabrina asked with a nervous laugh.

"I don't know yet."

"Well, whatever you do, it has to be quick," Sabrina told her, standing. "Not everyone wants a challenge, but if there is one, sides will be drawn. Brandon would have the entire town on his. That's a lot of pressure."

Picking up the mugs and a few plates from the kitchen, Nikki agreed silently. If she was going to help, she needed to get started.

Chapter Five

RJ was impressed with the number of articles written by Nicole B. Stratton. She had travelled to several countries, writing about what she saw and bringing awareness to the many cultures that were ignored around the world. It was obvious the woman was good at what she did and truly enjoyed it.

It also raised the question—why would she put that on hold to come back home? Why now? And would she be leaving soon?

The last question was purely personal. He wanted to see more of the woman and knew one taste of her was not going to be enough.

The alarm on his watch beeped and he glanced at the time. It was already late morning and he needed to get into town to open his shop, even if the people who came in the shop only wanted to check out the new Alpha's brother.

He stuffed the articles in his top desk drawer before logging off his computer.

He showered quickly before dressing in a faded pair of jeans and a black T-shirt. His custom boots and jacket followed. Locking up behind himself, he wondered what Nikki was doing that morning.

If she hadn't known who he was the night before, surely she did by now. It might make it more difficult to get closer to her but he was a determined man.

He wouldn't trade on his feelings for her to get information on her brother, but a woman with the integrity to write the articles he'd read couldn't be behind a hostile takeover.

And a challenge would be just that. Cameron had chosen his brother to lead the Pack. It angered him that the old Alpha's wishes were not being respected, in addition to the fact that he wouldn't stand for any threat against his family.

The hum of his bike was loud in the quietness of the yard. He drove slowly and carefully towards town. Brandon Stratton had already pulled him over once. It had been a tense battle of strength between the two men. RJ knew the sheriff had been testing his control. Pushing his buttons to see what he would do.

He had managed to hang onto his wolf and not give the sheriff what he wanted. After taking the speeding ticket, he had been almost certain he'd briefly seen respect in Brandon's eyes but couldn't be sure.

He took the side streets until he reached the back alley in which he parked. He entered his shop through the back door and flipped on the lights. The shop remained neat and clean from the night before.

His footsteps echoed as he crossed the front entry to the windows and doors. He opened the blinds, letting the bright sunlight in to gleam against the stainless steel countertops. He was just reaching for the 'Open' sign when he spotted her.

She crossed the street with long, confident strides. He smiled as he watched her. She was dressed in almost identical style to his. Faded jeans, a snug, fitted black T-shirt, with black sneakers. Her long hair was pulled back in a ponytail and he could almost imagine hanging on to her hair as she went down on him. His cock rose and he licked his lips in need.

He wasn't surprised when he realised she was heading in the direction of his shop.

Everything he had learnt from the internet made him think she would attack any problem head on. Hopefully he could get her on his side. Not against her brother, but against a challenge.

He unlocked the door and pulled it open when she was still several feet away.

Surprise crossed her face before she wiped it with a look of determination. She nodded at him as she passed beside him to enter.

He closed the door behind her, leaving the sign on 'Closed'.

She walked around the shop, taking in his pride and joy. He let her prowl and admired her as she roamed. After several minutes, she paused and turned to him.

"We have a problem," she told him.

"Just one?" he asked, crossing his arms.

She laughed. "One problem at a time, I think."

"Okay." He waved to one of the couches. "Have a seat."

She sat down and he chose one of the other chairs so he could be directly in front of her. He wanted to sit close but he wasn't sure if he did that he would be able to keep his hands off her.

It was better that he put some distance between them, for now anyway. She smelt clean and fresh. He closed his eyes briefly and breathed in deep, pulling her scent inside him.

When he opened his eyes, he saw her staring down at her hands.

"Which problem would you like to discuss today?" he asked. He didn't like the thought of her being upset. The urge to join her on the couch was strong once again.

"Our brothers."

He tensed. He didn't mean to but it was a reaction he couldn't hide. As soon as he did, she shifted away from him. He took several deep breaths in hopes of calming himself and putting her at ease.

"I have heard rumours," he admitted, not wanting to give too much away until he knew her stance. "It concerns me."

"It concerns you? That's all you have to say? Just an everyday nuisance?" she accused. "Don't you want to do something to stop it?"

He laughed. This spitfire of a woman was sure intriguing. "You've been here, what? Twelve hours? I have been here for weeks. In all that time, not one person has asked my opinion. And if they did, I would tell them that Cameron chose his replacement and the members of this community need to accept it."

She frowned and shook her head. "What's your brother going to do about it?"

"What's my brother going to do? Are you saying Brandon is going to challenge?"

"No!" she practically yelled. She caught herself and cleared her throat. "No, I'm not saying that. But there are people in this town who don't want your brother to be Alpha. He needs to address it."

He was amused. Even though the entire situation was serious, he admired the woman sitting across from him. "My brother plans on accepting the position of the Alpha of the Midessa pack as requested by the current Alpha Cameron King," he told her formally. "He does not have to prove his worth to anyone and does not have to ask permission. This has already been decided."

She snorted. "Nice. Nicely worded."

He was glad she appreciated it.

"And you know that was a bullshit answer. I didn't expect that from you. Maybe from Ben, but I thought you would shoot a little straighter."

He tensed and a growl slipped out. "What do you know about Ben?"

"Not much. Doesn't seem like anyone knows much more than he keeps to himself and he's very smart."

Her words filled him with pride. Ben was smart, even though that was why he kept to himself so much. Being bullied as a kid would do that to you. Dylan and RJ had done their best to protect him, but they hadn't always been around.

"Dylan hasn't been around much, either. Spending all his time with Cameron," she commented.

"He does have a new Pack to learn about," RJ replied easily.

"Then there's you. You placed yourself right smack in the middle of town, you mix with the community and stay visible. Like you're trying to take everyone's attention from your brothers."

She was smart. But so was he. "And you. The big-city girl comes home, asks around about the Cross brothers, and thinks she knows it all?" he questioned.

She shook her head. "No, I don't know it all. But I do know that in two days, one way or another, we will have a new Alpha. If there is a challenge of any form, it will tear this town apart."

He sighed because she was right again.

"And if he is challenged?" she asked. "What happens if that does happen?"

That was a tricky question. He knew what he thought Dylan would do but he didn't think she would like that answer. "I can't answer that. You would need to ask Dylan."

She pressed her lips together before sucking her bottom lip into her mouth in thought. His cock responded immediately as he stared at her mouth. Damn it, they were having a serious conversation and he still wanted to mount and claim her.

Just the thought that she was brave enough to ask questions no one else had made him want to strip her naked and pound into her.

She licked her lips and he stifled a groan.

The fantasy from the night before came back. Her on her knees in front of him, pleasing him with her mouth and hands. His cock was leaking against the front of his jeans and he shifted, trying to relieve some of the pressure.

Her cough brought his thoughts back to the current time. When he glanced back at her, she was staring at his lap. His erection was obvious under the zipper of his jeans.

"Really?" she asked, peeking up at him.

He grinned and winked. "What can I say?"

She chewed on her lip more and he groaned.

Her eyebrows drew together in confusion.

"Stop with the lip thing! You're killing me here."

Her eyes widened. "Hmm," she teased, and darted her tongue to swipe at her lips.

He wasn't a saint. His control could only be tested so far. He jumped off the chair and was on her instantly. He straddled her legs and pushed her back against the couch.

"You're playing with fire, Nikki Stratton," he warned. Any indication she wanted this to go forward and he would be all over her.

He jerked when she ran her hands up from his knees to his waist.

"Oh God, just kiss me," she told him, tilting her head back.

"Hell yeah." He celebrated for a quick second before leaning down and slowly closing the distance between their mouths.

She arched up, trying to meet his lips. He grinned as he cupped the side of her face. "Are you sure?"

She growled and tightened her hands, now resting on his upper legs. "Stop teasing," she demanded.

He had no idea where he found the gentleness with which he kissed her. Their mouths met and she opened under the pressure of his. Their tongues touched tentatively at first then more forcefully.

She responded beautifully, reaching up and pulling him closer so his hard cock brushed over her stomach. He moaned at the friction and she swallowed the sound.

He closed his eyes and let himself go, kissing and rubbing against the woman under him. It wasn't until he felt her push him back that he realised she had been yanking at his shirt trying to get off the cotton material.

He leant back quickly and ripped the shirt over his head before removing hers as well.

She traced the tattoo over his heart before leaning forward to lick at the eagle. He shivered at the feel of her tongue on his skin.

"Marine," she murmured against him.

As gently as he could with shaking hands, he held her head to him. She left the eagle to run her tongue down his pecs, over his nipple, to the tribal tattoo that covered his left side.

His erection pulsed in need as she continued on exploring. Finally, before he blew, he slipped off her and guided her to lie down on the couch.

He kissed her again, enjoying the taste of coffee and pure woman. It was heady, this need that she had awakened in him. He wanted to worship her from top to bottom.

Just as slowly as she had done to him, he learnt every inch of her. Using his hands and mouth, he teased her soft skin, causing goosebumps to pop up.

She lifted enough to help remove her white silk bra and pressed against his hand when he cupped her sex through her jeans. He could smell her arousal. She was wet, ready for him. She scratched her short nails down his arm as he snapped the button on her jeans and slowly unzipped her pants. He let her toe off her tennis shoes and he yanked her socks, jeans and panties down until she lay bared for his eyes to feast on.

He bent and placed soft kisses on her stomach before moving lower. At the first swipe of his tongue through her juices she cried out. When he ran his fingers between her folds, she gasped before he opened her and mouthed her plump pussy, causing her to buck and grab at his head. He pleasured her, drawing out her climax, until she dropped back on the couch spent.

"Not nearly done with you," he warned her as he got his jeans open and pushed them down. He fought with his boots and socks before finally managing to get free of them. She watched with heavy eyes full of lust.

He climbed back to his knees and scooted closer to her.

"Mmm, yummy," she said before crawling off the couch and pushing him back. He hit the floor still reaching for her.

"I knew you would be big and hard. Just perfect for me," she admired, and stroked his cock. He lifted his hips into her touch. "I have to taste you."

He cried out when she swallowed him down her throat. He tried not to buck, really he did, but she was using her tongue under the head of his penis and he couldn't help it.

"Uh!" he called out as she took him deeper.

She slipped her hands beneath him and gently urged him to move.

As carefully as he could, he plunged in and out of her hot mouth. His control was close to snapping when she moved one hand to his balls and rolled them.

It was too much too soon. He couldn't hold back any longer.

"I'm gonna," he warned, thrusting faster even though he wanted to be buried inside her. But that would have to wait.

She hummed her permission and sucked him down. He came, white explosions behind his eyes, and she swallowed.

She licked him clean before sitting up and propping her chin on her hand. "Well, that wasn't the way I thought this conversation would go."

He laughed and gathered her to his chest to bask in the afterglow. He held her close, stroking her hair and praying they would be able to find a solution to the Pack problem. One afternoon and he knew that the woman in his arms was his. He would not let her go.

Chapter Six

Nikki couldn't believe she had agreed to meet RJ at the old bar at the edge of town. She'd managed to avoid both her brothers after her morning romp with RJ but guilt ate at her.

She was supposed to be trying to find a solution to the challenge problem, not sexing up a member of the enemy camp.

But really, it wasn't like the Cross brothers wanted a challenge, right? They had just as much at stake as anyone else.

She and RJ had at least agreed that a challenge was the last thing anyone wanted. She would have liked to discuss more in the privacy of his shop but an old military buddy had called and RJ had needed to answer the phone. Plus, by that time she had already felt guilty about throwing herself at him.

She pulled up in front of the old barn that had been converted into a bar and sighed. She knew her brothers wouldn't understand but she just couldn't stay away from RJ. Not only was she hoping for a solution to the Pack issue, but she just wanted to spend time with him.

As she'd lain in his arms and he'd told her he wanted to see her later that night, she hadn't been able to meet his eyes. It wasn't that she regretted what had happened between the two of them but she did have to look out for her family.

RJ had forced her chin up and when she'd lifted her head, she had been able to clearly see how important it was to him. She'd reluctantly agreed to come all the way out here. Away from anyone who would question the two of them being together. Give them time, he'd said, to figure out their next move.

As she'd expected, his Harley was parked close to the door. She parked her Jeep and stepped into the warm night air. Even at ten in the evening it had to still be in the eighties.

The music was low and the smoke thick when she opened the doors. Not too many people there at this time of night on a Monday. She ignored the four men playing pool and walked to the back booth where her date waited.

Not that this was a date. Or maybe it was. She didn't have any idea. He smiled and slid out of the booth when she reached the table.

The kiss she received was just shy of erotic and had her toes curling.

"I'll get you a drink. What's your pleasure?"

She nearly said he was but swallowed it at the last minute. "Light beer on tap."

He nodded and guided her to the seat he had just vacated.

She put her purse against the wall and watched as he walked to the bar. He wore tight black jeans and now that she knew what was under them, her mouth watered for another taste of him.

He cocked his hip against the bar as he ordered, surveying the room. When two beers were set in front of him, he pulled out his wallet and paid, before turning back to her.

His white shirt stretched tight against his chest and she had to curl her fingers up to stop herself from reaching out for him. He wasn't the first good-looking man she'd ever run into or even dated, but there was something about RJ Cross that just sent shivers of need down her spine.

He plopped the drinks down and joined her in the booth. She shook when he tugged at the bottom of her black skirt.

"And just what do you have under this?" he whispered in her ear.

She sent him what she hoped was a sexy grin and reached for her beer.

"Ah, something to find out later," he teased.

If his hand kept going up her thigh, it wouldn't be much later. She took several large gulps to try to cool her heated body.

He chuckled and nipped at her ear. "Slow down, honey. I don't want you too drunk for what I have in mind later."

She almost choked on her drink.

He kissed the side of her neck before leaning back and reaching for his own beer.

Nikki took a deep breath in relief. She wasn't too far from jumping him there in the bar and that wouldn't be good.

"We need to talk about our brothers," she told him. She was determined to find some sort of solution.

He raised his glass and tilted it to her. "You need to convince your brother not to challenge Dylan."

"Yeah, why didn't I think of that?" Nikki rolled her eyes. "It's not that simple and you know that."

He shook his head. "But it is. Dylan was picked by Cameron King. The Pack needs to respect his wishes."

"The Pack is worried. They don't know your brother, your family, or anyone else. They have the right to be concerned," she shot back.

"If they believe in Cameron, why are they questioning his choice? I've met the man several times and I don't see him turning his Pack over to someone who will lead them down the wrong road. Do you even know why they don't accept Dylan?"

She shook her head.

"That's bullshit then. He's a good man, and he will be a great and fair leader."

"He's new and different."

He snorted and took a long drink.

She didn't want to fight with RJ but he had to see where they were coming from.

"So instead of using these last two weeks or even the few months we've been here getting to know the future Alpha or asking questions, they come up with a conspiracy to get rid of him."

"It's not a conspiracy," she argued, even though it did kind of feel that way to her too.

"They had their time to talk with Cameron. To ask questions. Instead they wait until days before the ceremony before they start speaking about a challenge?"

Nikki sighed. She could see where RJ was coming from. But that didn't help. "If Brandon doesn't challenge then someone else will."

With a jerk of his shoulder, RJ sat forward. "Fine, but it's all bullshit."

She laid a hand on his arm. "It's nothing against you or your family."

RJ snorted. "Yes, actually it is. Dylan is meant to be the Alpha. But dividing the Pack was never meant to happen. Even if Dylan wins the challenge, he will constantly be reminded he's not from here. How is that fair?"

"He had to know coming here something like this might happen."

"No," he interrupted. "We were told we were wanted here. That it had already been decided. Dylan doesn't deserve this."

"What about his inner circle? Is he only using the wolves he brought with him?"

RJ shook his head. "I don't know. I do know that Cameron and Dylan have discussed it, but that is something that we'd have to ask him. Why?"

"Just some rumours that Dylan is using this to bring his Pack up and leave the original Pack in the dust."

"Dylan wouldn't do that!"

Nikki pushed her drink away and sank back against the back of the booth. "This isn't going to work. If we can't agree, then we will never get the Pack to."

When he put his arm around her shoulders, Nikki cuddled into him. The kiss to the top of her head gave her hope.

"I think the majority of the Pack, both new and old members, are okay with it," he told her. "Just a handful of the people, really, have any concerns. Besides, we're more involved than the others. It's our brothers who will be hurt."

She gave into temptation and ran her hand over his chest. "So what do we do?"

"I don't know. Dylan is worried about it and it sounds like Brandon is too. Maybe they should just get together and have it out before the ceremony."

Nikki thought about it. "That is a good idea, unless they kill each other before the ceremony."

RJ's thumb on her bottom lip surprised her. "You're doing it again."

She swiped at his thumb before sucking the digit into her mouth. She watched his nostrils flare.

"Fuck, baby," he panted at her.

She grinned and let go.

"Can you get Brandon to our house tonight?" he asked, trying to get back to the point.

She hesitated before nodding. "Yeah, if I don't tell him where we're going, I think I might manage it. I'd have to bring Justin too. This is a family issue."

"Okay, that will work. Ben will be there, so three of you and three of us. It's fair and we can all sit down and hash this out. There is only one more day. We need to do it now."

She glanced at her watch. It was half after ten. "Midnight?"

"Yeah, that will work," he agreed. He dropped his hand back under the table. "We should probably get going."

"Yeah," she breathed as he nuzzled her neck while slipping his hand under her skirt.

She spread for him until he was teasing over the flimsy material she wore for panties. She was already wet for him. "RJ, please."

"Let's go!" He grabbed her hand and pulled her from the booth.

She laughed and stumbled as he continued to drag her through the bar. They hit the door and ran out into the night.

"Where are you parked?" he asked, lifting her off her feet.

She held onto his shoulders and wrapped her legs around his waist. "Who cares?"

He chuckled as he walked farther from the bar. "I see it."

She was busy kissing and biting at his neck so she didn't really care if he found the car or not. Just the taste of him was breathtaking. His salty skin called to her. Reminded her of how much she had enjoyed him earlier.

"Baby, if you keep that up we aren't going to make it to the Jeep."

"Uh-huh," she murmured. Really, all that they needed to do was get to a flat surface. She wanted him inside her this time. She squeezed his waist and he groaned.

Happily, she went back to sucking at his neck.

She grunted when her back hit the side of her Jeep.

"You drive me crazy," he told her and slammed his mouth down on hers.

She slid lower, rubbing against his hard body. "Want you...please...need you," she managed when they broke away to breathe air in.

"Christ." He glanced around the empty parking lot before opening the passenger door and pushing her inside.

She giggled as she fell back into the seat.

"Gonna be quick," he warned, leaning over her and pushing her shirt up.

"Don't care," she promised, already starting to unsnap his jeans.

They managed to move clothes out of the way enough so he was pressed up against her.

"Look at me," he demanded, just inches from taking her, his cock hard and pulsing at the lips of her pussy.

She lifted her head. His eyes held the power of his passion and she shivered. "RJ, now!"

He slammed inside, going deep with the first thrust. Her breath caught and she clawed at his back. Perfect, what she needed.

"Oh fuck, you feel good," he told her as he started to pound into her.

She tightened around him and lifted her hips to meet each wild, passionate plunge. This was what she craved, what she longed for on those cold lonely nights. Someone to take her. Someone to swamp out all of her feelings and just demand a response.

"Yes! Yes!" she cried out as he rode her hard. She ran her hands over every inch she could touch, his head, his shoulders, chest, and stomach. The ink on him rose and shimmered as they moved in sequence.

"Mine, all mine." He spoke each time he buried himself back inside.

She heard him talking but couldn't concentrate on the words. The feel of him inside her, the sight of the pleasure on his face, and the fierceness in his eyes was mesmerising. The pressure built until she couldn't stand it.

"RJ, please!"

He grabbed her face and their eyes locked. "Mine," he growled.

His eyes were almost wolflike and his teeth became elongated. She knew the wolf was close to the surface. Her own animal was clawing to get out. To be claimed.

"Yes," she told him. There was no doubt she belonged to him one hundred per cent.

He snarled, throwing his head back, slammed inside.

"Yes!" she cried again as she exploded. Her orgasm tore through her body. She clutched at him, pulled, tried to anchor herself.

He followed her over the edge, spilling his seed inside her, marking her with his scent.

Long minutes went by as they both tried to get their control back.

He planted both hands on either side of her head. He waited until their gazes locked. "You know what this means?" he asked quietly.

"Yeah…" She cleared her throat. "Yes."

"I will mate you, Nikki Stratton. And soon."

She had no doubt and that scared the crap out of her.

Chapter Seven

Freshly showered, nervous, and almost desperate, Nikki drove down the empty roads with Brandon beside her and Justin in the back seat.

She had expected more questions but the men must have seen something in her face that convinced them that when she said they needed to come with her, they did.

She needed to tell them about her and RJ. She should prepare them. Her fear was that her emotions were too all over the place to hide once she was in the same room with the man.

But every time she opened her mouth, she couldn't get the words out.

"Nik," Brandon called softly. "What is going on?"

She had to give him credit that he had remained quiet for so long. In only a few more minutes, they would pull up to the house RJ and his brothers shared.

"I need you to trust me, Brandon. To know that I love you more than anything."

He covered her hand that was on the wheel. She released her grip and held onto him. "You're scaring me," he said, kissing her hand.

"Brandon, please trust me." She made the turn to the Cross house and felt him tense next to her.

"What are you doing? Nikki, why are we here?"

She shook her head and continued to drive.

"Stop the car," he ordered.

It took all her willpower to remove her hand from his hold and put it back on the wheel to continue towards the house.

"Nicole Stratton, pull this car over!"

She whimpered at the tone, her wolf wanting her to obey the dominant with her.

"Please, Brandon." She pressed her foot down on the gas pedal, moving them quicker before she lost her nerve. The house came into sight, with RJ standing on the porch.

She pulled up in front of him and took a deep breath. "Just come inside. Talk to Dylan, work this out."

Brandon growled long and low.

"Oh shit!" Justin barked a laugh from the back seat. "This is actually a good idea."

Brandon snarled at him and wrapped his hand around Nikki's upper arm. "What were you thinking?"

She shook, his fury hard for her to handle, but she had to try.

"Get us out of here," he demanded, shaking her a little. He was still in control, making sure he didn't hurt her, but she still wanted to roll over for him.

"Too late," Justin piped up from the back seat. "Look."

They glanced towards the porch where two other men had joined RJ.

"Just talk to him," she begged her brother.

"Come on, man." Justin gripped Brandon's shoulder. "It's a good idea."

Brandon moved quickly, throwing his door open then slamming it closed. Nikki and Justin scrambled to catch up. They met at the front of her Jeep.

Nikki looked over the two men she hadn't seen before, but her eyes were drawn to her lover. His gaze flickered to her but settled on Brandon, his body full of tension. No one moved for several moments.

RJ watched as the three Stratton siblings stood together, Nikki placed between the two brothers just like he and Dylan had put Ben.

No one moved or spoke. He'd convinced Ben to help set Dylan up to meet with Brandon but now, with the tension flowing through all the shifters, he had to wonder if it had been a good idea.

Nikki's distress was evident in her face and it was all he could do to not go down and comfort her.

It was Ben who broke the silence.

"Please, won't you all come inside so we can talk?"

Brandon glanced to his siblings before he nodded and started to the house. RJ never took his eyes off Brandon, though. Brandon, for his part, looked loose and relaxed, but RJ could tell he was just as wary.

Ben turned and led the way inside. Brandon, Nikki, and Justin followed with RJ following, and finally Dylan.

The biggest room was the den and that was where they headed.

"Please sit and be comfortable," Ben invited.

Brandon took one of the recliners, Nikki sat on the couch, while Justin shifted nervously from foot to foot.

"I just put some coffee on, let me bring it in," Ben stated once everyone was in the room.

"Let me help you," Justin offered.

Dylan took the recliner across from Brandon. RJ squeezed his shoulder as he passed and sat on the fireplace hearth across the room. He hoped by taking himself out of the situation Dylan and Brandon could work something out.

"Thank you for coming," Dylan started until Brandon snorted.

"Like I had much of a choice?"

Nikki pressed her hands together in her lap, looking guilty.

Dylan sighed and leant forward. "It seems to me my brother and your sister had a little more sense than us. We should have met earlier."

Some of the fury seemed to leave Brandon as he took deep breaths. Brandon looked over at his sister, and RJ watched as they locked gazes. Brandon's eyes narrowed before he looked over to him. It was clear when Brandon realised something more was going on.

"You son of a bitch!" Brandon yelled and launched himself at RJ.

RJ took a hard knock back as Brandon's fist hit his chin. His head snapped back and he tasted blood in his mouth. He vaguely heard Nikki scream and Dylan holler as he shook his head. He managed to block the next punch to his head but missed the left to his stomach.

Dylan pulled Brandon off him and pushed him across the room to face off with him. From the corner of his eye, he could see Ben and Justin rush into the room.

"Brandon, stop!" Nikki tried to grab her brother but he pushed her back.

RJ growled but Dylan blocked his path. "No, we finish this now. If you have a problem with my family you come through me," Dylan told Brandon.

"Is this going to be how you run the Pack?" Brandon spat at him. "You have a problem and you send in one of your brothers to seduce an innocent?" Brandon accused.

"No!" Nikki gasped.

Dylan obviously was caught off guard because he took a step back and faced him. "RJ?"

RJ shook his head. "It's not like that. Come on, Dy, you know me." Dylan stared at him as he searched RJ's face for something. Finally, he nodded.

Dylan turned back to Brandon. "I do know my brother. And whatever you think, you have it wrong. But this isn't about them, it's about us. Do you want to challenge me? You want to do this now?"

Brandon still fumed. "Fuck you. This is about all of us. If I didn't want to challenge you before, you crossed a line tonight. She" — he pointed at his sister — "has nothing to do with this."

"Brandon—" Nikki started.

"No, I don't want to be the damn Alpha. I never did. But I won't let this Pack belong to someone with such little consideration and respect. This is just too much. Do you know what is going to happen in three months when we go public? No, none of us do. We have to trust our leader."

Brandon grabbed Nikki's arm and pulled her towards the door.

"Wait!" Nikki dug her heels in. "Just listen to me."

"We'll talk about this in the car or at home. We're leaving now." He tugged her again.

"We'll talk about this now," Nikki argued and yanked her arm from his hold. "RJ didn't seduce me or whatever you think."

"Nik, this isn't the time or place."

She shook her head and sidestepped his reach to stand by RJ. She didn't look at him as she addressed the room.

"RJ didn't do anything wrong. Dylan and Ben didn't even know we were coming up with this. Can we please just sit down and try this again?"

"Brandon..." Justin moved from the doorway to his brother. "We need to hear Nikki out.

Brandon looked torn but eventually he nodded. Ben gripped Dylan's shoulder and led him back to the chair.

Once Brandon and Dylan were settled back in chairs and Ben and Justin on the couch, Nikki bit at her lip. RJ wanted to reassure her, pull her into his arms, do something to help. But he stood silent while she worked out what she wanted to say.

He was so proud that the woman he would mate had stood up for what she believed in.

"First, let me clear up one thing. I went to RJ," Nikki told them. "I'm sorry, Brandon, but I couldn't let the Pack pressure you into doing something you didn't want. I understand you have to look out for the Pack. But you're my brother and I have to look out for you."

Brandon opened his mouth but promptly snapped it shut. Instead of speaking, he just nodded.

"I knew you didn't actually want to be Alpha. I also know that Dylan doesn't want to meet you in a challenge. A challenge would leave one of us"—she gestured between her and RJ—"without one of the people we love the most."

RJ held out his hand. He'd let her talk, but he needed her to know that he was behind her.

She clasped his hand in hers. "Yes, I didn't expect the complication of my feelings getting involved when I went to talk to him. But they did." She smiled up at him. "We have to work this out. It's about more than just the Pack. It's about our families coming together."

"Our families, Nik?" Brandon shook his head. "You've been here two days. You can't just come in and fix things."

"Why not? No one else was doing anything. You talk about what happens when we go public. You're expecting the worst. You always do," she accused.

"I've kept you safe, haven't I?" Brandon snapped back.

"Yes." Her voice softened as she let go of RJ's hand and knelt in front of him. "You have. But you also taught me to stand up for what I believe in."

Brandon ran a hand over his face roughly. "Even if I don't challenge, I know someone will," he said tiredly.

"Can I ask a question?" Ben asked from the couch where he and Justin had settled. "Who approached you to challenge?"

"I can't...I can't tell you. It wouldn't be fair to him."

"But it's fair to let him pressure you to challenge an appointed Alpha?" Nikki questioned.

"Let's start this way," Dylan offered from across the room. Everyone looked over at him and he smiled. "Let's look at the issues. Issue one is I support the shifters going public."

Brandon shrugged. "I see both sides of the argument. But I guess I have been lax in supporting it, so that is what's brought up the most. And I don't honestly think that is what this is about. I think they're using it as an excuse. They are more worried about losing the ear of the Alpha. Especially when you decide on your own inner circle. That will leave a lot of us out in the cold."

"Okay." Dylan leant forward. "Cameron had agreed to go public, and when I accepted the Alpha position I kept the agreement. I have also discussed my inner circle with Cameron and he has agreed. You can't tell me that Cameron would have been challenged."

"No, I don't think so," Brandon conceded.

"So what else is the problem? Me being a stranger? Cameron spoke to several of you, from what I understand, about bringing in an outsider."

"He did," Justin spoke up. "To all of his inner circle plus several of the younger wolves who were dominant."

"Did he contact the elders of the community?" Dylan asked next.

"Not until he'd decided on you," Brandon answered.

"Now, I'm not trying to get out of you who approached you, but I would bet it was one of the elders. Maybe an elder who is worried if you don't challenge me his own son will," Dylan guessed.

Nikki gasped. RJ raised an eyebrow and she shook her head. "You can't protect him forever, Brandon. I know he was your best friend, but he's not the same kid you grew up with."

"I know." Brandon sat back. "I know."

The room fell silent. "Have you tried talking to him?" Nikki finally asked.

"Yeah, couple of weeks ago. He says Dylan will take us in the wrong direction. But the thing is…he never said anything against going public." He looked over at Dylan. "I wasn't born to lead, I know that, but I don't want to see my Pack split in half either."

"I don't want to see that, either. It's not only me, but my family and my friends. I want this Pack to be strong and flourish," Dylan told him with conviction. RJ was proud of his brother.

"Then let's figure out what to do," RJ suggested and received nods of agreement.

Chapter Eight

The plan was simple. So simple it might just actually work.

Get everyone involved who would support them, and spread the word that the Pack needed to stick together and support Cameron's decision.

Cameron and Dylan went to the diner for breakfast before making the rounds around town together, while Ben and Nikki wrote articles for the paper to publish the next morning, RJ would speak to the new Pack members asking them to mingle with the older members, and Justin talked with the kids at the school and in his shifter classes.

Hoping the support of the Pack and bringing everyone together before the ceremony would calm the waters, they all worked hard to do their best.

Once Nikki had turned in her special edition article, about her hope for the future under Dylan and her support of the Cross family, she walked out of the office and headed downtown.

She waved at Sabrina and Max, who were posting flyers of the pre-ceremony barbeque on shop windows. Ben had come up with the idea of getting the Pack together before instead of just after the ceremony, and Nikki thought that was brilliant. The youngest Cross brother was smart as a whip…and, if she wasn't mistaken, taken with her own sibling, the middle child. Justin had been sending sly looks Ben's way also. It would be fun to see where that went.

She'd learnt from her time away that you couldn't judge people by how they looked or any preferences they had. If her brother was interested in Ben, she was a bit surprised but already liked Ben a lot. One thing Cameron had always preached was acceptance. She had a good feeling Dylan would continue with that lesson.

She crossed the street a few stores before RJ's tattoo shop. He stepped out, holding the door open as another man walked out. The stranger was shorter than RJ but had the same muscular build. His hair was buzzed and the Marine Corps tattoo down his left arm that matched RJ's had her figuring this was one of RJ's military buddies.

RJ glanced up when she got to the sidewalk and the smile he sent her was so bright she felt her breath catch. God, he was handsome.

He held out a hand and drew her in up against his body before taking her lips in a sweet, deep kiss. She moaned, pressing closer, feeling him wrap both arms around her waist.

A throat-clearing broke the sexual haze and she pulled back from RJ but didn't look at the stranger yet.

"I needed that," she whispered against her lover's lips.

"Me too," he agreed and turned her towards the stranger, who was grinning ear to ear.

"This is one of my best buds, Mike Jackson," he informed her. "Mike, this is Nikki Stratton."

Mike held out his hand. "RJ's barely talked about anything else on the phone. It's funny how your name keeps coming up in every sentence."

Nikki laughed. "Well, honestly, I'm not gonna complain about that."

RJ blushed a little and shuffled his feet. "Yeah, yeah, yeah."

Mike and Nikki shared a laugh at his expense.

"Ben and I finished our articles. They'll be in the paper tomorrow. I just hope we're doing enough," she shared.

"I think it's a good plan. Uniting both Packs. Even if there is a challenge, maybe the aftermath won't be so bad," Mike offered.

"I guess we'll see soon enough." She shrugged.

"We're heading over to the café for lunch, join us?" RJ asked.

Nikki glanced at her watch. She needed to meet Justin in an hour. "Sure, I have time."

They started down the street. RJ still had his arm around her waist and she enjoyed the casual touch even though she had never been one for public displays of affection. Maybe she just had never been with the right guy.

"So, Mike, where is your Pack?" she questioned RJ's friend.

"Northern California. I haven't been back in a couple years. The last mission...made me miss it, though," Mike admitted.

RJ stiffened against her.

"Mission?"

He shook his head. "That's something we'll have to talk about in private."

"Oh." Nikki wrapped her arm around his waist. It hit her that she really didn't know RJ well. Oh, she knew he was loyal to his family, was smart, good looking and hot as hell, but the real part of him, what was deep down? There just hadn't been time.

He kissed the top of her head. "There's time," he whispered.

She hoped there was. But with all of the drama that had happened since she'd come to town, it felt like she'd been there months already instead of just a few days. And she had plans, future assignments that she had moved aside to come home.

She pushed those worries away for now. She had more than enough on her plate. Besides, when this was all over, she wasn't even sure where she and RJ would stand. She shook the thoughts from her head and concentrated on the story Mike was telling about the mating ceremony he had come from. She listened as she learnt about the town of shifters and the new wolf and bobcat couple.

"A wolf and a bobcat," she mused. "I bet that was interesting."

RJ chuckled. "Gray is a good guy. Helped us out with a situation and still managed to get the girl."

Nikki grinned up at him. She got his point. "Well, talking about getting the girl…" She reached up to grab the back of his neck when she was interrupted by a growl.

"Well, looky here, boys. Nikki Stratton is back and playing in the gutter."

She twirled around and faced the speaker.

"Samson," she greeted politely. She nodded at his two friends.

He sneered back. "Didn't your brother teach you any better than to hang out with trash?"

She gripped the back of RJ's shirt when he moved forward.

"You got a problem, man?" RJ snarled.

She noticed Mike moved a little to the side and straightened his shoulders, bracing his feet. RJ vibrated in fury next to her. Crap, she didn't want a brawl in front of the café the day before the party to unite the Pack.

"Yeah, I got a problem. You. You and your brothers." Samson's lip curled.

Nikki stepped into Samson and RJ. "That's enough. Why don't you just keep going, Samson?"

He snorted. "I see where your loyalties are. Brandon knows about this?"

"Why? You gonna tattle on me?" she challenged. She wasn't afraid of him. Brandon and Samson had been best buds until they'd reached high school. After that time, Samson had changed, turned into a bully, and Brandon had spent less and less time with him. "Don't forget, Samson, I grew up with you. I know all your secrets, too."

Samson shook his head. "Bran was always too easy on you, should have turned you over his knee, maybe I'll do that myself."

RJ surged forward. "Touch her. I dare you."

Samson's eyes narrowed. "You think I'm scared of you? I'll touch who I want."

To prove his point, he grabbed her left wrist. She managed to hold off RJ with her right but barely. It was Mike who moved the quickest. He had Samson's free arm back and angled. Samson hissed.

"Why don't you just let her go?" Mike suggested calmly.

Samson released her and turned on Mike. "You'll regret that."

Mike shook his head. "Get out of here, man. You're making a scene. Just go and get control of yourself. Sober up some. I can smell the alcohol on you."

Samson brushed past them and headed off, cursing them and making threats. Nikki looked up into the wide café windows and saw several tables staring at them.

"Damn it," she muttered and dropped her head.

"Asshole," RJ grunted, still watching Samson as he crossed to an old Chevy truck.

"Hey." She yanked RJ forward by his belt loops. "Let it go."

He frowned and twisted his neck. "He fucking put his hands on you."

She held up her wrist. "And I'm fine. But now we have to go eat and make sure we show a united front."

He glanced up at the café. "Shit."

She moved up to her tiptoes. "We need to choose our battles. If that's how he acts tomorrow, we may have some problems, but I didn't realise how far gone he was. If he challenges Dylan, he won't win."

RJ threw his arm around her shoulder and herded her to the café door with Mike following behind. "Can't believe your brother was best friends with that dick."

She sighed. "He actually used to be pretty nice. They stopped hanging out when they were still in school here. My second year in college they had a final falling out. Bran never told me what about, though."

"Well, let's try to enjoy our lunch," RJ suggested, opening the door.

There was still a fire in his eyes but she let it go. It was going to be a long day.

Chapter Nine

RJ blew out a heavy breath as he locked the shop door for the night. Other than the encounter with Samson Lewis in front of the café, the day had gone pretty well. He'd spoken with every member of his old Pack who had come to town with them — almost fifty members. Several of the kids and teenagers had already made friends and found their place. The adults had all brought in new businesses or had found work. He hadn't realised how much his Pack had already started to mingle into the established one.

He felt better knowing that Dylan did have some support if in trouble. Just a few of the older families didn't want an outsider leading them.

But in the upcoming months they would need a strong Alpha in charge. The Alpha council had already set the date when the world would know for sure that shifters were among them.

"Hey, handsome," he heard behind him. "Can a girl get a lift?"

He spun around and grinned. Nikki leaned against a street lamp, her smile welcoming. He strode to her and laid his mouth over hers. She opened for him, wrapping her arms around his shoulders, and pressed close.

It had only been six hours since he'd kissed her goodbye but his blood boiled and need clawed at him.

He yanked her forward, his lips still devouring her, until his back hit the door he'd just locked.

She hummed and nipped his bottom lip. "We have a little time before meeting the others."

He liked the way she thought. He quickly unlocked the door and pushed her inside. She laughed and, walking backwards, started to lift her shirt over her head.

"First one naked gets to be on top," she teased.

He didn't care who was on top as long as he got her bared before him. So he pounced and helped her undress. They fumbled a little when her jeans caught on the shoes she still hadn't removed. They laughed and tugged them off together until she was finally undressed.

"Now you," she murmured and reached for his belt buckle.

"In a minute," he told her and gently pushed her back onto the couch. He fell on top of her and started to kiss her once again.

He mapped her body with his hands, learning where she was sensitive and how much pressure she liked. She arched into him, dragging her nails down his back.

"RJ…please."

He just chuckled and continued his assault, feeding on her ripe breasts, full and begging for attention. She liked the way he flicked her nipples with his tongue if the volume of her moans was any indication.

He trailed his mouth down her stomach as he slipped his fingers inside. Her pussy, already wet and swollen, called to him. He buried his face in her sex and breathed deep. Her scent beckoned to every part of him. Man and wolf both wanted to claim her. To mark her where no other person would ever lay a hand on her again.

He licked at her, slowly at first, but as she spread wider for him, he just feasted, nibbling until her shouts of ecstasy bounced off the walls. When she climaxed against his mouth, he sucked down her sweet essence.

But it wasn't enough. He pulled away from her and flipped her over. She landed with her knees on the floor next to the couch and her stomach pushed into the leather. He held her down with a hand on the back of her neck while he released his raging hard-on with the other.

His wolf howled at the show of dominance and submission.

And she arched her back, moaning and begging for him to take her.

So much, so much emotion, so much passion. There was no doubt that the woman under him was meant to be his future. He slid inside her little by little, drawing out both her pleasure and his.

Her body welcomed him.

He withdrew slowly then slammed back inside.

"Yes...yes," she urged him on, still drunk on passion.

He growled and let himself go, pounding into her, lifting her hips and claiming her body like he wanted to do to her soul. Nikki met him thrust for thrust. The slaps of flesh coming together and their cries of joy filled the room. His orgasm came too quickly. She yelled, clamping her inner muscles around his cock, and pushed him hard over the edge.

He collapsed over her back, panting in her ear until she started to giggle. He rose slightly and brushed her sweaty hair out of her face. She grinned up at him.

"Just keeps getting better and better," she said, her voice husky and pleased.

He laughed, pulled out of her gently and fell back down, leaning against the couch.

* * * *

RJ kept Nikki's hand in his as they walked up the steps to his house. He could hear voices in the living room as he led the way through to the den and had to smother a grin when he walked in and saw Justin leaning close to Ben on the couch. They were alone in the room and RJ knew what would happen if they thought they still were.

"Hey, guys," he greeted them and watched in amusement when they jumped apart. He heard Nikki smother a laugh and had to hold in his own.

Ben blushed and dipped his head. Justin, a little more comfortable, just sighed and leant back. "Great timing," he muttered in complaint.

Nikki brushed past him and patted his head. "Better luck next time," she teased.

Justin wrinkled his nose. "At least one of us got something."

This time both Nikki and Ben blushed.

"Hey, I thought I heard voices," Dylan said, joining them.

Everyone froze in place. Dylan walked halfway through the room before stopping. "What? What did I miss?"

Nikki cleared her throat, Ben was squirming in his seat, and Justin found his hands interesting.

"Okay, what?" Dylan asked again.

"Brandon's not here yet. I'll put the coffee on." Ben jumped up and ran out of the room.

Dylan raised an eyebrow and glanced at him. RJ just shrugged. He wasn't going to give Ben away. Ben would tell them when he was ready.

"Hmm," Dylan hummed. "Okay, you want to tell me about your run-in with Samson Lewis in front of the café instead?"

Damn. RJ thought about throwing Ben under the bus but just couldn't do it. He strolled over to his spot on the fireplace hearth where Nikki had already taken a seat.

"He started it."

Justin tried to hold back and a chuckle and failed. Nikki slapped a hand on her forehead while Dylan scowled at him.

"I know you did not just say 'he started it' like a four-year-old," Ben commented, coming back in the room.

RJ thought about once again about telling on his younger brother but that really would make him look like a four-year-old. "Well, he did," he complained.

Nikki elbowed him. "We were walking to the café when Samson came out and made some...rude comments."

Dylan leant forward and RJ sighed.

"Normally, you wouldn't lose your cool over some words. You have better control than that," Dylan stated, plainly knowing there was more.

RJ wanted to squirm in his seat like Ben had earlier. "Yeah, well..."

"What did he say, RJ?" Dylan asked directly.

"He was talking about me," Nikki told them quietly. RJ noticed she was also rubbing the wrist Samson had grabbed.

"And?" Dylan pressed.

"He put his hands on her!" RJ exploded and stood. "And had we not been dealing with this damn challenge, I would have taken him out."

Dylan raised his hand. "And you would have been right but there are ways to handle things. What would have happened if Mike hadn't been there?" Dylan asked.

"I would have fucked up what we are trying to accomplish with the Pack," RJ admitted.

"Which was his point," Dylan assured him.

RJ plopped back down and accepted Nikki's hand when she held it out to him. He kissed her palm, which calmed him a bit.

"One thing for sure. He is in no condition to challenge you. He'd been drinking, heavily, and is in no way as strong as you," RJ told him.

Dylan nodded. "That's why they needed Brandon." Dylan glanced at his watch. "Who should be here by now?"

"I'll call him," Justin said, pulling out his cell phone.

"So, if they've lost Brandon, does that mean they won't challenge?" Ben asked from across the room.

Dylan shrugged. "I don't know. Cameron tried to get hold of the elders but no one would answer. They've shut him out."

Nikki groaned. "I don't understand why they are trying to stir everyone up. There's only, like, six of them left. They don't even hold any positions in the Pack anymore."

"But they're still listened to and they advise Cameron. I think they're worried about losing that small amount of power," Dylan noted.

"Straight to voicemail," Justin informed them, slipping his phone back into his pocket. "He was heading into the station. You know how he is."

Nikki nodded. "Probably lost track of time."

"So, is everything set for tomorrow?" Dylan changed the subject.

"The food will be there in time. Toby, from the café, volunteered to man the grills with help from some of the others. Steve, over at the church, is taking over the tables and chairs they use for their parties. I'll meet with him to get everything set up," Ben told them.

"I'll catch up with Ben along with some of the older teenagers. They'll help us get everything done in time," Justin added.

They heard a car door and waited as Brandon walked in and joined them in the living room, still in uniform. Brandon nodded to Dylan.

"Sorry I'm late, but something came up."

Everyone remained silent at his sombre tone.

"RJ, man… I'm sorry. Someone broke into your shop and tore it up pretty bad."

RJ jumped to his feet before the others could even react.

"RJ, wait!" Nikki grabbed hold of his arm. He tried to shake her off but she held firm.

Brandon blocked his way. "I know you want to see, but I need to ask you a few questions first."

RJ shook his head. "No, we all know who did this." He looked back at Dylan.

"I'll call Mike and have him meet us there," Dylan said, taking charge. "You and Nikki go ahead with

Justin and Ben and head over. I'll ride with Brandon and explain on the way."

"Now, wait just a damn minute!" Brandon ordered loudly to the whole room. "I'm the sheriff and I have some damn questions!"

RJ could feel his wolf close to the surface. He wanted to find that coward Samson and smash his face in. He rolled to the balls of his feet in preparation of jumping around the sheriff. He didn't give a damn what the man said. He wanted to go, now.

"Brandon," Dylan spoke calmly. "Let RJ go. I'll explain everything."

Brandon sighed but waved a hand. "It's a crime scene so don't go in without me," he reminded.

RJ nodded and, as gently as he could, grabbed Nikki's hand to pull her with him. He didn't care if Ben and Justin caught up or not, but he wasn't letting Nikki out of his sight.

Justin hit the unlock on his SUV. "I'll drive."

RJ let Nikki manoeuvre him into the back seat while Ben jumped into the passenger seat. The doors had barely closed before Justin took off. RJ was glad the other man was moving. Energy pumped through his body and only the fact that Nikki was rubbing his arms and legs kept him calm at all.

"I'm sorry," she whispered, kissing the base of his neck.

He closed his eyes and took deep breaths. "My last mission was the rescue of the feline Prince Zachary," he started.

He heard the gasp from the front seat but Nikki just took his hand and gave it a squeeze.

"His cousin knew that Zach had mated with another cat—a bobcat who ran the unit I was in—and our departure was an opportunity," he explained. "Before we left for the mission, Casey asked a favour of me. I'd done all of the unit's tats but he wanted a special one for him and Zach. He wanted matching mate tats so that, when he wasn't with his mate, he could always see him."

He opened his eyes and pulled her close. "I drew their mate in cat form on each other's chest. Zach's lion over Casey's heart and Casey's bobcat over Zach's. They were the most important pieces I ever did."

"That's wonderful," she told him, running her hand over his throat to grab his chin. "I love it."

He nodded, glad she understood. "That's what I want to offer. That tattoo kept Casey sane while we were searching for Zach. He had his love with him in some way."

"He won't get away with it," she promised then kissed him.

RJ let her control the kiss and just enjoyed having her close. When she broke off to snuggle into his chest, he held her close.

Justin pulled up in front of RJ's shop and it was both too soon and not soon enough. There were several people outside in the street and on the sidewalk beside the tape the sheriff department had put up. The windows were all busted up and the door smashed.

"Hey," Nikki said softly, blocking his view. "We will rebuild. We will fix it, I promise."

RJ knew they could, but this hit deep. It was the only thing he'd wanted when the unit had decided to retire.

"I'll be here with you," she promised and kissed him one more time.

And that was the best thing he'd ever heard. He'd already gained so much more than he had thought. He had a new home, his brothers back, loyal friends and Nikki. He wouldn't have even imagined finding her. He hadn't been looking. But his future mate sat in the back of an old SUV, worrying and upset, because he was.

"I love you Nikki Stratton," he declared quietly, staring in her eyes.

She blinked. Opened and closed her mouth several times. "Holy hell!" she whispered. "I love you too." She seemed shocked by her own admission and it was enough to convince him.

"We'll do this together."

She nodded and slid out of the vehicle behind him.

Chapter Ten

Nikki watched as Mike broke away from the other spectators on the sidewalk and embraced RJ.

She was beyond pissed off that this had happened to the man she loved.

And wasn't that a kick in the ass. Somehow she had fallen for RJ Cross. She hadn't even seen it coming. RJ turned and held out a hand, and she quickly clasped it and let him pull her close.

"I don't want you going anywhere without me or Mike with you," he said once she was close.

"Excuse me?" She looked up at him. Where the hell had that come from?

"Just listen." He turned and cupped her face. "This is a direct attack on me. Add in that your brother has switched sides, and Samson's words earlier... I don't want you alone."

"RJ, this is my hometown. Everyone knows me and I have been on my own a long time. I have been in more hostile places than this. I can take care of myself."

"Just wait until after the ceremony," he pleaded. "If something happened to you...I wouldn't be able to hold in my wolf. I need to make sure you are protected."

She opened her mouth again to protest when Justin interrupted, "I agree. You're a target now. All of us are. You shouldn't be alone either, Ben," Justin added.

Ben frowned. "Now wait!"

"Enough!" Mike growled. "It goes for everyone in both families. No one from either family will be alone. Double up and figure it out."

"I couldn't have said it better," Dylan offered as he and Brandon joined them. "In fact, Brandon and I just spoke about the same thing in the car on the way over."

Nikki shook her head but she knew she was beaten. She might have been able to fight against RJ and Justin, but just the look on Brandon's face told her he was in full protective mode. "Fine."

Everyone else agreed and Brandon put a hand on RJ's shoulder. "I'll take you inside to look around but don't touch anything yet."

He nodded and glanced at her. "Come with me?"

She offered him the best smile she could manage. "Of course."

"I'll take Mike and get some wood to cover the windows and door," Dylan told them. "Ben, you and Justin hang out here and watch everyone who is out here. Samson might not be here, but I doubt he wouldn't have eyes and ears out to let him know what is going on."

Nikki kept a hold of RJ's hand as Brandon led them inside. On top of the windows and door glass being smashed, all of the furniture was upended. The leather couches and chairs were shredded. Ink was spilled over the counters, floors and walls. RJ's instruments had been broken and tossed around the shop.

"Son of a bitch," RJ grumbled. "Damn it!"

Nikki rubbed his arm with her free hand as he took in the mess.

"You have insurance?" Brandon asked from the door.

RJ nodded. "Yeah, of course."

"Okay, I'll give you a copy of the report as soon as I can."

RJ turned and Nikki saw the rage on his face.

"Listen, man," Brandon said holding his hands up. "This sucks. This is a violation and a challenge but we need to handle this legally. Also, I promise we will fix this. Everyone in this town will help get this place up and back open as soon as possible. But think before you react."

RJ spun around and stomped off, letting go of her hand. Nikki stayed where she was and let him pace.

"He'll pay for this," RJ snapped.

"He will. Let me handle this, RJ. It's what I do and I am damn good at my job. But what we *can't* do is let this distract us, let him separate us and what we are planning to do about mingling the Pack."

RJ growled and picked up one of the chairs before hefting it across the room.

"Feel better?" Brandon asked sarcastically.

"Bran!" Nikki complained.

But RJ started to laugh. "Actually, I do."

Nikki looked between the two of them as they both chuckled. She threw her hands up. "Men!"

RJ wrapped his arm around her shoulder. "I hate to admit it, but Brandon's right. This is just a distraction. We'll get it cleaned up."

Nikki resisted the urge to remind him she'd said it first. Instead, she just moved up to her toes and kissed his cheek. "Bet your ass, and we will replace that furniture right away."

"Furniture?" he asked with a raise of an eyebrow.

"So we can break it in properly."

"Nicole!" Brandon objected as RJ grinned.

She laughed and started for the door. "The sooner we get this place boarded up, the quicker we can start...practising."

She wasn't surprised when RJ beat her to the door while Brandon mumbled under his breath, following.

* * * *

RJ groaned at the loud beeping in his ear. He reached over and slapped the alarm off before burying his head back into the pillow.

"It can't be morning already," came the complaint from next to him.

RJ lifted his head and grinned at the sight before him. Nikki was wrapped under his bedspread with her head hidden under the pillow. He'd taken her back home with him the night before and they'd spent all night into the early morning hours practising how they would 'break in' his new shop furniture.

He chuckled while he scooted closer and edged the top of the blankets down, revealing her naked shoulder. He ran his tongue over her soft skin until she shivered.

"Ugh!" she said before laughing. "You can't want more already."

RJ smiled. He actually felt pretty sated but just waking up beside her had all kinds of ideas popping in his head. "Well, if you can't handle it..." he teased.

The pillow above her head slid off the bed as she burst up. "Can't handle? Me?"

He chuckled. "Well…"

She pushed herself up and crawled over him, causing him to roll onto his back. She straddled his hips and bent over him, her hair curtaining them. "Well what?"

"Oh, nothing," he said as innocently as he could manage.

"Hmm," she murmured as she brushed her lips over his. "Feeling better?"

He smirked and raised his hands over his head. "Feeling pretty damn good."

"Oh really?"

"Yes, as matter of fact…" He gasped when she grasped his cock under the covers.

"You're right, baby," she teased. "You do feel pretty damn good."

He sucked in a breath when she tightened her grip and she rubbed her body down his.

"As a matter of fact, you feel so good I think I'll have to taste."

He did his best not to buck when her moist mouth wrapped around his shaft. But damn, did she have a talented mouth and that thing she was doing with her tongue… *Oh damn!*

"Baby…" He buried his hand in her hair. "Damn."

She looked up at him from between his legs and deep-throated him again.

"Oh sweet Jesus!" he yelled, unable to keep quiet.

She continued to suck and lick until he finally lost control and plunged in and out of her mouth. She urged him on with a hand on his hip.

"So good… Yeah, suck me deep… Oh baby…"

Too soon he could feel the start of his climax. He tightened his hold on her hair and pulled gently. She popped off and grinned.

"Get up here," he ordered, already pulling on her before she started to move. "I don't want to come until I'm inside you."

She moaned, sitting astride his thighs. "Yes."

He held her around the waist while she positioned herself over him. She sank down slowly, drawing a moan from them both.

"God, you feel me up so good," she told him, arching her back once he was seated deep inside her.

He couldn't have agreed more. He held her tight and pushed his hips up. "Come on, baby, ride me."

She pressed her hand down on his shoulders and lifted up before sliding back down. She took her time, slowly rising and falling, teasing and taunting.

"Please, Nikki," he begged as she tortured him.

She laughed wickedly.

He slapped her ass playfully. She tightened around his cock and moaned. Oh, now this was interesting. He did it again and was treated to her gasp and her pace picking up.

"Yeah, baby, faster, harder," he encouraged and gave her another smack.

"RJ," she cried, tightening even more.

He braced his feet on the bed and thrust up each time she came down on his cock. They moved quickly, with him spanking her every few strokes, until it was just the sound of flesh against flesh filling the room.

RJ lifted up to sit and gripped her hips hard, pulling her down on his shaft deeper. "Come for me, Nikki, come on my cock."

She did. Crying out his name, she fell over the edge, pulling him over with her.

He dropped back down, keeping his arms around her as he struggled to catch his breath.

She nuzzled his chest and he knew he wanted to wake up like this every morning for the rest of his life.

Pounding on the door broke up the peaceful sated state he had fallen into.

"Come on, you two! Get your asses in the kitchen," Dylan ordered.

Nikki groaned.

"We're coming!" RJ called out to his brother.

"God, I hope not!" Dylan shouted back. "I'm surprised you haven't killed each other yet."

Nikki squeaked and started to squirm off him.

"He's just messing with us," RJ tried to assure her.

"No, I'm not! If you two go at it again, I'm going to make you sleep in separate rooms," Dylan argued.

"We'll be down in a minute!" RJ hollered, watching a blushing Nikki dart into the bathroom. His brother's laughter started to drift away and RJ rubbed his hand over his face. He was going to have to think of a way to get him back and soon.

Chapter Eleven

After a wonderful, if not embarrassing morning, Nikki found herself with Justin and Ben at the Pack clearing, getting ready for the barbeque before the ceremony. She was pleased with the number of volunteers and the progress they were making.

The tables had been covered with red and white cloths, the chairs set up, and six grills were off to the side ready to be fired up.

The teenagers of the Pack had finished setting up the table and chairs and started piling wood in the fire pits for later in the night. She grinned as Sabrina and Max began to load one of the tables with an assortment of desserts. It was all coming together. They just had to get through the day and hopefully by morning they would have a new Alpha and the Pack would be complete. Then she had to figure out what she was going to do.

When she'd made the trip home, she hadn't known anything about what she had now found herself in the middle of. Finding a mate hadn't even been on her radar. Now she couldn't imagine returning to the city without RJ. But she could tell that RJ was home here—with his brothers, with his Pack—and she couldn't ask him to leave. So where did that leave them?

"Penny for your thoughts," Ben said softly, coming up behind her.

She turned and smiled at the youngest Cross brother. "Do you think we'll be able to actually pull this off?"

Okay, that wasn't what she had actually been thinking, but it was close.

Ben looked around and nodded. "I think so. Even if Samson tries something, without Brandon there to back his play I don't think much can come from it. The Pack respects Brandon and that was our biggest concern. He would have support just because he has earned it. Samson doesn't have that going for him."

"Brandon never wanted to be Alpha," Nikki reminded him.

"No, he didn't. But if you hadn't come down, I don't think we would have been able to come together like we did. All Dylan and Brandon needed to do was get together and talk about the future of the Pack. To see that they both shared the same ideas on our future."

Nikki laughed. "Yeah, well, leave it to the men to be stubborn and almost fight instead."

Ben chuckled and Justin caught her eye as he moved from the group of teenagers to talk to Max. She glanced over at Ben.

"So you want to let me in on what's going on between you and Justin?" she teased.

Ben blushed and shifted on his feet. "Uh…well…"

Nikki turned to face him with a smirk. "Should I ask what your intentions are with my brother?"

Ben shook his head, his eyes going wide. "No! It's not like that! I mean…we haven't really decided…"

She threw an arm over his shoulder and turned them so they could see Justin trying to steal a cookie from one of the platters an older Pack member was placing on the table. She slapped at his hand, but he danced away, laughing.

"Just treat him right. I think the two of you are perfect for each other," she told Ben sincerely.

Ben sucked in a breath. "Really?"

Nikki hugged him closer. "Yeah."

"I've never felt like this before," Ben confessed. "He makes me laugh. Makes me feel like there is something besides work. He's just so friendly and free."

"Good. Make sure he treats you right also. I'd hate to have to kick my brother's ass."

"Speaking of kicking a brother's ass, may I ask why you are hanging on mine?" RJ's voice came behind them.

"Because he is so damn cute!" she told RJ as he pulled her away from his brother and into his arms.

"Not cuter than me, though, right?" RJ asked and winked.

"I…I think I'll go see if Justin needs some help," Ben said quickly and left them alone.

Nikki didn't even glance after the other man. Her entire focus was on the one in front of her. "I wouldn't really say you were cute," she taunted.

"No?" he breathed against her neck.

She wrapped her arms around his waist, pulling him closer. "No. Sexy, maybe. Hot, for sure."

"Mmm, sexy, I like that," he told her, licking a path from her ear down her neck.

"Oh yeah, sexy as sin." She shivered when he started to nibble.

"Haven't the two of you had enough of each other yet?" Dylan asked sarcastically as he joined them.

RJ sighed and loosened his hold. "Maybe if you would stop cockblocking me," he groused.

Dylan laughed. "My sympathies."

"Where's Brandon?" RJ asked, looking around. It had been agreed upon that Brandon and Dylan would partner up for the day so neither man would be alone.

Dylan nodded to the parking lot. "He's going over something with his deputies. He wants everyone on high alert. Hopefully the ceremony will go off without any problems, but I don't see Samson just giving up. That attack on your shop last night shows how pissed he is."

"Hey, where's Mike?" Nikki asked RJ. Mike was supposed to stay with RJ for the same reason.

"He had some calls to make. I left him in the truck."

A commotion from the parking lot had them stiffening up. Nikki laughed nervously when a dozen small school-aged children came running into the clearing.

"Damn," Dylan groaned rubbing the back of his neck. "We need to calm down or we'll have heart attacks before the ceremony even starts."

RJ kissed the side of her neck before pulling Dylan by the arm. "Come on, let's get a drink."

Nikki watched them go, smiling. They stopped to talk to several people, both new and old Pack members, before they made it to the drink table. She saw Justin and Ben sitting at a table sitting close together off to the side.

"I never thought I would see you smiling at someone like that here at home."

Nikki sighed and turned to face Brandon. "I didn't either," she admitted. "You know I was pissed when you ordered me home."

He nodded. "Yeah, you didn't hide that well."

"What would have happened if I hadn't come?"

Brandon shrugged his shoulders. "I hope I would have gotten my head out of my ass before I did something stupid like challenge Dylan, but I don't know. I got caught up in all the politics."

"You have it worked out now?" she asked, stepping closer to her brother. He was a good man so she did believe he would have figured it out. No matter what happened, she was proud of him.

"Dylan asked me to be his Beta. He wants Max and RJ as his enforcers and a couple others from both Packs in the inner circle. Everyone he named made sense and Cameron agreed with his choices. I do believe he will make a good Alpha."

"Well then, congratulations," she said with a hip bump against him.

He grinned. "Thanks, but it's not over yet. Stay close tonight."

Nikki sighed but he cut her off.

"I mean it. This will be the last chance before anything done against Dylan will be against the Alpha. It's all or nothing tonight."

"I know, Bran," she assured him. "I'll be careful."

He nodded. "Cameron just arrived. I have to go over a few things with him."

He left her quickly and she rolled her eyes. Brandon in full protective mode once again. She spotted RJ and made her way over to him to steal some more kisses.

* * * *

RJ could feel the excitement in the air. The Alpha ceremony would start soon and the Pack was in full celebration. Cameron, Dylan and Brandon stood in the middle of the clearing, preparing for the circle. Justin and Ben were working the crowd like pros and Nikki was in the middle of a group of women around her age. They laughed and squealed, and he couldn't hold back a smile as she shook her hips and danced away, laughing.

He caught her eye and the look in hers changed, moving from happy to heated with passion. He jerked his head to the edge of the crowd and she nodded.

He captured her in his arms as they came together on the outskirts of the clearing. Their lips met, breath mixed, and he devoured her. She broke away panting and rested her forehead on his chest.

"I've been watching you," she informed him, slipping her hands down his back.

"I know," he whispered back. "I've been watching you too."

They kissed again until she shivered in his arms. It was getting too hot, too fast.

"I want you," she admitted, mouthing his collarbone. "I always want you."

He moaned and looked around for any semi-private place. They were surrounded by Pack members. No one was paying attention to them now, but it wouldn't be long before they drew some unwanted attention. Especially if she kept teasing him with her tongue…

"We can't…" Damn it, there had to be somewhere close by.

"Ladies and gentlemen, Pack members," Cameron's voice rose above the crowd. "It's time."

"Oh God!" Nikki whimpered and pushed him away. "They better hurry and get this over with."

Her chest heaved, her eyes wild, and he could smell her arousal. He reached for her again but she shook her head. "If you touch me again, everyone is going to get a show," she promised.

He dropped his head and stifled a groan. He had better control than this. They would get through the ceremony then he would take her to the first private spot they found and pound into her.

"Please join me at the circle as we welcome our new Pack members and begin the Alpha ceremony," Cameron invited.

RJ led Nikki around and through the crowd until they stood next to the circle beside Brandon, Justin and Ben. Dylan knelt in the middle of the circle with his head bent.

"Woodrow Wilson once said, 'The ear of the leader must ring with the voices of the people'. I have tried to listen to each member of this Pack and always advise with all of your best interests in my heart. My time has passed and another's has begun."

RJ looked at his brother with pride almost bursting from his chest. Nikki slipped her hand into his and gave it a squeeze. The feelings of happiness threatened to overwhelm him.

"I know in my heart that my replacement will be able to lead the Pack in the right direction and protect you as the shifter world moves forward with plans on going public."

There was a stirring behind Cameron but RJ's view was blocked.

"The future of the Pack will rest on the shoulders of this man before me. I want each—"

"Excuse me, Alpha Cameron!" someone shouted from the crowd.

Pack members shuffled around while Samson led a small group forward to stand at the edge of the circle across from them.

Samson was backed by the elders and their families and a half-dozen men he'd never seen before.

There was a gasp in the crowd and he heard the murmur of words like 'feline', 'cats', and 'shifters'.

RJ searched for Mike and saw him moving forward. He looked down at Nikki's pale face.

"You and Ben go with Mike," he whispered to her, waving a hand at the man.

"RJ, no!" She gripped his hand tighter.

"Please, baby."

Mike arrived to pull Ben and Nikki back. Both fought but a look from Brandon had them grumbling back into the crowd.

"What is the meaning of this, Samson?" Cameron demanded and he faced the other man. Dylan stood and RJ, Brandon, Justin, Max and a few others fanned out behind him and Cameron.

"You have your pick for the future and we have ours," Samson told him, motioning to one of the big strangers next to him.

"You have no authority to choose the next leader. I am Alpha and the choice is mine," Cameron stated, bracing his feet apart and standing to his full height. While aged, the man was still a powerful force.

"You just said you listen to your Pack," Samson challenged. "Your Pack has a different vision than you."

Cameron took his time looking around his Pack. All of the Pack members that had already been at the ceremony had separated away from Samson, leaving a wide area between them. "I believe the majority of the Pack respect my wishes."

"But not all. This is a Pack decision, one that will affect us for many years," one of the elders spoke up from behind Samson.

"So instead of following my choice you bring forward a man, a feline shifter we know nothing about?" Cameron inquired with a nasty twist of his lips.

"Fred has led his small group of felines for several years," Samson argued. "He is just as qualified as Dylan Cross."

There was more rumbling in the crowd but Cameron held up a hand.

"What exactly do you suggest?" the Alpha asked.

"Simple. A challenge. Dylan and Fred. Winner takes Alpha position."

RJ went to step forward, having heard enough. There was no way he was going to let his brother fight some feline they knew nothing about. Dylan cut his eyes over to him and shook his head. He was going to ignore his brother when Brandon gripped his shoulder.

"Dylan needs to handle this," Brandon said quietly.

RJ shook his head. This was unbelievable. They had a problem with Dylan leading so they brought in a cat shifter no one even knew? Dylan had been in town for months getting to know his new Pack.

And it didn't matter what anyone said. RJ would not be convinced that the fight would be fair.

"I accept the challenge," Dylan stated, his voice strong and proud over the crowd.

"No!" Ben cried from the crowd.

RJ agreed with his brother. "Absolutely not. How can we even ensure it would be a fair challenge? There is no one here to judge the feline," he protested.

"It's a good thing I made it in time, then," another voice rose from the crowd.

RJ turned and saw the members of his military unit standing with Mike, Nikki, and Ben. The Prince of the felines stepped forward.

"I believe I am able to judge the challenge fairly. I also have the ability to take down one of them if they choose to use means not approved for the challenge."

Activity picked up when everyone recognised the power of the strongest cat in the world.

Cameron nodded and waved the Prince forward. RJ met the gaze of his friend and the Prince's mate, Casey Williams. He cut his eyes to Nikki in silent meaning. Casey looked surprised before he smiled. He nodded and placed his hand on her shoulder. RJ knew Casey would protect her.

"The terms," Prince Zachary called out.

RJ walked with Mike, Brandon and Justin to his brother's side.

There would be a challenge and he'd be damned if he was going to lose his brother. He would give the man every single piece of information he had learnt over the years of fighting next to the cat species.

Some of his best friends were felines, but this was a fight he wouldn't let his brother lose. He just hoped Dylan knew what he was doing.

Chapter Twelve

Nikki couldn't believe what was happening around her. The parents of young children had been ordered to take the kids away and anyone else who didn't want to witness the challenge was free to leave until it was over.

It didn't surprise Nikki that most of the Pack stayed. This would affect the entire Pack. She wasn't sure what exactly Samson's plan entailed, but she knew it wouldn't be good. Bringing in an unknown feline shifter to lead a Pack of wolves? It was beyond crazy.

"If you will step over here with me," the man who had introduced himself as Casey asked.

She looked back over at RJ but his attention was wholly on his brother.

"Please, let RJ help his brother now."

She followed with a sigh to where she would still be able to see but there was no one behind them. Mike had already explained their appearance. He'd been on the phone with the unit leader off and on since RJ's shop had been destroyed. That was when the unit had decided they needed to be there.

So the Prince of felines and two other men had shown up.

She stood beside Ben and they both watched helplessly as Dylan and the feline Fred entered the circle.

"This is wrong," Ben whispered, grabbing her hand.

"I know." She held on tight.

Cameron and Prince Zachary stood between the two fighters as the others backed out to give them room. RJ stood with his arms across over his chest, directly across from Samson.

Samson sneered at him but the way the man's eyes darted back and forth revealed some of his worry. He'd also had a heated discussion with Fred before the man had stepped into the circle.

Obviously, the arrival of the Prince had been a shock to them. Nikki just hoped it would keep the challenge legal and fair. Everyone knew that the Prince would have no problem bringing either man down if they cheated but what about the damage before that?

The challenge started without any ceremony. Cameron and the Prince waited until both men had stripped and shifted before they backed out of the circle.

The tiger roared but Dylan just shook and growled. Nikki had never seen anything like it before. Dylan in wolf form was impressive. He was fully black and big. However, the tiger was huge. The feline swiped at the wolf, who just darted out of the way. Okay, so Dylan was quick—that was good.

The two animals came together with a clash of fangs and claws. Nikki had to close her eyes several times as the fight continued. The sound of bone-crushing hits and blood spraying was just too much to handle.

Ben started to shake beside her and she wrapped both arms around his waist to hold onto him. Their guards even stepped closer to them.

Dylan bit at the tiger while the massive feline claws scrapped down him. All attention was on the two fighters so no one noticed Samson until it was too late.

Samson had shifted and he howled before he launched himself at RJ outside the ring.

RJ only had enough time to cover his face before he landed on the ground with the wolf on top of him.

"No!" Nikki screamed and started towards him.

She was caught around the waist and lifted off her feet.

"Don't," Casey ordered, holding her tight.

Nikki panicked. The other cats that had arrived with Fred started to shift and so did the wolves with RJ. Brandon, Justin, Max, and even Mike. RJ still fought to hold Samson off so he could shift himself.

"Do something!" she yelled at Cameron and the Prince.

"We can't," Prince Zachary told her, his face revealing regret. "As long as they don't cross into the circle they are not interfering with the challenge."

RJ managed to get away from Samson long enough to start stripping off his clothes. Mike lunged at Samson but was blocked by a cougar protecting the wolf.

Inside the circle, Dylan growled out a warning as another two felines tracked RJ's shift. As soon as he was in wolf form, they attacked.

The distraction worked for the felines. The tiger was able to pounce on the wolf and pin him down for several moments. Luckily, Dylan managed to avoid the powerful jaws but only barely.

Nikki didn't know where to look. Both her brothers, the man she loved, and her future Alpha all battled while she was held back.

"Let me go! Let me go!" she demanded, digging her nails into Casey's arms. She had to do something. Her entire world was being threatened and her wolf was raging inside.

"Don't shift," Casey told her sternly. "Hold on. RJ needs all of his attention. If he has to worry about you, it could cause him to get distracted."

Nikki knew Casey was right but she just couldn't hold it in. Her body shook with the effort to hold in her animal.

"Calm down," Casey urged quietly. "It will be okay, just breathe."

Nikki followed his instructions. She didn't want to be the one to put the ones she loved at risk. She wouldn't be putting just RJ in danger, but Brandon and Justin too.

Dylan had somehow figured out how to get the tiger off him and was taking quick bites before backing up. The tiger was starting to tire.

Nikki watched in shock as Samson was knocked from going after Justin and the wolf flew. RJ followed, growling and stalking.

RJ was just magnificent. Inside, her own wolf started to calm as she watched him, noting he was okay.

"Good, that's better," Casey told her, loosening his hold.

She had forgotten he still had a grip on her.

Inside the circle, the wolf finally managed to pin the tiger with his jaws locked into the feline jugular. Dylan shook his head, biting down, and the tiger fought even harder.

"If you wish to submit, start to shift," Prince Zachary stated firmly. "Or Dylan can end your life."

A collective gasp travelled through the Pack as the tiger started to shift back to man. Dylan released his hold and back away a few steps but stayed in wolf form.

It was only a few seconds before Fred lay in the centre of the circle, panting.

"The challenge is over," Prince Zachary declared. "Dylan Cross is the winner and new Alpha of the Pack."

A cheer rose from the Pack, drowning out the howl of one lone wolf. Nikki turned in time to see Samson coming at her while RJ's back was turned as he looked towards his brother.

Her wolf had had enough. She ripped out of Casey's hold and finally let her animal take control.

She only managed to get out of her pants before she was on all fours and changing. Samson knocked into her and she could hear RJ and the others start forward.

She snarled at them to stay back and faced her foe. She wasn't going to let anyone else get hurt. She launched herself at Samson just as the other wolf did the same. They slammed together, but Nikki was smaller and quicker. She turned in the air to put him under her and as they hit the ground hard and rolled, she clamped down on his throat.

He kicked at her, the claws of his back legs digging into her stomach, but she wasn't letting go. She bit down until blood started to flow. Samson went limp in her hold and whimpered.

"Nikki." Dylan knelt down next to her. "He submits to you. You need to release him."

She shook her head, tearing more at his throat. Didn't Dylan understand that all of this was Samson's fault?

"He will be taken care of," Dylan assured her. "Let him go now."

She didn't want to, she really didn't want to, until she caught another scent. The scent of her mate.

She dropped him down to the ground and stepped on him to get to the other side. RJ was still in his shifted form and was crouched down, pawing towards her.

She fell down in front of him and turned onto her back, exposing her belly for him. She didn't want to challenge him—she wanted something else.

He nuzzled her neck and belly and she let him. He licked the wounds she had gained in the battle but they were already starting to heal. When he encouraged her to stand, she followed his direction.

"Please, everyone, let us get back to the celebration. Brandon, can you take care of our visitors?" Dylan spoke above the crowd.

Nikki didn't get to watch what was happening around her. RJ was nudging her away from the pack towards the woods. He nipped her hindquarters to hurry her along. She took off in a trot once she was sure what he wanted.

Away from the Pack and alone, he stopped and head-butted her. He started to shift back to human and she followed suit.

She stood and stretched and found herself yanked up and into his arms.

"God, baby," he breathed against her. "You scared me."

"RJ!" She grabbed the back of his head and brought his lips down to hers.

They kissed, mouths mating, claiming and biting as every emotion she'd felt came back full force. The strength of her love, the worry, the fear—she let go of it all and devoured him.

They fell to the leaf-covered ground, rolling around naked, hands mapping each other's bodies, need pulsing through them.

"Please," she begged. She needed him like never before.

RJ slipped down her body and buried his head in her sex. He didn't waste any time—opened her up with his fingers and started to lick her pussy.

"Oh God! Yes!" she screamed. She grabbed the back of his head and arched up into his mouth. He feasted and teased her with his fingers until she was panting and tingling.

She came, crying his name. He tore himself away and flipped her around. She had barely managed to settle on her hands and knees before he was thrusting inside.

Her inner muscles clamped down around his hard cock, holding him in deep.

"Never again! Never again will you be in danger," he promised as he continued to pound inside.

She met him, pushed back into each of his frenzied plunges.

"You're mine. No one else will ever touch you!"

"Yes!" she cried out. "Yours! Yours!"

"My mate!"

"Claim me!" she demanded. "Now, do it now!"

His hips snapped and he yanked her head back to reveal her throat. He bent down and closed his teeth over her. He bit down and the mating mark sent her into the most intense orgasm she'd ever experienced.

He rocked into her, hammering her though her climax, until he stiffened and emptied his seed deep into her. They collapsed together and she started to laugh.

He rolled over and grinned down at her. "Damn, baby."

She brushed the hair off his forehead, staring into the eyes of her future. She wouldn't put herself in danger, but she wouldn't sit back and let her loved ones suffer either.

She brought her mouth down on his. "I love you."

He closed his eyes briefly. "I love you too."

She let him gather her close as they lay beneath the canopy of the trees under the moon and the stairs. She had found her mate. There was no doubt she would be coming home to the pack and would stay by RJ's side for the rest of their lives.

And she was okay with that. She was home and loved. She couldn't ask for more than that.

Chapter Thirteen

Three months later

RJ locked the door to his shop before sliding onto his bike and heading home. He waved at Brandon as he passed the sheriff's office. Brandon lifted a hand with a smile on his face.

The last few months had proved that Brandon had been a great pick for Beta of the pack. He was protective and kind, and he was a voice of reason to Dylan when he was needed.

The unmated inner circle members had moved into the Alpha house, so since Dylan and Brandon were now roommates along with a few other Pack members, it was a good thing they were getting along.

The Pack had dealt with the issue of Samson and the elders well. They had arranged for them and any who others who wished to join them a place with a Pack they would be happy at. Well, as happy as possible. The elders had accepted the move while Samson had stormed off without a word. He had moved out of his home, and they had not seen or heard from him since.

The attack on Nikki still angered him, but she had handled herself well and all of the Pack kept a watch out for Samson's return. He would not be welcomed back.

The drive home was now familiar and he grinned at the sight of the front porch light on. He parked his bike in his usual spot right next to the old Jeep.

"Honey, I'm home!" he called out, stepping in the front door.

"In here," Nikki called back.

He made his way to the kitchen of the house that had seen many changes over the last several months. Dylan had moved into the Alpha house, which had left RJ and Ben in their home. It wasn't a week after he'd moved Nikki in that Justin and Ben had told Dylan about their relationship and Ben had moved into Justin's and Nikki's childhood home. He'd just had lunch with his brother and was happy that Ben had found what he wanted and needed. Justin was perfect for his little brother.

"Hey, baby." He greeted Nikki with a quick kiss as she sat at the kitchen table in front of her laptop. She'd just returned home from doing a story on one of the big cat sanctuaries that was need of funds.

She saved her writing in Word and pulled him back down. "What kind of greeting was that?"

He ran his tongue over her lower lip and nipped until she opened for him, then made sure she was breathless before he pulled away this time.

"Mmm, better," she told him with a smile.

He was already hard and pulled her out of her chair. "I don't know, baby, I think I can improve on 'better'."

He leaned her back over the papers she had over the table until she wrapped her legs around his waist. She arched up and rubbed against his swollen shaft.

"Oh, I have no doubt," she teased, gripping him through his jeans.

He bucked into her hold and let her push him back. She knelt before him, mouthing his cock through his pants.

"Yeah, baby, missed you," he expressed sincerely.

"Me too." She opened his jeans to expose his cock to the warm air then hummed as she jacked him off. "Missed everything about you, but especially having you hard in my hand...in my mouth."

She deep-throated him and he had to slam a hand down on the table to avoid going weak in the knees. God, but she had a talented mouth.

She sucked until he was gripping her hair and tugging. "Want inside you."

She popped off his dick with a grin. "Good idea."

He found himself in the kitchen chair she'd abandoned while she yanked her shirt over her head then pushed her sweats down her legs. He reached for her as soon as she was bare in front of him.

On her left breast, just over her heart, was the image of him in wolf form. His own mate tattoo over his heart had been one of the best presents to himself.

He licked at her tattoo as she shivered in his arms.

"I dreamed about you every night I was gone," she informed him, straddling his legs.

It had only been a few days but he'd not been able to breathe correctly when she'd been away.

"Next time you'll have to come with me," she told him, bracing one hand on his shoulder while she held his cock with the other.

He was relieved she had said it first because he didn't know how he could let her take another assignment that would take her away from him.

All thoughts flew out of his head when she started to lower down and her hot pussy engulfed his cock.

Their moans mingled and he caught her lips to devour her mouth as she finally took him all the way in. She rose and he dug his hands into her hips. On the next slide down, he plunged up to meet her.

"Oh yes, RJ, please," she mumbled against his lips.

That was all he needed to hear. He held her tight as he continued to thrust up into her willing body. She rode him hard, digging her nails into his arms, arching and trembling for him.

Too soon she cried out and gripped his cock hard as she climaxed. He pounded into her, drawing out her pleasure until she shook. He stood, laying her back on the table, and took control. As he slammed deep inside her, she scratched and moaned, urging him on. His hips snapped, drawing them closer and closer to the edge.

She ripped at the collar of his shirt until she could bite down on his shoulder.

Her scream was muffled against his flesh as her orgasm hit. This time she tightened around him, not giving him any choice but to follow her into ecstasy.

He pumped his seed into her until he didn't have any more to give. He claimed her mouth, thrusting his tongue in and out, knowing he would never have enough of his mate.

Once the need to breathe demanded he break away, he pulled back enough to look down at her, beautiful and naked, laid out before him while his jeans were around his ankles and his torn shirt hung off his shoulder.

Nikki's watch beeped and she looked at the time with a sigh. "We have just enough time to clean up before the news comes on and the others get here."

He nodded and helped her up.

* * * *

RJ settled on the couch in front of the flat-screen television and accepted the bottle of beer from Nikki. She held her own bottle and settled next to him. Justin and Ben sat in one of the overstuffed chairs beside them, while Brandon sat in the other, and Dylan paced behind them.

The news was turned up loud so they wouldn't miss a word.

At exactly seven o'clock, the picture on the screen turned to the private room full of reporters.

"Ladies and gentlemen…the President of the United States of America."

They all watched as the leader of their country stepped up to the podium.

Nikki gripped his hand and they exchanged worried glances. This wasn't the only place where the shifters' existence was being revealed to the public. There would be similar announcements made in other countries, until it was finally known around the world that some of the mystical creatures in movies and books were very real.

The shifters were now out in the open.

About the Author

Crissy Smith lives in Texas with her husband, daughter, and three Labrador retrievers. The three dogs love to curl up under her computer desk and nap while she writes. It doesn't leave a lot of room for her but what's a woman to do?

When not writing or reading, she enjoys hunting, camping and shooting. But she has a girly side too and is addicted to pedicures and coffee.

She has been writing since she was a teenager and still loves everything to do with the paranormal. Her stories and characters all have a place in her heart. She loves the alpha male, the dominant werewolf, or the Master vampire which find their way in most of her books.

Learn more about the characters she has created at her website where they have their very own page. It will be updated from time to time to let you know what's going on with them. Also you can find out who will be in the next book.

Crissy Smith loves to hear from readers. You can find her contact information, website details and author profile page at http://www.total-e-bound.com

.

Total-E-Bound Publishing

www.total-e-bound.com

Take a look at our exciting range of literagasmic™
erotic romance titles and discover pure quality
at Total-E-Bound.